WHAT ARE FRIENDS FOR?

A P.J. SMYTHE NOVEL

WHAT ARE FRIENDS FOR?

CAROLINE TAYLOR

FIVE STAR
A part of Gale, Cengage Learning

GALE
CENGAGE Learning™

Detroit • New York • San Francisco • New Haven, Conn • Waterville, Maine • London

GALE
CENGAGE Learning

LIBRARY OF CONGRESS CATALOGING-IN-PUBLICATION DATA

Taylor, Caroline, 1943–
 What are friends for? / Caroline Taylor. — 1st ed.
  p. cm.
  ISBN-13: 978-1-59414-956-6 (hardcover)
  ISBN-10: 1-59414-956-9 (hardcover)
  1. Single women—Fiction. 2. Documentary films—Production and direction—Fiction. 3. Chick lit. I. Title.
 PS3620.A9358W46 2011
 813'.6—dc22   2010048400

First Edition. First Printing: March 2011.
Published in 2011 in conjunction with Tekno Books and Ed Gorman.

Printed in the United States of America
1 2 3 4 5 6 7 15 14 13 12 11

For John

ACKNOWLEDGMENTS

The details of this story spring from the imagination, and I have taken enormous liberties with the geography of Annapolis. That said, I owe much to Dave Slater for introducing me to two indispensable Annapolitans: Geoff Oxnam, who corrected numerous faults in my grasp of nautical terms and issues and who told me about the Maritime Republic of Eastport; and Chris Dollar, who helped me find the right places for my characters to live, work, and eat. The Banner Building and the building that houses MoneySource are completely fictitious, but the streets and neighborhoods are for real. With the understanding that police searches are not nearly as careless as I have described them, I apologize profusely to Annapolis's Finest. I remain indebted to the late Andrea Gaski of the U.S. Fish and Wildlife Service for her insights on illegal wildlife trade and to Robert Wade for tips on skip tracing. Thanks also to Dana West, Susan Schwartz, and Nancy Nicholas for their helpful advice on the initial manuscript.

CHAPTER ONE

Did you ever have a best friend you felt like murdering? I do. Those love-hate flames are burning so strong in me right now, if Alicia were anywhere within spitting distance, she'd be charred beyond recognition. But she's not. She's in Europe skiing. And that's no accident. She knows exactly how I feel.

Oh, sure. She's done her best to make up for the mess she got me into. And I know she must be feeling just a little bit guilty (not to mention surprised) at how the whole thing nearly wound up being a complete disaster—especially for yours truly.

You see, thanks to Alicia Todd—as in Todd's Landing, which was what people in colonial times called the place that is now downtown Annapolis—Ritchie—as in Maryland's forty-ninth governor—I nearly got myself killed. Twice.

Of course, it's partly my fault. I'm such a sucker. Alicia knew that I knew I owed her from way back, and she used that to get what she wanted from me.

The whole thing was her idea to begin with. But Alicia's ideas are often way out of touch with reality. Even her self-image is out of whack. To everyone else, she's a gorgeous, wealthy society deb whose biggest challenge of the day is deciding what to wear to the next charity ball or which polo-playing yachtsman's heart she's going to break next. Even I think she comes across that way, but it's all an act. I should know. I grew up with Alicia. I slept over many a night, spent summers at her beach house, went through the whole boy-girl thing and, later, the where-to-go-to college thing (although only one of us had choices).

This is a driven person. She wants to make a name for herself because, deep down, she's scared that some day the money and privilege will evaporate, and she'll become invisible. Still, I have to hand it to her. Whereas other poor little rich girls might opt for the Paris Hilton mode of handling inherited wealth, Alicia does her part, carrying out the duties expected of someone in her position. Her mother relies on her to shoulder some of the burden. And that's why Alicia has a wardrobe full of designer clothes and a shoe rack that would make Imelda Marcos turn in her grave. She also has a heart as big as her bank account. She's helped me out of more scrapes than I can remember. I, in turn, have tried (unsuccessfully, so far) to get her to abandon her calling, which is to be a documentary filmmaker.

Well, that's not exactly true, is it? After all, if I'd said "no" the first time Alicia approached me with her lunatic idea, I wouldn't be sitting here debating the relative merits of poison versus "accidental" drowning. Not that I'd actually go that far. Or would I?

Let's see: My uncle (who raised me practically from birth) is furious, not to mention embarrassed (although perhaps also a tad grateful that I'm still among the living). Bobby, my ex, is after me for money he thinks I owe him and may show up any day demanding payment. I've lost my (would-be) lover, and a former flame is behind bars. And if all that isn't enough, my car is now nothing but a tiny, compacted cube of twisted metal, soon to be recycled into something perhaps more useful, but not nearly as much fun.

I blame Alicia for all of this. Well, perhaps not the Bobby thing. If I'd known at the outset that his middle name was "Me First," I probably wouldn't have married him. Okay. Not exactly true, but it seems true in retrospect.

In retrospect, I should have said no to Alicia. But, by the time things got really out of hand—with me a prime murder suspect—I was so deeply immersed in my "role" that I forgot I wasn't a hard-boiled private eye determined to bring a killer to justice.

CHAPTER TWO

It was a bright and windy Tuesday, and I was California dreaming when a tall, dark, and handsome woman walked into my office. Trailing after her drifted the scent of something faintly woodsy. She wore gray from head to foot: a gray sweatshirt with GEORGETOWN written across the front, gray sweatpants to match, gray running shoes with the familiar swoosh in navy, and a gargantuan gray canvas backpack, which she shrugged off her shoulders like a featherweight shawl.

Finally, somebody had seen the ad in the Crabwrapper (aka the *Capital*). Alicia would be thrilled. I pressed the button activating the hidden video camera. "What can I do for you?"

"*You're* P.J. Smythe?"

Okay. Most people wouldn't expect to encounter a petite blonde in a ponytail in the private investigation business. But it didn't seem to bother Ms. Amazon. She plopped down into the worn leather chair opposite my desk, lowered the backpack to the floor, and propped her feet on the only corner of the army surplus wooden desk that wasn't already scarred from the shoes of others. Her inky black hair was short and carefully tousled by a cut that probably cost her more than I made in a month. She had amber-colored eyes under short, thick brows, and a faint dusting of freckles skittered across the bridge of a turned-up nose. The sweats and her height made me wonder if the woman might be a Washington Mystic, although perhaps not one of the starters. Shrink her down to my size, and she'd be called cute. I settled for "arresting."

Dragging a yellow legal pad out of the drawer, I grabbed a pen. "What can I do for you, Ms.—?"

"Remington," she said. "Vivian Remington. I'm with the Wetland Protectors Alliance, and we'd like to hire you to document a theft and possibly retrieve the item for us." She flipped her business card across the desk.

"Document a theft? Does that mean you know who took it?"

She glanced briefly toward the filing cabinet in the corner and then back to me. "We want to be discreet."

"Discreet." I wrote the word in caps on the second line of the yellow pad, following her name.

"The item—if I don't get it back real soon—could be embarrassing."

"And the item is . . . ?"

"A fur coat."

"Did you call the police?"

Vivian sighed. "I can't—it wouldn't be wise to put her on the spot just yet."

"Her? As in—?"

"I know who stole it. A prominent Florida politician who happens to be on our board. She's got a thing for other people's belongings—clothes, jewelry, you name it. I guess I thought she'd never have the nerve to . . ."

I tuned out, my brain stuck on the word "politician." Not only were the high and the mighty way out of my league, they were probably not what Alicia had imagined when she set the wheels in motion to film, as she'd put it, "a novice private investigator, learning on the job." I tapped my pencil on the desk and took a deep breath. No guts, no gravy. "Okay, one of your board members stole your fur coat. Did you ask her to return it?"

"No." Her face turned rosy, which made the freckles stand

out. "We have a history. A bad one. I'm sure that's why she's now on our board."

The woman sounded paranoid, so I changed tack. "I'll need a description of the coat," I said, pencil at the ready.

"It's full length ocelot."

"Ossa-what?"

"Ocelot." She spelled it out as though I was a dimwit. "It looks like leopard. Spotted, you know? With a bronze-colored satin lining. It's also endangered."

"How could a coat be endangered?"

My new client rolled her eyes. "The fur comes from ocelots and is forbidden to be traded under sight-ease."

I felt like I'd wandered into a foreign country without a translating dictionary. "Sight-ease?"

"The Convention on International Trade in Endangered Species. We call it CITES. I'll give you some background information." She poked away with the stylus, no doubt making a little note to herself.

Beside the tiger I'd doodled on my yellow pad, I made my own, lower-tech note: "Why am I DOING this?"

Leaning back in my chair, I stared at the speckles of ochre paint on the walls that had been revealed when the white coat somebody had carelessly slapped on top had begun to blister and crack. Did the place Alicia had chosen for my "office" have to hark back to the thirties? "How did this personage get her hands on your coat?"

"It's not mine," she snapped. "The Fish and Wildlife Service lent it to me for a demonstration I planned to give to people traveling abroad to inform them about what they can and cannot buy overseas and bring back into the country. It was with a pile of stuff I used for the demonstration—brochures, a poster, some coral beads. I was doing an inventory. The only thing missing was the coat."

"You're sure it wasn't just misplaced somewhere . . . ?"

Another roll of the eyes from Ms. Remington. "I didn't have to search. One of my colleagues told me he saw the woman carrying the coat out to her car."

"Let me guess. You couldn't exactly accuse a board member of theft."

She nodded. "And the Feds are gonna hand me my lunch if I don't return it real soon."

"You'll have to pay for it?"

She shuddered. "That's the least of my worries, although back in the eighties ocelot coats could cost as much as forty thousand."

I wrote "40K!" on the legal pad. It was more than I could hope to make in a year in my real job—the one that paid the rent and bought gas for my car. "You think she's going to try to sell it? How could somebody get away with that if it's against the law?"

Remington's brows arched upward, forming a peak at the center. "There's always a market for these things. Look on the Internet. I saw an ad the other day from somebody in New Zealand, claiming the coat was a part of his mother's estate. Uh-huh." She drummed her fingers on her knee. "I keep checking every day, but I figure she's got other ideas. She's trying to set me up so that I'll be accused of stealing it. They'll arrest me even if I tell them she took it."

"So call her up and demand that she return it."

Vivian rolled her eyes. "Like she'd even talk to me. Besides, I'm pretty damn sure she took that coat to get back at me for— Well, it's really none of your concern."

"Then give me her name and number, and I'll tell her you want it back." How hard could this be? There was a witness to the theft, after all.

The dark head fell forward as though Remington had suddenly discovered an embarrassing stain on her sweats, which meant I couldn't read her expression when she said, "I don't think that would be a good idea."

"Do the other board members know about this?"

"No. Only me. And I want it to stay that way until you produce the documentation. Or the coat."

"Because they wouldn't believe you otherwise?"

She looked at me. "It's a reflection of my stewardship. I had this valuable item on loan. I let it get out of my hands. If they think I failed on this score, they will begin to believe I don't measure up in other areas, and that could ruin our whole effort." Her eyes slitted. "I'm sure that's her real objective."

I leaned back in my chair, crossed my arms, and ran the conversation back through my muddled brain. "She joined the board with the explicit objective of wrecking the Alliance? I thought board members had a—"

"They do. But I don't have any proof. Only suspicions. Strong ones."

"What about your witness? The person who saw her carry it out of the office?"

"He's on a climbing expedition in Nepal. Completely out of touch for at least the next month—by which time, the damage will be done."

I scanned my notes. "You said this board member has it in for you. Why's that?"

Remington gave me a thin, tight smile. "It was Jim's idea to put her on the board, okay? Jim's my boss. When I found out, I was furious; but I couldn't complain to him because he didn't know . . . Okay. Here's the deal: In my last job back in Florida, she was my supervisor. She borrowed—" (two fingers in each hand curled to form air quotes around the word) "—a laptop and a DVD player, claiming she needed them to work from home. She never returned them—probably still has them, in fact. She borrowed—" (again, the air quotes) "—my field glasses—they were Zeiss, top of the line—for a vacation trip to the Rockies and never returned them to me. When I asked about them, she flew into a fury, claiming the glasses were the Foundation's property and accusing me of thievery. Naturally, I hadn't kept the receipt, so it was her word against mine.

"Long story short, she made my life hell, so I went over her head and complained to the big boss. Next thing you know, she's submitting her resignation so she can spend more time campaigning for the state senate."

"No kidding?"

"Hah. The Foundation fired her, and she knows I'm the one who made it happen."

"If you think this coat-stealing might be some kind of petty revenge, you should either tell your boss or, at the very least, seek legal counsel."

Remington grimaced. "I thought of that. But the only lawyers I know already have dealings with the senator."

"And those people are . . . ?"

"Meredith, Geitrich, and Smeal. Perhaps you've heard of them?"

Annapolis was too small not to have heard of that particular law firm. Top of the line, to borrow Vivian's words—although how an outfit like hers could afford them . . . "Look, Ms. Reming—"

"Call me Vivian."

"—ton, I'm not sure I can be much help here. I don't know the lady. She doesn't know me. How's this going to happen?"

She shrugged. "We can arrange for you to meet the senator. On Saturday, there's a black-tie reception in Washington for the Florida Legislature. Senator Sutherland and several other colleagues of hers are the honorees. It's so cold right now, she might even be stupid enough to wear the damn coat. Take a camera, just in case. Or—" She paused at the look on my face. "—you're the expert, of course. Maybe you can just cozy up to her at the party, you know, do whatever you think is necessary."

"It'll cost you," I said. "Five thousand up front." (This was to discourage people who just wanted me to find a missing cat or catch a cheating spouse—subjects that Alicia felt lacked sufficient gravitas for her film.)

Remington whipped out a checkbook and began to write. Damn. I should have asked for twice that. Drawing the pad closer, I made a note of the fee. "I'll need some information about your legislator too, starting with her name."

"Marguerite Sutherland, state senator, Republican, from Kissimmee. She's got a pretty good record on the environment. I suppose that's why Jim thought she'd be a good addition to the board."

I shuddered. Florida reminded me too much of my own mortality, not to mention my former husband, Bobby Crane. The last time I'd seen him, he'd threatened to sue me for alimony if he ever found out that I was actually making a living. No worries there yet. "Wait," I said, my head spinning from the contradictory information I'd been getting. "So she did run for office. And now she's on your board because your boss thinks she's pro-environment."

"Right."

"Then you catch her stealing that ossy—"

"Ocelot."

"—coat, which will get you in trouble with the Feds. And maybe—as you put it—that's what she wants. Which would be a major breach of her fiduciary duties, so doesn't that mean that you have a duty to—"

"I can't." Remington sighed and leaned forward in the chair. "Look. That's why I'm hiring you. To document what she's up to. Right now, it's only at the rumor stage, and I could get into big trouble if . . . you know."

There was a momentary lull in the conversation as I did a quick sketch of a loon on my yellow pad while silently grinding my teeth because, obviously, I didn't know. I put the pencil down. "I don't think I can help you."

"Why?"

"I don't know a thing about endangered clothing. It would be almost impossible for me to get anywhere near this Florida senator, a complete stranger, let alone get her to hand over the coat—especially when you don't want me to just come right out and ask for it." Even as I spoke, I could feel Alicia's wrath breathing down my neck. "Don't screw up" had been her only piece of directorial input so far.

"Surely it wouldn't be too difficult for you to catch her wearing the coat or, failing that, perhaps get a picture of it hanging in her closet."

"Look, short of breaking and—"

Remington held up her hand. "Only if you absolutely have to."

"No way. I don't do B and E. It's against the law."

"That didn't stop you before."

In the ensuing silence, I picked up Remington's card and tossed it back across the desk, sticking my tongue out at the hidden camera as I did so. "I guess you know more about me than I do myself. But, whatever. You need to find somebody else to help you."

Remington gave a little half smile as she crossed her arms. "UVA. Back in 2003. Your little brush with the law. Didn't it involve illegally entering somebody's home?"

I slapped the yellow pad. "Somebody's been feeding you a line of bull. I don't know why, but it's not true." Oh, yeah, it is.

"Gareth Swenson," she said. "We were in grad school together last year. I ran into him the other day, we had a drink, I asked him if he knew anyone who might help me solve my little problem, and he showed me your ad in the *Capital.* He said you'd be the perfect choice—given your, uh, previous experience."

"He's wrong. I don't break and enter."

Picking up the card, she flipped it back at me. "I can't help thinking a certain Alexander Boyd Smythe wouldn't want to know about your shady past."

True. If my uncle found out, the first thing he'd do would be to fire me. Then he'd disown me. Then his heart would break. "That's blackmail."

"Call it what you wish. I can be discreet if I get what I want. And I want proof the bitch stole that coat."

I took a deep breath and let it out slowly. "If I got caught breaking and entering, you'd be in big trouble too."

This had gone far enough. Beyond far. I tapped my foot impatiently, trying to figure the odds of surviving Alicia's rage if I stepped out of character and told Remington the real story. Then I realized it might not be the "client" who was attempting blackmail, that all that bullshit about meeting up with Gareth Swenson in grad school was a load of hooey. Alicia was perfectly capable of feeding Remington the information just to keep me in the role she'd assigned until she got whatever footage she needed.

With a sigh, I leaned back in my chair. Okay. I would play it out till Remington left. Then I would throw in the towel.

For starters, I was not a party girl. Nor could I picture myself playing private eye pretending to be paparazzi with a powerful Florida politician or stiff-arming her into 'fessing up to a crime, let alone handing over stolen goods. And there were other problems. I didn't own one shred of clothing suitable enough for a Washington reception where legislators and lobbyists and lawyers and all manner of powerful people mingled while drinking martinis and stuffing their mouths with caviar and smoked salmon. My mouth began to water even though my tastes ran more to surf 'n turf.

On the other hand, maybe I could pull it off. I could get lucky. And the food would be free, a real plus. I put Remington's business card and her check into the desk drawer and sat there as she hauled her backpack up off the floor and slung the strap over her shoulder.

"One other thing," I said to her departing back. "Where did you run into Gareth Swenson?"

She turned with another half smile. "City Dock." At my look of surprise, she added, "Don't worry. He thinks you're a psychotic bitch."

January 20, 2003

She slips the credit card into the crack near the doorknob. Nudging the plastic forward, she feels the latch give, and turns the knob. That sure was simpler than she'd imagined. *After this, he'll buy a more sturdy lock.*

Crossing the darkened room, she lowers the Venetian blinds and hits the switch on a nearby table lamp. Next, a quick peek at her watch. There are eighteen minutes to go. Gareth will not be hiding drugs in any obvious places. Looking up, she catches sight of her face in the mirror over the false fireplace. Her gaze drops to the two of them, framed in pewter and sitting on the mantel. Beer steins in hand, their heads are tilted together in a *Star Trek*–like mind meld, and they're laughing like lunatics on the lam. Back in the days when love ruled.

In the kitchen, she dumps the flour out of its metal canister and finds three baggies at the bottom. They're filled with a fine-grained powder that's much whiter than the flour. Ditto with the sugar and coffee canisters. Nine baggies total. But wait: She's getting a bit ahead of herself. Moving back to the front door, she takes a quick peek up and down the empty hallway outside No. 503, pulls the disposable out of her pocket, and shoots the brass-plated numbers. Back inside, she clicks off another shot of the kitchen stash. Next, a shot of the notepad next to the telephone. It's Gareth's handwriting, reminding himself to call Barbara tomorrow. Bastard. He doesn't have a sister, and his mother's name is Josephine.

She wanders into the bedroom, eleven minutes now. There's a lipstick-smeared tissue in the trash basket beside the bed. Dark red. Not a shade she would ever choose. So why is she trying to save the cheating sonofabitch?

In the bathroom, she takes the toothbrush she's used once or twice and drops it into the pocket of her jacket. Taped to the inside of the toilet tank top are eight more baggies. Not smart, Gareth. The cops always check toilets. Click, and then flush.

Click again on the monogrammed brush on the bureau. GWS in some florid script etched into the silver back. Pocketing the camera, she heads back to the kitchen and flushes the contents of nine baggies down the garbage disposal, along with some coffee, flour, and sugar. But only a little bit. Let the jerk have to clean the place up. In fact, let whoever shows up first wonder who's been here and what happened to the drugs. With an angry swipe, she shoves an armful of the floury mess off onto the floor. Oops.

Back in the living room, with four minutes to spare, she's photographing the damned proof that, yes, she knows this guy (or thought she did)—hoping the flash off the pewter and glass won't obscure the two lovebirds—when the phone rings. Her heart thuds as the answering machine kicks in, and the caller says, "Hi Gareth. It's Linda. You left your sweater at my place the other night. Why don't you stop by and pick it up? It's all I'm wearing at the moment."

Grabbing the picture, she heaves it at the mirror. There is a loud crack as the glass shatters. Behind her, the door to the apartment flies open. "Police!"

CHAPTER THREE

A faint trace of Vivian Remington's woodsy perfume lingered in the doorway like a ghostly watchdog as I shut the door, locked it, and shut down the camera. Then I phoned Alicia, who, conveniently, was not answering.

Cursing myself six ways from Saturday, I crossed to the window and lowered the blinds. In the darkened room, the only thing I could see was the peeling day-glo label on the four-drawer filing cabinet, which read "ARN - NG! C - NTENTS MIG - IP!" Trust Alicia to get all the scenery right, anyway.

I tilted my chair back, trying to gather my thoughts into some coherent form, but the gnawing sensation in my stomach from too much coffee and a bad trip down memory lane had the hackles rising at the back of my neck. My venture into vandalism and subsequent—what I liked to think of as morally responsible—blackmail were supposed to have been long since relegated to the dustbin of Foolish Experiences While in College. I'd paid a big price for that lesson, not being able to find what my uncle called serious employment because I could not honestly check off the "never arrested" column on most job application forms. The one exception was MoneySource, where I hadn't been asked to fill out an application because my uncle owned the place.

So, instead of being grateful to be employed, here I was, playing hooky from work, pretending to be a private eye. But then, what are friends for?

"You'd be a natural," was the way Alicia had put it over drinks at 49 West. "You've certainly got more curiosity than the average human being, you're an excellent liar, and you're not stupid."

What a gal. "I think you're nuts" had been my response.

"Look, I'll pay for everything. I've found the perfect place for your 'office,' and I'll front for you with your uncle—even pay you if he won't."

"What he'll do is fire me."

The raised eyebrow. The index finger on the right cheek. Alicia was the one who should have been in front of the camera.

I swallowed the last of my wine and ordered another. She had me there. My uncle wouldn't fire me because I was good at my job.

I make my living lying. It's not what I want to do, but you have to start somewhere. I'm a good liar, mostly because I've had lots of practice. But I've never been one of those people who lie so often they wind up not being able to tell the difference. It's just that lying is a really effective way to do my job, so I fib a lot—and I get results.

Lying has also made it possible for me to minimize, if not totally defeat, my uncle's overly protective gestures. He raised me, he employs me, and he's on my case twenty-four/seven about things like my car, my love life (or lack thereof), and my career aspirations. The only person I've never successfully deceived is Alicia. She has some kind of spooky lie detector hard-wired into her brain.

"Look," I pleaded. "Why don't you do a documentary on payday loan outfits? Now there's a place where you could really uncover some unsavory—"

"And bite the hand that's feeding you?"

"MoneySource is different."

Again, the raised eyebrow, this time followed by a heavy sigh.

"Right. So, as I was saying. My objective is to show how somebody with gumption—that's you, by the way, P.J.—can get a handle on the job by doing it. It's part of a series. I've done show jumping, sailing, skiing, teaching literacy, ESL. Now I want to do detecting."

"How about waitressing?"

"Overdone. And, besides, that's so easy a moron could—You did see *Waitress,* didn't you? Great flick. But it's been done. I'm blazing new territory."

Yadda. Yadda. I'd heard the spiel so many times, I could say it along with her. And, yes, perhaps I shouldn't have had that second glass of wine because it did seem to have affected my judgment—never my strong suit—and I wound up going along with my best friend's idiot scheme.

I tried Alicia's number again. Then I buzzed her house and got one of the servants who took a message. The question was would I break my promise, now that I realized just how tricky the thing could get. Did I know anything about hobnobbing with the high and mighty? No.

"That's why it's called learning on the job," Alicia would say.

And failing miserably.

I sat up, my headache gone. Would Alicia be that mean? Was that her aim? To film me stumbling around a complicated case of a missing coat that happened to be endangered and the big factotum thief who couldn't be asked outright to return it? That would be *so* evil.

Like the time back when we were in high school and both of us crazy in love with Tom Eldridge. A skinny blond with freckles and light blue eyes, he was not the kind of guy I thought Alicia would find interesting. He didn't do sports. He wasn't class president (Alicia was) or homecoming king with Alicia as queen. Tom was the school prankster. I fell for him soon after he got away with taping a sign to the front of mean old Ackerman's desk that said "I HAD BEANS FOR LUNCH. APPROACH AT YOUR OWN RISK." It was sixth period before the teacher found out what had his students snickering behind their textbooks.

What Alicia saw in Tommy, I was never sure. She could have dated anybody, after all. Guys were always hanging around her locker, offering to carry her books. This actually spilled over onto me once or twice when the smarter guys figured out I was Alicia's best friend. So I became the repository of their coded messages for her. "Do you think Alicia likes 'mums?" (Translation: Does she have a date for Homecoming yet?) "Gary Towson? You *do* know he's the designated dope dispenser, don't you?" (Translation: Tell Alicia she should hang out with me, not Gary.)

Of course, neither of us actually pursued Tom Eldridge. It wouldn't have been cool—at least I'm sure that was Alicia's reason. I just didn't have the courage, even though I'd known him since he sat behind me in grade school and would yank my braids whenever the teacher had her back turned. So I pretended I didn't notice he was around, except we often sat next to one another in English and he would have me in stitches the whole time we were supposed to be pretending we understood Shakespeare.

It took about a week of showing up for class and finding the desks surrounding Tom Eldridge all occupied before it occurred to me that he might be avoiding me. I mentioned it to Alicia. After all, I mentioned everything to her, and I assumed the opposite was true on her part.

"Want me to find out?" she offered.

"No! He'll think I care."

"You *do* care."

"But I don't want him to know. You know. In case . . ." I was so chicken, I couldn't even finish the sentence. I made her promise never to talk to Tom about me.

Unlike me, Alicia was not the timid sort. She didn't exactly break her promise either. Instead, she did what teenagers the world over do. She asked one or two of Tom's friends, and they told her he thought I was okay, but I had B.O.

"You're kidding!"

Alicia held her hands up. "Hey, I'm only the messenger."

I sniffed my forearm. "Do I really stink?"

"Of course not, silly. You know guys. They can't just say they don't like you because you're short" (which I was) "or don't wear the latest . . ." Here, Alicia's voice trailed off because she knew I couldn't afford the phat styles and had often been the recipient of her castoffs, always delivered with a "thought I'd really like this, but it's just not right. Would it work on you?"

A week later, Tom Eldridge took Alicia to the junior prom. Two weeks afterward, while I was dipping out ice cream on the boardwalk at Ocean City, she and Kelly Jason, the varsity quarterback with a Clemson scholarship, became an Item for the summer.

It was only after school resumed in the fall that I overheard a couple of Alicia's lacrosse teammates in the locker room following practice.

". . . what she usually does to ditch the competition."

"No way."

"Way. Like, she even did it to—" (the words were drowned out by the slam of a metal locker door) ". . . even believed it, asking her, like, did she really have B.O.?"

"Geez. And then she goes and dumps him."

Okay. Did I know they were talking about Alicia? Was the "him" who got dumped Tom Eldridge? Did other girls go around smearing "the competition" with the B.O. label? Did guys routinely use B.O. as a reason for not liking some girl? Yes. Yes. Yes. Yes.

I should have had it out with Alicia like real friends occasionally do, but I couldn't bring myself to confront her on the basis of something I'd overheard. I certainly didn't want to quiz the dumpee for fear I'd discover that, in fact, he *did* think I smelled bad. So, instead, I moved on like a mature person would under those circumstances. Alicia was insecure. She was spoiled and always had to have her way. But she was my friend. And Tom Eldridge was history.

Chapter Four

The card that constituted my ticket to the Washington reception was engraved, and that made me wonder briefly if I could persuade Alicia to go and pretend to be me. She'd be much more comfortable attending a black-tie reception. The only problem was, she was going to be directing the cameraman, some geek she'd met in a cinematography class. How she'd wrangled an invitation I would probably never discover—unless I thought about it for two seconds, kicking myself for being so suspicious, but also remembering why I had to go to the danged thing and show Alicia Todd Ritchie that I could, indeed, learn on the job.

Which was why I was stuck doing homework when I should have been tracing skips. I looked up the Wetland Protectors Alliance Web site. On it were lots of interesting facts about the Everglades and the Mississippi River Valley and the Chesapeake Bay. Under "About Us," I'd discovered that the alliance was a consortium of environmental organizations—Audubon, Sierra, National Wildlife, and others—that had banded together to protect recent federal legislative victories on Everglades restoration from being undermined by less environmentally concerned groups like the sugar industry, agribusiness, and commercial fishing interests. I could join for as little as ten dollars. And, sure enough, Senator Marguerite Sutherland was on the board of directors.

The Fish and Wildlife Service site confirmed that it was a

crime to import items made from tortoiseshell, coral, ivory, reptile skins, and the fur of endangered big cats, including ocelot. A Google search took me to the site for an organization involved in protecting big cats where I found pretty much everything Vivian had told me during the initial interview and not a whole lot more. And, yes, there were a couple of links to sites where people seemed to be selling old, previously used, recently reconstructed, ocelot fur coats, most of which, the nearly impoverished owners claimed, had been lying around in grandma's attic for the past thirty or forty years.

So Vivian at least had been truthful, and I knew a few more useful facts. But my heart wasn't in it. Nobody likes to have their arm twisted or their fortitude questioned. Anyway, I'd already spent nearly eight hundred smackers (thank you, Alicia) on a skin-tight black silk halter-top number with side slits practically up to my undies and no back, a pair of strappy sandals with stiletto heels, and a tiny black leather bag with a gold-plated shoulder-length chain. So might as well party on.

"Black is so passé," said Alicia as I shimmied into my dress. She'd dropped by to help me transform myself from pint-sized urchin into petite blond bombshell. "This looks so off the rack. You should have—"

"I like it," I said, twisting around to see if anyone could tell I wasn't wearing a bra. "Anyway, it's the closest I could get to the 'classy dame' look."

She raised a brow. "Point taken." Then she stepped back, a tiny crease forming between her brows. "Maybe you could have found something more Lauren Bacall at a costume store."

Alicia, who could have been Lauren Bacall's twin except for the vast difference in their ages, was tall enough to wear a glam gown with football-player shoulder pads. I, on the other hand, would have wound up looking like a kid playing dress-up.

Speaking of playing, it was time to ferret out some important details. "Don't you think it's far too coincidental that our 'client,' Ms. Remington, went to grad school with Gareth Swenson?" I asked her.

Alicia grinned, humming the *Twilight Zone* theme. "Annapolis is still a small town."

"UVA is huge."

"Not at the graduate level, I bet."

I turned and grasped her by the arms. "You know this is insane, don't you?"

"Persephone Justinalia Smythe. Don't you dare wimp out on me. Chances like this don't just arrive every day."

Alicia was one of the few people with whom I'd shared the ugly secret of my hideous name. What had my mother been thinking? I'd promised to kill Alicia if she ever uttered it in front of anyone but my uncle, who was the only other living person to know what P.J. stood for.

"And anyway, this could turn out to be my best attempt. Maybe it'll even get to Sundance. With you in the leading role."

"If I wanted to be a movie star, I'd be in Hollywood," I retorted. "The way things are going on this gig, you're going to wind up making me love my real job. And, speaking of Hollywood, don't you think it's really, really odd that Vivian Remington didn't have any reaction to finding herself suddenly in the midst of a film noir B movie?"

"She's so worried about that coat, she probably didn't notice."

"You should be glad she's clueless."

"I am, even though I did put a lot of effort into set design."

"For a documentary set in 2010. I don't get it."

Alicia gave me the beady-eye treatment. "A lot of people just getting started on a shoestring budget have to settle for the bare minimum, you know."

"Okay, whatever. But wouldn't Windows 95 be more realistic as your so-called 'bare minimum'?"

Alicia groaned. "Would you cut the crap, P.J.? I'm the one who's making this film, and it's my artistic vision we're dealing with here, okay? You'd think this was a dental appointment, the way you're carrying on. So shut up and let me play fairy godmother."

Cursed as I was with very fine dirty dishwater blond hair—ash blond is the usual euphemism—a ponytail was just about all I could manage. But Alicia, whose own naturally wavy golden hair belonged in a shampoo commercial, seemed to have innate hairdresser talents. She twisted my limp locks into a chignon at the base of my neck and stuck a billion hairpins into it to hold it in place. Wearing her diamond studs and tennis bracelet, I looked halfway decent and, in fact, far more grown up than I felt.

"Have you got tip money?" she said as I slung the handbag over my shoulder.

"Tips?"

"I know. That's for your escort to worry about, but you're flying solo tonight."

"Unless you want to trade places and let me direct the filming."

"Not gonna happen." Alicia shoved a handful of dollar bills into my handbag. "This is for the Cosmos Club valet, and leave something for the ladies' room attendant."

With a tremendous sense of foreboding, I set out for Washington in my uncle's two-year-old car. I wanted to make a good impression by arriving at the Cosmos Club in a silver luxury sedan, but I also had no choice. Uncle Alex had said he was not going to go sleepless wondering if my beat-up 'seventy-one Volkswagen might break down on the outskirts of Washington where drivers who pull off to the shoulder with car trouble are routinely run down and killed.

You will have a wonderful time, I said to myself, as I cruised down Route 50 in the direction of Washington. You will meet a sexy man who will flirt madly with you throughout the evening. The senator under suspicion will collect the stolen fur from the coat room and hand it over—case solved. Lesson learned. Roll the credits. Oh yeah, baby. She'll have fun fun fun till her uncle takes the Lexus awaaaay!

At the Cosmos Club, a uniformed valet helped me out of the car, jumped in the car, and pulled away. There was no turning back. With a determined smile pasted on my face, I sailed up the steps and through the door and nearly tripped over a luscious-looking lawyer.

CHAPTER FIVE

How did I know he practiced law? He represented my uncle. His name was Neal Patterson, and every time he visited Money-Source, my insides would start to tingle and I'd develop an embarrassing stutter and turn bright red and generally comport myself like a love-struck teenager.

Neal grabbed my elbow to break my fall. "Hey, P.J. What brings you to Washington?"

I could feel my face burning already. "B-business," I said. My pulse was racing the way it always seemed to on the few occasions I'd seen the man in my uncle's office. I forced my trembling lips into a semblance of a smile. Instead of looking over my shoulder for something more appealing, he turned the full force of his baby blues on me and beamed.

Picture a young George Clooney, black hair not yet salt-and-pepper but on its way, judging from a spattering of white just above his ears. Eyes as blue as a June sky. A long nose, just a tiny bit slanted to the left, probably from having been broken once upon a time. And a smile straight out of a toothpaste commercial. Yummmmmy.

Ever since I'd first laid eyes on my uncle's lawyer, visions of Neal Patterson had haunted my dreams, which usually involved him rescuing me from a monster or a fire or a terrorist bombing and the two of us pledging our eternal love. I would awaken with a smile on my face and a feeling of sweet lassitude. Then when I realized it had only been my overactive subconscious,

I'd be cranky the rest of the day. Now there he was by my side like a proud escort. Only, of course, that wasn't true.

"You're meeting someone?" he inquired.

"Y-yes," I said. "Her name's Marguerite Sutherland."

"Neal, darling!" I turned to see a slender young woman with shoulder-length glossy black hair, ruby red lips, and very white skin thrust her willowy self between us. She was wearing a floor-length white organza gown tied in back with a scarlet bow that set off her tiny waist. She threw her arms around him, kissing first one and then the other cheek. "Sorry I'm late."

Why was I surprised? No. Make that just a teeny bit disappointed. As I turned away from the darling couple, I noticed a man across the room staring at me. He looked vaguely familiar with his chiseled face and square jaw, but the buzz cut didn't ring any bells. He didn't look happy, either, as he made his way through the crowd to my side.

"So we meet again," he said. "Better circumstances this time, wouldn't you say?"

"I'm sorry. Do I know you?"

He smiled and clasped his hands behind his back. "I guess so. We had a rather traumatic break-up back when you were a senior in college."

Gareth Drug-Dealer Swenson in the flesh. I would have recognized him if he hadn't shaved off what used to be shoulder-length, dark blond hair that he'd worn in a ponytail. He also appeared to have exchanged the rimless round glasses for a pair of green-tinted contacts. New ones, I judged, from the telltale redness surrounding the iris.

Up to now, there'd only been two men I'd really fallen for, so how likely was it I'd run into one of them at a black-tie affair? I realized that no way would my ex-husband Bobby be there, making things even more weird, but I searched the crowds anyway before turning my attention back to Swenson. "I don't think I want to talk to you."

"Ah. Let me guess. Vivian Remington has already been in touch." He sneezed, pulling a white handkerchief from his breast pocket.

I backed up to avoid catching the germs. "I think I've persuaded her I can solve her problem without breaking the law."

"Good. I didn't mean to suggest otherwise, P.J. And, by the way, I don't have a cold. I'm allergic to all this perfume." He waved a hand in the direction of the crowds swarming around the buffet table. "That's a real eye-catching ad you put in the *Capital.* I'd no idea you'd become a private eye—although your particular penchant for, shall we say, finding things that other people don't want found, is probably a great asset." He grinned, revealing the same slightly tilted front tooth that I'd once found endearing.

Why did Gareth's supposed compliment strike me as sinister? "Well," I said, groping through my stunned brain for the kind of response a genuine P.I. would give, "you're not expecting me to thank you for the referral, are you?"

He shrugged. "Maybe not. But I think you should know that it's exceedingly annoying—not to mention rude—for you to be staring over my shoulder as though you're looking for some knight in shining armor to rescue you from my evil clutches."

As if. I jerked my gaze back. "Does Vivian know about your criminal past?"

Gareth stiffened. "Certainly not. You may find it hard to believe, P.J., but I too have matured since college, and I no longer care to risk running afoul of the law."

Although not above telling a friend where she could find an amateur B and E artist. "Good for you," I said, my eyes searching the room for signs of a senatorial-looking woman.

"And speaking of the past, I assume you've destroyed those

damning pictures you claim to have taken the night you trashed my apartment."

"What's it to you?"

"A lot, P.J. I'm just about to get appointed to a high-level government position, and I don't want to worry about someone dragging up my—" He sneezed again. "Sorry."

"You know I wouldn't do that." I insisted. "I could have turned you over to the police, after all."

Gareth narrowed his overly green eyes. "I'd like to think you mean it, but I would be even more sanguine if I knew those pictures no longer existed."

"I didn't get rid of them."

"Look, P.J. That was all so long ago. Do you mind letting me have them now?"

"I do." I turned to the side, once again scanning the crowd.

"Who are you looking for?"

"I don't suppose you'd happen to know which one of the guests is Marguerite Sutherland."

"I'll introduce you." Placing his hand at the small of my back, Gareth guided me across the crowded room. We were approaching a woman who appeared to be in her mid to late forties. Her auburn hair danced about a rounded face in a riot of curls, tamed only by one strategically placed diamond clip. "Good evening, senator," he said. "I'd like you to meet P.J. Smythe, an old friend from college."

"Pleasure to meet you." She smiled, brushing my palm with her fingers in what I assumed was meant to be a handshake. Like many women in public life, Marguerite Sutherland had kept her figure trim, shown off by the drape of her floor-length, golden-hued brushed satin gown. She had brown eyes, circled with too much aubergine eyeliner, and her lips had been plumped by at least one too many injections, giving her a pouty baby-doll look out of keeping with the lines etched between her brows and at the corners of her eyes. I certainly didn't want to kiss her, but Gareth planted two pecks on each side of her face, offered to refill her wine, and left the two of us standing there sizing each other up.

"What is it that you do?" Senator Sutherland inquired, to get the obligatory Washington question out of the way.

Pretending didn't seem to be the right thing to say. "I'm a photographer. In fact, I just finished shooting a member of the Maryland House."

The senator raised an eyebrow. "Really? Is he still alive?"

I laughed. "Just a term of art. I aim for candid shots, you know, showing the person interacting with other people—like here, for example."

"How interesting."

"I brought my camera." I said, reaching into my handbag. "I try to capture moments like this as a way to help you hold onto precious memories. If you like, I could shoo—uh, take some pictures of you while you're here."

"Perhaps." She patted her hair and smoothed her dress. "Although I hardly have time for such non—"

"Oh, of course. I heard you were in the Florida legislature. It must be interesting work."

"Demanding. Truly demanding. But rewarding too. It's a diverse state and a real challenge to see that my constituents are well served." Swallowing a yawn, she took a discreet peek at the tiny diamond watch on her wrist. I was betting she needed bifocals to read it.

"Well, don't mind me," I said, waving the camera. "I'll just—"

An arm grabbed my elbow. "Could I see your press pass?"

I turned to see a gentleman in black tie with a label that read "Event Staff."

"I don't have one," I said. "I'm not with the press."

"Then no pictures, please." He stood there while I stuffed

the camera back into my bag, my face as crimson as the carnation in his lapel.

"I'm so sorry," I said to the senator. "I had no idea . . ." My eyes darted around the room, searching for Alicia and her cameraman, wondering if they too had been stopped. But no. There she was, standing right behind the large lady in the silver lamé gown, whispering in the ear of a chunky guy with a handlebar mustache who was standing next to her, holding a camera. Both of them had press badges pinned to their clothing. "Perhaps another time?"

"Perhaps," said the senator. Her gaze drifted over my left shoulder, which made me feel almost invisible, and then she said, "Oh, thank you Gareth darling. You're such a dear."

Taking the stemmed glass from Swenson's outstretched hand, Sutherland downed half the contents in a gulp and sent a thousand-volt smile over my right shoulder. Turning, I noticed that the object of her attention was none other than Neal Patterson, minus Snow White.

"Darling," she gushed. "So good of you to come."

Neal smiled and gave a little half bow. As they exchanged air kisses, I realized that my teeth were beginning to hurt from so many darlings. Stepping back, I gave the senator a little wave. "I'll be in touch."

Casting a speculative look at Gareth Swenson, Neal pinched my arm above the elbow in a surprisingly territorial gesture. "Let me get you something to drink, P.J. I don't know about you, but I'm starving," he muttered as he guided me through the throngs in the direction of the buffet table.

Grabbing a handful of shrimp, I popped one in my mouth and dipped another in some red sauce. As Neal reached for a napkin, I noticed his watch. It was thick and gold and had a little crown-like logo at twelve o'clock. In fact, he was a real snappy dresser, all in all. His tux fit like it had been personally tailored, and the watch must have cost mega-bucks. Probably standard dress for a lawyer with Meredith, Geitrich, and Smeal, which put him out of my league. Still, nothing ventured, as my mother used to say.

"What's your connection with Marguerite Sutherland?" I said, as he handed me the napkin.

"What's yours?"

"You go first."

Rolling his eyes, Neal took a sip of wine. "Some of the firm's clients have interests in common."

"Such as . . . ?"

"Do you know that guy? The one who introduced you to the senator?" A muscle at the side of Neal's face started jumping as if he were trying to suppress a pang of jealousy. In my dreams.

"Yeah, from back in college, although I can't figure how he got hooked up with a legislator from Florida." I took a sip of wine.

"Politics, I suspect. She's a party loyalist, and I hear Gareth Swenson is on the short list for a big job at DEA."

The news made me swallow wrong, and I began coughing.

"Hey, take it easy." Neal patted me on the back till the attack subsided. "Swenson used to work for us."

"Really."

"Yeah. Wasn't going to make partner, so they let him go."

Harsh. But then wasn't that typical of lawyers?

"What's your interest in Senator Sutherland?" he asked, snagging another shrimp.

"Work." I reached for a cheese stick and popped it into my mouth, nearly choking when I realized Marguerite Sutherland wouldn't be the sort ever to set foot in a place like Money-Source. "Uh, I'm freelancing—sort of a favor for a friend of mine who's involved with a nonprofit over on Clay Street, and they hired me to, uh, document something that would be useful to them."

"Ah. Vivian Remington's organization."

"You know her too?"

"Why yes. I've been advising her."

Who didn't he advise? Except for my uncle, who could hardly afford the stratospheric rates charged by a firm like Meredith, Geitrich, and Smeal, most of the firm's clients were huge corporations more than willing to pay whatever it took to find— or create, through discreet lobbying—loopholes in securities and corporate laws. So what was Neal doing working for a do-good nonprofit like the Wetland Protectors Alliance?

"Aren't you, uh—?"

"Too expensive?" He laughed. "I figured that's what you were thinking. But the firm likes to take on a fair portion of pro bono stuff, and I like working with Vivian. She's really amazing."

My eyes morphed from gray to green as I snagged a slice of rare roast beef and a tiny roll. "You don't need to hover around me like a chaperone. I can circulate perfectly well on my own."

"What if I'm hanging around because you look particularly fetching?" The dimple in his cheek flashed in tandem with the sparkle in his baby blues. "You know, I think this is the first time I've ever seen you all dressed—"

"It's not my thing," I explained. My face was probably as red as the cocktail sauce.

"Yes, well . . . does your uncle know you're here?"

What? Did I look under age? Through the red haze clouding my vision, I struggled for control. Then I caught a glimpse of the Florida senator heading for the door. "I believe Ms. Sutherland is about to make her departure, so pardon me if I say a few words of farewell." I spun on my heel, nearly ripping the hem out of my dress, stumbled briefly, and made a beeline for the spot where I had seen the woman disappear around the corner into what probably was the ladies' room.

Sutherland was standing at the sink as I walked in, steam still pouring from my ears. "Hello again," I said, pulling a lipstick from my handbag. My hand was shaking so badly, any attempt to actually apply the stuff would have been disastrous. "A real mob out there, huh?"

She laughed. "Yeah. I hardly got two bites to eat. Which is just as well." She bent down and removed first one and then the other gold lamé sandal. "These things are killing me. Why aren't women allowed to wear sensible shoes to these affairs like the men are?"

"Good question." I pushed an errant strand of hair behind my ear, wondering if a darker shade of lipstick might add a few years. "You know, I'd really like to photograph you—maybe sometime when the legislature's not in session?" We were interrupted by the chimes on her cell.

"Yes?" she said curtly. "Oh God. These guys are supposed to be smart, but what are the signs?" She paused briefly. "No. I'm not asking you. Anyway, why are you calling at this hour? I told you not to bother me when—Okay. Well, maybe I did say that, but you should've had the sense to . . . Look, now is not the time. Just get rid of anythi—" She stopped, looking at me. "I'll get back to you later." The crease between her brows deepened as she snapped the phone shut and shook her head. "Try to get competent help in this town."

I nodded in what I hoped came across as sincere sympathy. "We were talking about taking your picture. Could we get together sometime soon?"

"Do you have a card?"

I pretended to fumble around in my handbag, and then I shrugged, giving her my best ditsy blond bimbo smile. "I must have left them at home. How about I give you a call?"

"If you like." Opening her tiny sequin-studded evening bag, the senator pulled out a thin gold compact and began to powder her nose.

I reached for a tissue and blotted my lips. "I'll be in touch sometime next week then."

"Whatever." Snapping the bag shut, Sutherland slipped her feet back into the sandals, spun around, and headed for the door. A toss of her head sent the diamond hair clip flying over the wall of the nearby stall where it hit something metal and plopped into the water.

"Oh!" I said, but the senator was already out the door. I noticed that she'd forgotten to leave a dollar bill in the plate for the attendant. No doubt her handbag was too small to hold cash once she'd stuffed the cell phone into it.

I was big enough to seize the opportunity, however. After putting one of Alicia's dollar bills in the plate, I went into the stall, retrieved the clip, rinsed it carefully, and dried it with a paper towel. Then I slipped it into my purse and headed for the front entrance where I saw Senator Sutherland with a large fur coat draped, lining side out, over one arm. It made a nice contrast with the old gold color of her dress. And, yes, there was Alicia's guy with the camera trained right where it should be.

Sutherland was smiling up at a tall, distinguished gray-haired gentleman in a black tie. He might have been Mr. Governor himself, for all I knew. With a bawdy laugh, he pinched her on the ass and winked. Instead of slapping his impertinent face, the senator giggled and playfully pushed his hand away. "Shall we go, darling?" And there I stood, my mouth agape. Was this how our elected officials comported themselves in public?

"Wait!" I called out. "I think you lost something." Grabbing a fistful of skirt, I dashed forward. I should have known better than to run across a marble floor in brand new shoes, for I lost my footing and began to skid. A hand grabbed my elbow, and I turned to find Gareth Swenson smiling down at me, his eyebrows raised in mock concern.

"You don't have to tackle that man to get his attention."

I could feel my face heat up as I shook his hand off. "I was trying to catch *her.*"

"Well, I happen to know they're heading over to the Palm. Shall I take you there?"

On a cold day in hell. On the other hand . . . "Actually, I could use a bite to eat."

January 21, 2003

"I'm in jail."

"Uh-huh. And I'm in bed. So why are you calling at this ungodly hour?"

"No. Really, Alicia, I'm not kidding."

"My God. What happened?"

"They're charging me with breaking and entering and destruction of property."

"I'll get you a lawyer."

"Thanks, but you need to call Gareth Swenson first."

"Can't that wait? You'll be out on bail as soon as the lawyer can arrange things."

"Listen, Alicia. Call Gareth. Tell him I have pictures" (mentally cross fingers that this is still true) "that I took while I was at his place. Incriminating pictures."

"Of what?"

"He'll know what I'm talking about."

"Does this have anything to do with—?"

"Gotta go. They're telling me my time is up."

"Take care of yourself, girl. What an awful place to be!"

No kidding. Her cellmate, a drunk prostitute, throws up all over her feet and doesn't even apologize. But at least they let her clean off the vomit and move her to an empty cell where she stares at the ceiling, wondering how on earth she's going to explain herself to Uncle Alex.

"He's asked them to drop the charges," says the ruddy-faced lawyer the next morning as the jailer hands her the tray of belongings that include her watch, a toothbrush, and the disposable camera.

"If I were you, young lady, I'd get some counseling on anger management."

That's the least of her concerns. Right now, she needs to find a higher-salaried job so she can pay off the lawyer's fee and not have to explain to Uncle Alex why she needs more than tuition assistance for the upcoming semester. Worse, she now has an arrest record. The only good thing is that Gareth did the right thing for once. No, make that the prudent thing.

Chapter Six

What was I doing? I hated Gareth Swenson. Back when I knew him, he'd been a liar and a cheat. And those were his good qualities. Of course, that didn't say much about my judgment, but I was young. In addition to despising the man driving me to the Palm, I was also furious at Neal Patterson. "Does your uncle know you're here?" Sheesh.

Then there was Alicia. Tonight, when we met up back in Annapolis, I would make it totally clear I was quitting. I'd played along with the Washington soirée idea because . . . well, because a girl likes to dress up every now and then (especially when somebody else is paying for the outfit), and I didn't get too many—make that *any*—opportunities to play Cinderella.

"You seem anxious, P.J. Something wrong?"

"I'm fine," I said, recrossing my legs. What was in it for him, playing chauffeur? Surely Gareth knew it would take more than delivering me into Marguerite Sutherland's august presence to even the score between us—although it would help a teeny bit. Maybe he had some business of his own to transact.

As we circled the block looking for a parking space, he caught me up on his life, how he'd traveled around Europe and the Far East for a while, cadging food and lodging from others like him who weren't quite ready to capitulate to the Man, and then deciding that beating the Man at his own game would be more lucrative. He'd gone to law school at UVA, no doubt financing it from the profits on his undergrad sideline, and that's where he'd met Vivian Remington.

So, at least that part of Vivian's story was true—unless Alicia had also enlisted Gareth in her project. Well, whatever. After tonight, I'd be out of it.

We arrived at the Palm right on the heels of Marguerite Sutherland and her distinguished-looking escort. But the gods of luck deserted us at the door once the haughty maître d' learned we hadn't booked a reservation. He shook his head when Gareth flashed a couple of twenties, and that's when I noticed the raised eyebrows from a few of the female patrons as Sutherland's friend helped her out of the spotted fur coat and handed it to the coatroom attendant. For a number of reasons—number one, political, and number two, its modern cousin political correctness—Washington was not a fur coat town. In fact, Sutherland's coat looked so Hollywood fifties, some of the observers were stifling giggles.

Thwarted in our efforts to rendezvous with the Florida Senator, Gareth and I headed to I Ricci across the street where the menu was so pricey, I decided I'd limit myself to a small dessert. We were seated near the window, where I had a bird's-eye view of the comings and goings at the Palm.

As soon as the waiter had taken our orders, I asked Gareth how he knew Marguerite Sutherland.

"Pure politics, my dear. She's got contacts on the Hill that I need to cultivate."

"Isn't she just a state senator?"

Leaning forward, he lowered his voice to a loud whisper. I could smell wine on his breath. "Don't let her hear you use the word 'just.' That woman has more irons in the political fire here than Karl Rove did during the last administration."

"I hate Washington."

He laughed. "So what's new with you, P.J.? I understand your marriage didn't last too long."

"About as long as Annapolis did as the nation's capital."

"Ah. Too bad. He run out on you?"

I shrugged, feeling my face flush. "We all make mistakes. I should've known better."

"Ain't that the truth." Gareth leaned back and tapped his long narrow fingers on the tablecloth. "Wasn't he a sailor?"

"Yes. Bobby Crane. You might remember him from college. Majored in drinking."

"Better than the stuff I was into."

No kidding. I found myself tensing to fight off the charm Gareth had been dishing out since we walked in. "And you swear you're out of it for good?"

"Cross my heart." Taking a sip of his coffee, he raised his eyebrows and grimaced. "Luckily, I wised up fairly early. Some of my, uh, partners didn't do so well."

"As in jail?"

He nodded. "Worse, even. One of them died. An overdose."

Considering the number of useless drug deaths that were probably on Gareth's conscience, I couldn't bring myself to say anything sympathetic, so I turned my attention to the tall, well-dressed couple who were jaywalking across the street in front of me, headed into the Palm. I recognized the handsome gent in the tux. He was holding the arm of the Snow White knock-off who'd kissed him at the reception. "Oh," I said, as they strolled under the awning and entered the restaurant.

"Say, isn't that the fellow who snatched you away from me earlier this evening? Don't tell me he was your date."

"Hardly." My face was warm again. "He's an Annapolis lawyer I just happen to know." I watched, fascinated, as the waiter finished flambéing Gareth's concoction and handed it to him with a flourish. It looked yummy. "Okay," I said, the prelims dispensed with, "What are you up to these days?"

"Mostly knocking on doors," he said. "Marguerite's helping

me—Well, you know how that goes. She's so busy, I need to be sure I stay on her radar. We're okay for now, financially, but my wife—"

"You're married?" I put my coffee cup down with a clink. "Any kids?"

"Not yet," he said. "She's, uh, well actually, she's battling cancer."

"Oh. That must be hard on—"

He held up a hand to silence me. "Not nearly as hard on me as it is on her. She's in remission right now, but the doctors aren't real optimistic, and the bills for this designer drug she takes are killing us."

"And you're unemployed?"

"Nearly. I'm doing a couple of things for Marguerite. Just helping out. And, like I said, I've got something lined up in the Obama administration. All it'll take is a word or two in the right ears on the Hill, and I'm on my way." He leaned forward, placing his hand on top of mine. "If somebody ever got their hands on those photos you took back in Charlottesville, it would kill any chance I have for that job." He paused, staring across the room. "But worse, that would mean I couldn't afford Sarah's drugs."

"I can't give you the pix, Gareth, mostly because I don't—" I forgot what I was going to say as I spied Alicia and her camera-toting sidekick standing on the sidewalk across the street. "Oh!" I said. "There's a friend of mine. Haven't seen her in ages." Placing my napkin beside the plate, I stood up. "Do you mind? I'll only be a sec." Without waiting for his reply, I sped through the door and crossed the street.

The crease between the brows, the impatient, side-to-side wave of a hand. I was not to approach. Well, tough. I threw my arms around her. "Alicia! How long has it been? You look terrific!"

Swiping her index finger across her neck, Alicia signaled to the camera guy to stop filming. "This isn't part of the story, Ramón." She pulled me under the shelter of the Palm's green awning. "What the hell are you up to, P.J.?"

"You tell me," I said. "I think I need to see the script."

"There isn't one. This is a documentary."

"No," I said, tapping my foot. "It's a set-up. How many rocks did you have to turn over before you uncovered Gareth Swenson?"

Her eyes widened and her head jerked backward. "What? You think I somehow put him together with our client?"

"Absolutely. You couldn't get any responses to that stupid ad in the Crabwrapper, so you enlisted Gareth and then Remington—or vice versa, maybe."

Alicia crossed her arms. "Never happened. I don't know Vivian Remington from shit. You're so paranoid, P.J. Ever since—"

"Ever since you got this ridiculous idea, I've been feeling snookered. I won't be a pawn in whatever game you're playing, Alicia."

"You can't quit now!"

"Oh, yeah?" I snorted. "Watch me." I spun on my heel and headed back to I Ricci where Gareth proceeded to capitalize on my brief absence by extracting a promise to have lunch the next time he was in Annapolis. I found myself hoping for a blizzard followed by an ice storm that would shut down traffic between the two cities for weeks, if not until the first spring thaw.

Like a surprising number of state capitals in America, Annapolis is small. Its population barely exceeds 35,000, although growth has speeded up immensely because of the city's proximity to Washington and the appeal of all that waterfront acreage on the Severn and South Rivers, not to mention the Chesapeake Bay. By the year 2050, America's sailing capital will most likely be nothing more than one of many suburbs of greater Baltimore-Washington. Only Washington, being the most important capital in the most important country in the universe, would have to come first. Then people would probably start calling it D.C. East—which reminded me that I was still feeling deceived.

I loved Alicia. Except for the incident in high school (still subject to doubt), she'd been loyal, generous, supportive, and a lot of fun to be around. So maybe it was me. Maybe I was overly sensitive, unwilling to take the big risks necessary to rise above the daily grind. After all, what harm was in it? Leaving aside my suspicions about Alicia's role in things, as far as Vivian Remington knew, I was a legitimate private investigator. She hadn't asked to examine my credentials (fake though they might be), so caveat emptor, right? Her story checked out so far—at least in terms of the ocelot coat and how she knew Gareth. Either that, or Marguerite Sutherland was also part of the game. Naw. I'd checked her out on the Internet. She was indeed a Florida state senator, complete with a photo closely resembling the woman I'd just met. All I had to do was tell Remington I'd seen Sutherland wearing the coat, collect my pay (which Alicia said she would donate to charity), and spend the next sixty hours getting caught up on my real job.

Traffic was light, so I took the car up to ninety and set the cruise control. What are luxury cars for if not to see how fast they can go? I'd thrown the killer shoes into the backseat, and the radio was blasting out a country song about growing up poor and making it good by being bad. I sang along with Reba, figuring I could audition as her next backup if I got in enough practice. Somewhere along the way, it occurred to me that it just might be illegal to drive barefoot even if my foot wasn't touching the pedal. The way my luck had been going, I'd get pulled over for speeding and then thrown in the slammer for Driving While Shoeless. I felt a flush creep up my neck as I pictured the expression on my uncle's face when he got the one phone call the cops would allow, once I'd been arrested. Better to drive conservatively, I told myself, and slowed down to a sedate seventy, the unofficial speed limit on that portion of Route 50.

When I got home to my one-bedroom apartment on the ground floor of a row of not-yet-renovated townhouses off Murray Avenue, I noticed that I had indeed torn the hem on my dress and that it had a greasy splotch right on the midriff where my stomach must have brushed across some kind of mayonnaise-based sauce when I was reaching for the roast beef.

I'd been lucky to find the place, which was just the right size for somebody my height and not much bigger. Covering an area equal to the entrance hall at Alicia's Severn River estate, the living room held only enough space for a beige Naugahyde sofa that Uncle Alex had given to me plus a TV in the corner. The dining room was just a passage to the kitchen where I could simultaneously wash my hands and grab food from the fridge without leaning in either direction. The remainder of the space held the bathroom with its pantry-sized shower stall and my bedroom, which was big enough for a double bed, a dresser, and a chair.

I threw the sandals in the general direction of the closet, draped the dress over the chair, and fell into bed. Two minutes later, I got up, removed the earrings and bracelet that Alicia had let me borrow, pulled all the pins out of my hair, brushed my teeth like a good girl, and donned the teddy bear t-shirt I always slept in. On Monday, I would call Senator Sutherland's office and arrange to return the diamond hair clip. Then I would call Alicia, apologize for panicking, and tell her I was ready to get back in the saddle. Thirty minutes later, I wished I had laid in a supply of sleeping pills because all I could think about was Neal Patterson treating me like a precocious teenager. I couldn't help wishing I could be there when he told my uncle he'd seen me in Washington. I couldn't help wishing he didn't have a girlfriend, either. The man might be a patronizing jerk, but it would still be heavenly to gaze into those blue, blue eyes and kiss those scrumptious lips while running my fingers through his hair.

Okay. I was horny. I'd had a couple of amorous adventures since the divorce from Bobby, but otherwise I'd been living the life of a nun. Alicia had tried fixing me up with guys she knew, but I just couldn't seem to connect with polo players and yachtsmen on any level other than the obvious—and who needed that? I couldn't afford to move in those circles anyway. Which made me wonder if Neal Patterson didn't also own a sixty-foot yacht and a string of ponies. I could ask my uncle, except it would tip him off and before I could say "get off my case," he'd be inviting Neal out to the house on Tuesdays when I usually cooked dinner for Uncle Alex and his poker buddies. I shuddered, pulling the comforter up to my chin, thankful that tomorrow was Sunday. I would sleep in and then do a load of laundry, maybe even buy some groceries. Oh. And try to remember where I'd stashed those photos of Gareth Swenson.

Before long, I found myself standing in front of a bank of microphones telling the world about Gareth Swenson's dirty little secret and how he shouldn't be elected president. "I've got proof!" I held up the photographs I'd taken all those years ago. But the crowd was turning away, bored and restless for some real news. Only Gareth Swenson remained, a knowing smirk on his face. "You need to learn how to manage your anger," he said, disappearing into the fog-like mist as I poled the wide-bottomed, shallow boat, drifting through a tree-filled swamp, making my way past Spanish moss that floated across my face like icy rain. I could barely see where I was going, and my hands were so cold, I was afraid I'd drop the pole. I kept thinking it might snow any minute. Except, even in my dream, I knew it didn't snow in the Everglades.

I sat up.

CHAPTER SEVEN

The breeze stirred the curtains at the street-level window, which would have been fine except it was February, and no way would I have left a window open with the outside temperature in the low twenties. My tendency when frightened was to freeze as though if I didn't move or breathe, an intruder wouldn't notice I was there. I heard no sounds of movement. After about five minutes of a pep talk designed to self-motivate, I slowly slid open the drawer in the nightstand, removed the .38 special that I didn't have a permit for, and sat there wondering what to do. I didn't want to open the chamber to check for bullets in case the intruder could hear it click, yet without bullets, the gun wasn't going to be much protection.

Still no sounds, other than my own shaky breathing, which was far too loud. I tiptoed to the doorway, peeked around it, and saw nothing unusual in the hallway. Then I picked up one of the sandals I'd worn to the reception. Those stiletto heels had to be good for something besides foot malformation.

Walking near the wall so the floor wouldn't creak, I made my way down the icy hallway to the kitchen, where I saw the door that led to my postage stamp-sized patio standing open in the predawn light. Was someone out there still? I counted to a hundred before it seemed safe to approach the doorway. I took a cautious peek and immediately noticed several large footprints on the damp flagstones, heading toward the wall separating my little piece of paradise from the neighbor's. Boosting myself up onto the wall, I saw the same footprints crossing the neighbor's patio. Okay. Whoever had been in my apartment was now gone, but when had he been there and why?

After shutting and locking the door, I looked around the closet-sized kitchen. Not a thing had been moved, including yesterday's spoon and coffee mug, still sitting in the sink where I had left them. In the living room where I only occasionally used the sofa, yesterday's *Baltimore Sun* was strewn across the threadbare carpet in pretty much the same way I'd left it. (Yes, I was approaching thirty, but I still had to read the comics lying on my stomach on the floor.)

Back in my bedroom, I noticed that nothing, including Alicia's jewelry and the senator's diamond hair clip, had been stolen. I shut and latched the window. Opening the chamber of the .38, I saw that it was empty, just as my uncle had taught me. "You don't want some intruder grabbing a loaded weapon before you can get to it, do you?" he'd said. He knew a lot about guns because he'd started his career repossessing cars in some of Baltimore's roughest neighborhoods—not that he'd actually carried a gun then, or so he claimed.

The box of ammo was still at the back of the drawer. I put one bullet in the chamber, just in case the intruder returned, and then made a mental note to visit a firing range sometime in the near future. Oh. And, before that, clean the gun.

I couldn't go back to sleep. Adrenaline-pumping visions of Neal Patterson had been replaced by adrenaline-pumping thoughts of an intruder invading my space and rummaging through my belongings while I'd been sleeping. Or had the intruder paid a visit while I was chatting up the Florida state senator in Washington? I'd been so eager to exchange the fairy godmother's evening dress for more comfortable sleepwear that I hadn't really paid much attention to windows or doors.

On Sunday I went out and bought a heavy deadbolt for the

patio door and a broomstick that I could wedge across the bedroom window to keep anyone from entering silently. Then I headed downtown to the tiny office that Alicia had rented in the Banner Building on West Street.

It wasn't a large building, maybe six stories at most. The words "BANNER BUILDING" were etched in stone over the entrance, and that meant no new owner had a prayer of putting his own name up. That was why the building seemed so sad and dejected—like the good ol' days were never going to come back, so why bother getting all dressed up? The dingy stone facade needed a good scrubbing. Ditto the windows—inside and out. The lobby featured a threadbare carpet that had once probably been blue but was now nearly black with grime. The place looked like it hadn't seen a vacuum since the repeal of Prohibition. Near the elevator, which I would never use for personal reasons, stood the lobby's only piece of furniture—one of those floor-model ashtrays full of sand, probably dating from yesteryear when all of the building's tenants had been cigar-smoking men. I wondered how often the thing was emptied. It could probably be measured in months, rather than days.

I hoofed it up the stairs to the fourth-floor office. It was im-maculate. The problem was that Alicia had deliberately decorated "the set" to look like a pigsty. Now, all the yellow legal pads were stacked neatly in the middle of the desk. The coffee cup I'd been using no longer rested in the ring created by what appeared to be years of coffee spills on the desk's scuffed wooden surface. Instead, it had been rinsed out and turned upside down on a paper towel. Did paper towels even exist back then? Alicia would be furious. She'd carefully researched every detail of thirties-era offices. Somebody had put the covers back onto the vintage adding machine, Underwood typewriter, and ditto machine. Well, maybe she'd forgotten about the cleaning crew. They probably cleaned every office in the building, regardless of how weird it looked. Note to Alicia: Buy a deadbolt.

I ripped the cover off the typewriter, rolled a sheet of paper into it, and began to type, "The quick brown fox jumped over the . . ." What was it? Something with a Z in it, I was sure. But that was just fooling around. I'd come here to give Alicia a peace offering.

I crumpled the paper and tossed it into the wire mesh basket. Rolling a fresh sheet beneath the platen (would she be bitchy and ask where's the carbon copy?), I started typing. By the time I finished—far later than I had planned—my fingers were aching, and the typewriter eraser was only a nub. The resulting product wasn't beautiful—some of my erasures had put holes in the paper—but it would do. It would have to. I must have broken the typewriter. Whenever I hit a key, it made only a very faint impression.

Flexing my fingers, I heaved a sigh and called Alicia. Not home. Not answering her cell. Damn. I called again to leave a message, and her mother answered.

"Well, hello, P.J. We haven't seen you lately. Why don't you come for supper?"

"I, uh, well, actually, that would be nice. What time?"

We fixed a time, and I put the phone down. Shit. I loved Alicia's mom, but she was extremely challenged in the culinary department, and Sundays were the cook's day off. Oh well. I should return Alicia's jewelry, plus we needed some face-time.

And that's what I got, plus several drops of saliva as she spewed venom at me. "If it weren't for my mother liking you so much, I would have canceled the fucking invitation," she yelled. "What makes you think I want to see you? Do you have any idea how much work I've put into this project? No. Of course you don't. It's all about you all the time. You'd think I asked you to sell your first-born, or commit a fucking crime, the way you're carrying on. But, no. All I wanted was to give you a chance to do something more interesting—more fun, for God's sake—than that disgusting job you have, snatching money away from people who can barely afford to put food on the table."

Face crimson, she paused to catch her breath. I handed her the results of my typing exercise. "Here. I thought you'd want this since I've been thinking about the whole thing, and I guess I just want to say, if you'll still have me, I'm game."

"Huh." Alicia plopped into a chair and began to read:

REPORT

At the request of Vivian Remington, I attended a black-tie reception in Washington, DC. on Satruday, to ascertain whether ~~she~~ a Florida state senator and member of Remington's employer's board of directors might have ~~s~~ in her possession an ocelot coat that Remington alleges was stolen from a demonstration she had given to show travelers the kinds of goods that are illegal to import from abroad.

The senator, a ~~a~~ woman by the name of ~~Marguettie~~ Marguerite Sutherland, was wearing the coat, according to my own observation. I shall report this to the client on Monday, at which point the matter should be settled.

Respectfully Submitted,

P.J. Smythe, Investigator

"Yes!" Alicia laughed, her fist in the air. "This is good. Did you make a carbon copy?"

See? Never enough. I rolled my eyes. "You're lucky I didn't do this on my computer at work."

"Well, doesn't matter. You need to redo it for Vivian Remington and give it to her on Monday. Let me know the minute you've set up the meeting, because I might be able to sneak somebody in there to film it. Oh. And, after you've retyped your report, give me the carbon so I can scan it for a close-up."

"How about I do it on a computer in a typeface that looks like Pica?"

She crimped a corner of her mouth. "No. I want to be as authentic as we can. I've had enough trouble—"

"Oh, yeah. I meant to tell you. The Banner Building's cleaning crew must have added your office to their list. When I got there this morning, it was all straightened up."

"As in . . . ?"

"Well, the writing pads were all in a neat stack on my desk. And my coffee cup had been washed and placed on a paper towel. And the machines were all covered up. Plus, I think they might've washed some of the grime off the window. It seemed brighter. And there's a clean desk blotter . . . what? You think I'm making this up?"

"There is no cleaning crew at the Banner Building. I looked into it, just to be sure. I was told there aren't enough tenants to justify the expense."

It was my turn to collapse into a chair. "That can't be. And don't look at me that way. You know how much I hate housekeeping. Although . . ."

"What? Spit it out."

"Somebody broke into my apartment. They didn't take anything, but they left my bedroom window open, and I found footprints on my patio."

"Weird. Really weird." She sat up as the bell rang, summoning us to the dining room. "But probably coincidental. Definitely coincidental."

"Or you just want me to think so."

She shot me a sideways look. "Get off, P.J. How many times do I have to tell you: There. Is. No. Conspiracy. I am not setting you up."

We seated ourselves at the kitchen end of a mahogany table the size of a tennis court and took turns smiling politely at Mrs.

Ritchie, dishing out the chitchat, sipping our wine, sampling the cardboard-tasting tomatoes drenched in olive oil, and in general behaving as one would expect of well-brought-up young ladies.

The minute Mrs. Ritchie disappeared into the kitchen to get the main course, Alicia continued as though she'd never been interrupted. "Look. You live in a dicey neighborhood. Maybe some low-life found the window open and—"

"No way would I do that. Not in these temperatures!"

"Well, whatever. But they didn't find anything worth stealing."

"Oh yeah?"

Mrs. Ritchie returned, bearing a platter of chicken covered in a creamy sauce that failed to hide tiny dribbles of reddish juice, ominous signs that the meat was way underdone. Stifling a groan, I selected the smallest piece, hoping it would be more thoroughly cooked, and then nearly gagged on the sauce, which I'd assumed would be savory and turned out to be sweet, like the kind of white sauce you serve with gingerbread.

"Oh, you young women. You're always dieting," said Alicia's mother when she noticed us both rearranging the food on our plates. "Well, I was there once too, you know. I suppose you're not going to join me in some dessert?"

"Just coffee," said Alicia. "You, P.J.?"

Since I'd just (sort of) had dessert, I nodded and smiled. "I'd love dessert, Mrs. R., but can't do it tonight. A girl's gotta be careful." Not.

The door swung closed behind Mrs. Ritchie's back. "Your studs and the diamond bracelet were sitting there in plain view, along with—" I stopped. Why did Alicia have to know about Senator Sutherland's diamond hair clip?

"Then how do you explain it? I bet you left the window open."

I knew I hadn't. It was hard enough to keep the place warm, and I certainly could not afford a higher electricity bill.

Back in my apartment, I locked the door and checked that the broomstick was still wedged across the window. A logical person would notify the police. I punched in the numbers and then hung up the phone. What could I report? Somebody had been inside my apartment, but nothing had been stolen. Somebody had straightened up my so-called office, although that was really Alicia's problem and clearly not a crime. As for the two things happening on the same weekend, I told myself not to get too worked up about it, if only myself would pay attention.

CHAPTER EIGHT

There should be a law somewhere that says if you're stuck in a job that sucks, you at least do not have to endure things like freezing rain, black ice, burnt coffee, or Mondays. Alicia's remarks last evening while she'd been "venting" were right on target—which was why I hadn't bothered to defend myself.

I slid into work, hating life and feeling sorry for myself. Not that anyone cared. I pitched my coffee down the sink in the restroom and stuck my tongue out at the mirror image of myself. "You think you got it bad, girl? What about the poor people you're about to beat up on?"

At least one thing I'd done right was not to wreck my uncle's wheels on the way to work.

"You have a good time?" he asked as I handed over the keys.

"Fine," I said. "Thanks for lending me the car. It was great."

"Better than that bolt bucket you call wheels."

"Gets me where I need to go," I said, like I always do whenever he disses my car. "Uncle Alex, do you know anybody who fixes typewriters?"

"We got rid of those Selectrics in the eighties."

"No. It belongs to Alicia. I ate over at her house last night, and her mother was telling me one of the charities they support uses them, and they're down to the last one that actually types."

He rummaged through his Rolodex, pulled out a card, and handed it to me. "Tony will fix anything—computers, cars, stereos, you name it."

"Thanks." I left without telling him about the break-ins. Partly it was because it had been a no harm, no foul situation—except for scaring me half to death. But mostly it was because Uncle Alex would want to check it out himself, and then he'd discover what we were up to in the Banner Building and he'd go ballistic about the time I must be wasting—time that should be spent getting caught up on my work.

Skip tracing for MoneySource involved spending a lot of time on the telephone and the Internet, trying to track down deadbeats. It was unethical, and in some cases illegal, to misrepresent myself. And that's why I'd mastered the fine art of toeing the line, even touching it, but never once foot-faulting. That's what made me the most successful tracer at Money-Source. And no one questioned my methods. Not even Uncle Alex.

I never actually said I was a police officer or anything as precise as that. I preferred to convey a less threatening impression—someone from the unemployment office or the phone company. "We've got a man coming down the block to upgrade the phone lines," I'd tell the deadbeat's neighbor. "We need to get inside the house next door to disconnect some things before we begin the work. No one seems to be answering. Do you suppose they're not at home?"

And bingo. The neighborly neighbor would give me the guy's work number.

The singing experience I'd gained in college had given me great breath control and the ability to pitch my voice from high and whiney to low and authoritative, depending on the circumstances. I could also do a fairly credible Bal'mer accent, courtesy of Uncle Alex, and a passable Alabama drawl, thanks to a succession of college roommates who'd hailed from the Deep South.

My reward? More skips to trace. It was beginning to be a

drag, even though figuring out how to find the losers had always had a certain element of challenge to it. I'd learned to think like a deadbeat. Like the time I discovered that Eugene Richard Hobson, a ninety-day delinquent on a MoneySource car loan, was the same person as Richard E. Hobson, who'd just borrowed money for a deep freeze from The Cash Store in Baltimore. They had solid information about Hobson's employment as an off-the-books cabbie. Without his car, Hobson could earn no income, and that meant he wouldn't be able to pay off any of his debts, even if he managed to morph his identity into H. Eugene Richards.

I knew all about new identities, having once upon a time called myself Paula Jo. You can't help walking different—in my case, as Paula Jo, I strutted like Paris Hilton—and talking different—pitching my voice lower and adding a tiny southern drawl. It only lasted a few months. Nobody was hurt. And Uncle Alex never found out.

I flagged the Hobson file for my uncle's attention. Maybe he'd try to negotiate a reduced payment schedule with the flake—even though it would involve paying more interest. And, yes, that did produce a tiny twinge of regret somewhere deep in my conscience. My uncle would have said, "He shouldn'a bought a freezer till he paid off the car."

The only problem with that logic was that I knew what it was like to be at the sales end of the finance business since my uncle had once given me a job collecting payments from walk-ins. "Always ask them if they need more money," he'd say.

Who doesn't need more money? I'd hated soliciting the customers. I knew they could barely afford payments on their current loan, so why increase it and make the payments higher? When my uncle found out that I never solicited as I'd been instructed, he quickly moved me off the front desk and began to teach me the rudiments of skip tracing. "Their signature on the loan means they've promised to pay it off," he told me, "so don't get all sappy on me when they break that promise. And don't you ever forget that I am running a business, not a charity."

Not for the first time, I found myself trying to figure out how I could liberate myself from having to work for my uncle, to whom I owed much more than the job that paid my rent. My mother Rhoda, Uncle Alex's younger sister, died of ovarian cancer when I was fourteen, leaving me an orphan in his care. Obviously, I'd had a father, but his name had never crossed my mother's lips, and I knew nothing about him. Uncle Alex was the one who'd bandaged my skinned knees. He taught me how to ride a bicycle and was now teaching me how to pick locks (although he wasn't aware of it, since it was mostly me sneaking a peek over his shoulder whenever he deigned to let me tag along on a repo). Some of his gray hairs, I am sure, grew in following several near-death experiences teaching me how to drive, and the bags under his eyes surely resulted from a couple of sleepless nights after I got a two-day suspension in high school, the one and only time I'd been caught toilet-papering the boys' gym. (Tom Eldridge, who'd done the same thing to the girls' gym, skated.)

A grateful niece would never let the work pile up the way I had. I'd wasted a large part of the morning playing telephone tag with Vivian Remington, opting finally for an e-mail, the response to which was automated, announcing that she was away from the office and not back until Tuesday. "No excuse now," I muttered to myself as I eyeballed the stack of skip traces on my desk. It was so massive it practically buried the telephone. In one pile, I put the traces that simply needed a friendly nudge in the form of a suggestion to get that payment in or face the consequences. In another pile, I put the hopeless cases—the actual physical skips who'd disappeared from the address on the loan agreement (if, indeed, that had ever really been their residence) and no longer worked where our loan folks had verified employment when the loan was handed out.

Just as I'd suspected, several of the deadbeats in the first pile happened to be home and answering the phone. It was called unemployment. Not good news for collecting any money from the poor folk, but at least they knew what they had to do if they wanted to keep the bedroom suite, plasma TV, or whatever. Most of them did, it seemed, and, by the end of the morning, there were more files in the out box than in the "to-do" pile. I'd even managed to forget about the strange happenings over the weekend.

But enough of the good works. It was time for lunch. I went to McDonald's where I devoured a Big Mac, fries, and a vanilla shake. As I carried my tray away, the woman behind me in line said to her friend, "Look what all that skinny girl ordered. I do that, I be big as a house."

"Girl, you lookin' that way now," said her friend.

Was it my fault? I probably had one of those revved-up metabolisms that burned off fat early in life but returned later in the form of killer high blood pressure. Besides, I didn't usually get three squares, so whenever I did eat, I made up for lost time.

Back in my cubicle, I pulled out the file for Samuel Rayfield Lewis, discharged army sergeant, father of five children with three different mothers, borrower of four thousand dollars to consolidate his debts, and now missing from the address on the loan agreement. The collateral was a 1995 Yamaha motorcycle on which Lewis lavished more attention than any woman he'd ever hooked up with. No big surprise there. He was four months in arrears, nearing the embarrassing-for-me "write-off" stage. I figured he was once again unemployed.

I'd discovered that, instead of debt consolidation, Lewis had used the money to buy jewelry so that he could impress the woman who would probably soon be the mother of his sixth child. Once the Internet coughed up information about the whereabouts of Lewis's latest lady friend, I could access my own e-mail, not that I ever got much other than personal stuff. But maybe there would be something from Neal Patterson to cheer me up—a message telling me how, after seeing me last Saturday, he wondered if we might meet for coffee. No. Have dinner and then catch a movie. Except, I hadn't bothered to do the laundry and had nothing clean, let alone sexy, to wear. I'd have to go shopping. But I couldn't afford to go shopping . . .

I opened the Lewis file and reviewed its contents. The last time Sam had disappeared owing us only five hundred on a personal note, he'd kept in touch with his woman by placing ads in the personals along the lines of, "Mature SBPM seeks maternal SBF," and then a telephone number. Obviously, he didn't mind fielding calls from interested SBFs, but like a lot of deadbeats, he'd been stupid enough to use the number of the pay phone in back of the school where he had work as a part-time custodian. All I'd had to do that time was tell Jake and Rake, my uncle's muscle, where they'd be likely to find him and do whatever they could to persuade him to get current on his payments.

Okay. The conditions of my employment at MoneySource were definitely constricting. Despite my successes at finding deadbeats, I was not permitted to go on any chase calls in what my uncle considered to be unsafe neighborhoods. My uncle did not believe in having me personally meet any of the people I'd found. And he'd made it clear that stakeouts were not an appropriate line of work for a woman, especially the precious little niece whom he'd raised from childhood. He only relented on pickups or repos where he knew the people were not at home, and even then he usually tried to make me wait in the car.

Needless to say, my self-tutoring in lock-picking wasn't proceeding at a very fast pace.

In case Lewis was up to his old tricks, I pulled out the most recent edition of the *Washington Post* and turned to the back pages of the "Style" section to find the Personals. On my way there, an item in the gossip column caught my eye. Along with a photo of Senator Marguerite Sutherland, there was this juicy tidbit: "Noted with interest at Saturday's Cosmos Club reception for the Florida Legislature was the obvious affection of Big Sugar's most important grower, Juan Carlos Francisco, for Florida State Senator Marguerite Sutherland. Could it be Cupid—or the usual quid pro quo—bringing the state senator, a divorcee, and the wealthy Hispanic widower together?"

I clipped the item and put it in my pocket so it wouldn't accidentally get mixed up with the fresh stack of loan agreements that some evil person had dumped into my in-box while I was at lunch. All of them were stamped "SKIPPED." All of them required my attention. Reminding myself that it paid the rent, I spent the next two hours slaving away on the telephone and emerged at closing time with one possible location, two definites, and no message in the Personals with a telephone number that matched anything in the Lewis file. Maybe Lewis had wised up since the last fiasco. On the other hand, maybe he was using the old name switcheroo, and I'd have to look for Ray S. Lewis and Samuel L. Rayfield and Lewis R. Samuel before I hit pay dirt.

It stopped raining long enough for me to grab a couple of chocolate chip cookies from the Courthouse Carry-Out and make it back in time to check my e-mail. I'd steeled myself not to see anything from Neal Patterson, but instead found one from Gareth Swenson, who'd apparently gotten my address from Vivian Remington. He reminded me that we were going to have lunch to "catch up" and wanted to know when I might be available. How about never? I knew what he wanted, and I wasn't ready to hand them over just yet. I deleted the message.

The message from my ex was even harder to cope with. A sailing fanatic, Bobby was planning to stop over in Annapolis on his way to Hampton Roads and wondered if I'd put him up for the night. Like I ever needed to see him again.

Bobby Crane made my jaws hurt. At first, I'd been attracted to the charming yachtsman whose daredevil attitude had made him a much-sought-after crewman for numerous ocean races. Bobby was one of those crazy braves who climbed up to the top of the mast to check for wind shifts. Fear was not a part of his emotional makeup, and that made living with him scary. He was also one of those thick-skinned, happy-go-lucky sailors who believed everybody loved him and would take care of him just for the privilege of it all. That was on a good day when he had money in the bank and crewing offers to turn down. But, unlike most of the rest of us, Bobby did not thrive on dry land. He had a short temper and a tendency to spend all of our money on booze. Or sailing.

I remembered my shock at discovering what had happened to the six hundred dollars we'd received as a cash wedding gift from Aunt Rosalie. I'd been planning to use it to buy curtains and rugs to make our dismal duplex look homey, but before I knew it the money had disappeared and Bobby had a new GPS system and marine navigator.

Of course, to Bobby, our whole relationship had been my fault. Even while we were dating, he'd made it clear that "his life, his love, and his lady were the sea." My attempts to be a faithful "Brandy" had failed, probably because I hadn't been working in a pub serving whiskey and wine to sailors where I could at least drown my own loneliness while on the job. Fortunately, it had only taken a few months for me to realize our marriage was doomed.

I thought about a lot of places I could tell Bobby to bunk for the night—like a park bench, for example—and then decided the best course was to delete the message and pretend I'd never seen it.

There were two other messages: one from Alicia, reminding me to let her know when I'd be seeing our "client" and another from the client herself: "Let me know when you can brief me tomorrow on your meeting with Senator Sutherland."

You bet. Except I couldn't get that dadblasted typewriter to type up the report (with carbon copies) that Alicia was expecting me to produce. Steeling myself for the ordeal that lay ahead, I left a note, promising my uncle that I would finish the skips the following afternoon. Then I hoofed it over to the Banner Building, stopping only once along the way to buy a vanilla ice cream cone with fudge sprinkles on top.

After paying the locksmith Alicia had hired to put in a dead-bolt (he declined, politely, to let me watch what he was doing), I tried typing up my report to Remington. Nothing. What was wrong with the bleeping machine? I slammed the carriage return so hard, it tipped over the cup holding pencils and pens, spewing them across the surface of the desk.

Taking a deep, calming breath, I pulled Uncle Alex's rolodex card out of my pocket and called Tony, the repair guy. While I waited for him to show up, I played around with the adding machine, discovering as I did so that my checkbook would be in balance if I didn't make so many subtraction errors. I could pretend to investigate the case of the stolen fur coat, but short of demanding the item from Senator Sutherland (verboten) or asking her outright if she'd taken it (which would only elicit a lie, I was sure), I knew of only one other person I could pump for information. And that's what I kept telling myself as I punched in the numbers, realizing as I did so that the call to Tony had eaten all the remaining battery power. With a sigh, I picked up the receiver of the heavy black telephone Alicia had provided and laboriously dialed one number after the other, wondering if the Caller ID message at the other end would be flashing "ROTARY DIAL! ROTARY DIAL!" I was immediately transferred to Neal Patterson's direct line.

"Hi," I said, trying to unstick my tongue from the roof of a suddenly Saharan mouth. "This is P.J. Smythe, Alex Smythe's nie—"

"Hey, how are you? It was great to see you last Saturday. What can I do for you?"

"It's about Saturday . . . Those, uh, m-m-matters you said you've been advising Vivian Remington about? Do they have anything to do with a missing fur coat?"

"A what?"

"I take it that means no."

"I'm sorry, P.J. I can't reveal client confidences."

"Well, how about Senator Sutherland? She did seem awfully friendly."

"Not as friendly as she is with Juan Carlos Francisco, I gather." His laugh made the corners of my mouth turn up.

"Didn't you tell me she's also a client? Do you know her well?"

"Why do you ask?"

I hate it when people answer a question with one of their own. Yet, simply saying "because" would probably come across as extremely juvenile. So why not blurt out the truth? Naw. That would be too easy. "Just curious," I said. "She seemed awfully pleased to see you, so I wondered if you're also good friends." I could hear a pencil tapping on a desk. He was probably figuring out what he could say without violating attorney-client privilege. Lawyers sucked.

"Not really."

"So it's strictly business, right? Other than going to Washington receptions, that is."

"That, too, was work. You'd be surprised what we lawyers have to do that falls into the category of work. But, no. If you're asking, close friends, I've never had lunch or dinner with Marguerite or even been invited to her home. So we don't have what you'd call a social relationship."

"Okay. Just curious. Did Vivian mention anything to you about the senator's wardrobe?"

"What're you getting at, P.J.?"

"Just answer my question, okay?"

"I have never discussed *any* item of clothing with Vivian Remington. And now that I've said that much, you owe me an explanation of where this bizarre line of questioning is headed."

Nowhere, it appeared. Now it was my turn: "I'd like to tell you, believe me. But there's the issue of client confidentiality at this end too."

Neal started laughing again. "I had no idea you were so much like your uncle."

Shit. My uncle would kill me if he knew what I was up to. "This conversation is also confidential," I reminded Neal. "No spilling the beans to anyone. Especially him. Okay?"

"Sure. I understand your freelancing might make him feel you don't think he's paying you enough."

"Something like that." I dropped the phone into the cradle and hurled my pencil across the room just as a short stubble-faced guy in a "Rachi Rocks" t-shirt came through the door.

"Whoa," he said. "You need something more sure-fire than that to scare off folks." He had pale blond hair, light blue eyes, and the build of a wrestler too many years away from the ring.

"And you're selling what?" I asked.

"Typewriter repairs," he replied. "I'm Tony Marrero. You called me, remember?"

I planned to stick around while Tony played with the Underwood, but he lifted the cover and started to laugh. "You've run out of ribbon."

Putting a hand up to my ponytail, I said, "Excuse me?"

"Not that kind of ribbon." His face had turned pink. It took a while before the chuckles subsided and he could answer. "These babies here" (he gestured at the typewriter) "only work once. Then you gotta replace 'em. Where do you keep the spares?"

If I told him I didn't know, he'd just have another laughing fit. I opened the center drawer, but it held only a chewed-up pencil and a large dust bunny. The drawer to the side held two reams of paper, a stack of envelopes, and a book of first-class stamps. Damn.

"Why're you using an antique like this anyway? You afraid of computers?"

"Of course not." With as much nonchalance as I could muster, I moseyed over to the filing cabinet and opened the top drawer. "In case you didn't notice" (I threw my arm outward), "this is an authentic—to the last detail—re-creation of a 1930s office. My colleagues and I are doing a time-and-motion study to compare office routines of the thirties with today's fast-paced, multitasking environment in an effort to examine the parameters of—"

"Okay. Okay. I gotcha. You know how to change the ribbon?"

My face got hot. "Actually, I don't. My colleague—you might have heard of Dr. Alicia Fotheringill from Hopkins?—anyway, she's the one with the techno-savvy. I'm the statistician."

At that point, Tony had joined me at the filing cabinet and was peering into the top drawer. "There," he pointed.

I picked up the package and peeled off its cellophane—yes, cellophane, not plastic—wrapper, and Tony showed me how to do it, which was surprisingly easy—much easier than replacing the cartridge in a fax machine or printer.

"So, you wanna go for a pizza?" he asked as he wiped his hands with a tissue I'd found in the bottom of my purse.

I smiled. He was cute, but no Neal Patterson. "Thanks, I can't."

"Got a hot date, huh?"

I wish. "Just some things I have to do," I said, which was true. I did have to call Alicia and give her a heads-up on tomorrow's meeting with Vivian Remington, and then I had to type up that report (*with* carbons). I was also practically out of clean plates and needed to do a load of dishes.

Pizza for one somehow sounds so lonely, but I couldn't get the notion out of my head once Tony had put it there. An hour later, reeking of onions and pepperoni, I waddled through the door of my apartment.

"Have I met this Neal Patterson?" I could hear classical music in the background and the rasp of a nail file as Alicia attempted to refine what I suspected was probably an already perfect manicure.

"I hope not. He's just your type." Dragging the phone closer to the refrigerator, I pulled out a Carta Blanca, popped the cap off, and took a deep swallow. Whew, that was good. I tucked the phone into my neck and began to rinse the dishes before loading them into the dishwasher.

"And that is . . . ?"

"Good-looking. Intelligent. Educated. Well-dressed. Smooth as silk. A real hottie—only he's already spoken for, apparently."

"Too bad, but you should know that you're stereotyping my taste in men. I actually prefer beefy, sweaty rednecks who shoot pool and swill beer."

"Now look who's stereotyping!" I sank into the kitchen's only chair and put my feet on the Formica table. "Gareth Swenson wants to have lunch with me."

"Are you going to?"

"Shit, no. He wants those pictures I took back when I got into all that trouble at UVA."

"So blow him off. It might mess up our thing, you know. We should keep him out of the picture. Why don't you offer to mail him the pictures?"

"I was told he's being considered for a post at DEA."

There were peals of laughter at the other end. "You are kidding, aren't you?"

"I wish. But, Gareth also seemed to know Senator Sutherland. In fact, he introduced me."

"Stranger things have happened at events like that, I guess. But tell me about Mr. Tall, Dark, and Handsome. Any hope you can pry him loose from his current commitment?"

"You know me, Alicia. I'm not the type to intervene. Besides, the girl's gorgeous. Looks sort of like Snow White—or maybe that's just what she was wearing."

"Oh, yeah. I saw that woman. She is attractive. Only maybe not so faithful?"

"Really?" My feet dropped to the floor. "Do tell."

"She was coming onto some geeky-looking guy with horn-rimmed glasses wearing a really tacky tux with a pink cummerbund—I'm not talking about your Prince Charming, am I?"

"Doesn't sound like it. Neal doesn't wear glasses, and his outfit was really elegant, not at all flashy. So . . . Snow White is not so pure, huh?"

"Don't take that to the bank yet, but if we're talking about the same brunette in the white gown with the red sash, then she was all over this guy."

I pumped my fist in the air, remembering as I did so that brief interlude when my suspicious ears thought they'd heard Neal say that I looked fetching.

"Well, maybe they were both there to work. Neal told me he wasn't there to party."

"He is a lawyer, and I bet Meredith, Geitrich, and Smeal pay him plenty."

"You're not kidding. He looked like a million dollars."

"I bet he lives in Hillsmere, owns a sailboat, and drives a Bimmer."

Stereotyping again. "Too upscale for me, huh?"

"No way, girl. I'm just saying that MGS lawyers are top of the line. You can expect to be treated like a royal princess when Neal Patterson finally gets around to asking you for a date."

I couldn't help crossing my fingers, but it was time to change the topic. "Okay, enough of that. Other than giving Remington my report tomorrow, is there anything else you think I should do?"

There was a heavy sigh and the sound of fingernails tapping a table. "Look, I've already crossed the line by asking you to give her the damn report. I'm only supposed to be observing. You're the one who's doing the actual work. So think about it. What would Philip Marlowe do?"

I suppressed a snort. Philip Marlowe would not be so stupid as to let the client, not to mention the film director, call the shots. "Beats me," I replied. "We'll just have to see what happens tomorrow, won't we?"

Before calling it a night, I rummaged around in my dresser drawer checking that Marguerite Sutherland's diamond hair clip was still among the cache of jewelry that I kept hidden in my undies. I would have to make arrangements to return it soon. Or not. Vivian Remington had said the woman had sticky fingers. Maybe she'd shoplifted the bauble. But where was the thin gold band that had once belonged to my great aunt Rosalie? Uncle Alex had generously suggested that Bobby give it to me when we were wed. Funny how the fact that Bobby couldn't even afford to buy me a wedding band hadn't even registered in my love-struck brain when it should have set the alarm bells off big time.

He'd been so charming. He treated me as though he thought I'd hung the moon. He couldn't have been after my money because I had none. And it wasn't my talents as a song siren either. Back in college, Gareth Swenson had swooned at the dulcet tones I produced—"just like Tony Tennille" he'd said—but Bobby seemed oblivious to music in any form.

Sex. That was it. We could not keep our hands off each other. He kept saying he couldn't get enough of me. And because we were always ripping each other's clothes off, I'd believed him. And then, poof. It all just evaporated.

Just like that pesky ring. Where was it? I emptied the drawer onto the bed, threw all the underwear to the side, and pored through the remaining items. Marguerite Sutherland's diamond hair clip. Check. A pair of gold hoop earrings that Uncle Alex had given me when I graduated from college. Check. My mother's faux pearl choker. Check. I'd never worn it because I never wore anything dressy enough for pearls.

The phone rang, and I made a dash for the kitchen.

"Drop it while you can." The caller's voice was high-pitched and childish. There was a click, and the line went dead.

I kept telling myself it was some kind of kid's prank or maybe even a wrong number, but I couldn't help grabbing the .38 and heading for the front door to make sure somebody hadn't planted a pipe bomb or some sort of incendiary device there. Nothing. The back patio was bare, except for a thin sheet of sleet that was congealing into ice. I slammed the door and locked it. The crank caller had disturbed my peace and would probably keep me awake for hours, but I had a gun. I went to bed with the loaded .38 tucked beneath the pillow beside me.

January 22, 2003

He's sitting on the low brick wall across the street from her dorm when she heads out for her 8:30 class. She walks briskly up the street, but he steps in front of her and grabs both arms.

"You bitch."

"Leave me alone." She struggles to free herself, but his grip tightens, guaranteeing future bruises.

"Your little temper tantrum the other night cost me a lot of money, and I'm not talking about the broken mirror." His breath smells sour, like someone coming off a binge-drinking episode whose last worry is brushing his teeth.

"It's more like you owe me," she says, peering over his shoulder, realizing that no self-respecting student would be up this early. "I didn't tell the police anything."

"And that's why I dropped the charges," he says. "But now I've got to recoup my losses. Or, rather, you have to recoup my losses."

She stares at him, incredulous. "I don't think so." There is such fury in those bloodshot eyes. This isn't just some loud argument on the street; this is danger.

He drags her across the street where his beat-up Chevy Nova is double-parked. Digging in her heels, she resists with all her power, but he is nearly six feet tall and much stronger.

He shoves her into the car. The moment he starts moving around to the driver's side, she jumps out. Dashing down the sidewalk, she calls out for help.

In a flying shoestring tackle, he throws her to the ground, smashing her knees into the pavement. The cement scrapes a layer of skin off her nose as the contents of her purse spill out onto the sidewalk.

"Hey, buddy, why'nt you pick on somebody your own size?" The voice comes from a man who seems to have appeared out of nowhere and whose extra large work boots are planted just beyond her head. The sound of running footsteps tells her that Gareth has escaped as a gloved hand reaches down and pulls her to her feet.

"That scrape's not too bad," says her rescuer, who is a very large, very black man with the warmest chocolate eyes she's ever seen.

"How can I thank you?" Her voice trembles as she reaches a shaky hand up to her nose.

"Don't worry about it." He picks up her scattered belongings and hands them over. "You oughtta report that guy to the campus police."

She does not take the Good Samaritan's advice. It would only complicate things.

Back in the safety of the crowded student union, she lifts the telephone and calls Gareth's number. "You forgot that I still have evidence of your crime," she tells the answering machine. "If you ever bother me again, I'm going to turn you in."

CHAPTER NINE

The temperature had dropped a good thirty degrees overnight, and the single-digit wind chill that morning made me decide that only my fur-lined leather jacket would keep pneumonia at bay. I'd bought the jacket back in college with money my uncle had given me as a reward for having a three-point grade average three years running.

Fortunately, whatever muse was behind Alicia's "artistic vision" did not oblige me to wear some thirties-era costume to coordinate with the Banner Building office's décor. What a challenge that would have been. Vivian might have been blind to the surroundings, but the sight of me wearing a shirt and tie with a wool suit and a vest with pocket watch would have raised all sorts of questions—including my sexual orientation, not that it would be relevant. On the other hand, if I'd dressed like one of the classy dames in Chandler's novels, Vivian would have assumed I was P.J. Smythe's secretary.

At the Spartan but cozy offices of the Wetland Protectors Alliance on Clay Street, I asked to see my client. The receptionist's look of horror made me wonder if Vivian had an archenemy who coincidentally happened to look like me. "In a minute," she snarled.

I kept my eyes focused on the floor for what seemed an eternity. There were voices raised in anger somewhere down the hall. One of them sounded like Vivian Remington, urging the other person to "keep it down," but that only seemed to make that person angrier because I heard a man practically yell out, "I was only doing what I was asked."

"Yeah, right," said Vivian. "Just following orders. How *could* you?"

"I did ask for a raise, only you couldn't be bothered," came the angry reply. "Anyway, it wasn't—" Somebody slammed a door, drowning out the remainder of his reply.

The screeching of wheels needing oil on a cart being pushed in my direction obliterated most of Vivian's words. All I heard was "—ber, you're lucky we didn't call the police."

"You'll regret this," he said angrily.

"Don't threaten me, Marv. It won't work."

"We'll see about that."

Another door slammed, and I looked up to spy Vivian's gray running shoes coming toward me. Today's outfit was a pair of gray sweatpants covered by a black and gray sweatshirt with a red, white, and blue lollipop-shaped campaign button with the words "LICK BIG SUGAR" on it pinned to her right breast. As she led me down the hall, I could feel the twin laser beams of the receptionist's death glance boring a hole in my back.

"Was it something I said?" I asked Vivian, shrugging a shoulder in the general direction of the receptionist.

She laughed. "It's your jacket. A lot of folks who work here are animal lovers in the extreme. They'll wear wool because the sheep aren't killed in the process, but leather and especially fur are beyond the pale."

Well, golly. How was I to know? I removed the jacket and folded it to hide the fur lining.

Vivian's office, permeated with the woodsy scent she seemed to favor, was so crammed with books and papers that I wondered how she could find her desk. She picked up some papers lying on the chair behind the desk and swept up another pile that had buried the chair beside it.

I sat down while she pulled a prescription bottle out of the commodious backpack that seemed to serve as her purse. She popped the cap, examined the contents, snapped the cap back on, and set the bottle in the middle of her desk.

"I think Marguerite Sutherland wore your ocelot coat to the D.C. reception," I said.

The dark head jerked up, and yellow eyes gleamed. "No shit? That certainly was nervy. You got it on film?"

"They wouldn't let me take pictures unless I had a press pass." *And why didn't you think of that, Viv?* "Anyway, it appeared to be spotted fur, and the lining was reddish brown. It looked expensive. Of course, I'm no expert."

On the wall behind Vivian's desk was a huge poster of a smiling woman with one alligator-shod foot on the step above her as she approached the camera. She was wearing a full-length spotted fur coat and dangling a strand of black beads enticingly in front of her. The words at the bottom read "She's Killed To Dress."

"Cool poster," I said, drumming my fingers on my knee. "Is that ocelot?"

Vivian laughed. "Yep. Some guys here played a joke on me using that picture. They digitally altered the shot to put my head on the model and then made it look like I was wearing nothing but the coat."

"What does it mean, she's killed to dress?"

She laid her lifestyle toy on the desk. "The Customs Service and U.S. Fish and Wildlife display these posters at U.S. ports of entry to warn tourists not to bring in goods derived from endangered species. Fur coats from endangered big cats are off limits, as is her necklace, which is black coral. So, to wear that stuff, she's, in effect, abetting the killing of ocelots and coral."

I didn't know that coral could be killed. "How can travelers tell what's okay to import and what's not?"

Vivian handed me a brochure listing banned items. "These are distributed at all ports of entry in the United States and the Caribbean."

"One more thing, Viv," said a voice from the doorway. It was the same voice I'd heard arguing with her earlier. I turned around to see a gaunt, very pale guy with spiky purple and yellow streaked hair, wearing bib overalls over a shockingly white t-shirt. I couldn't help staring at the rubber-soled sandals on his feet. After all, the outside temperature was barely above fifteen.

"What do you want, Marv?" Apparently, Vivian was not pleased to be interrupted.

"Merely a nanosecond of your priceless time," he said with a sneer.

"I've got company."

"Duh." He shot me a baleful glare.

With a groan, Vivian got to her feet, motioning me to remain seated. "One second and counting, Marv."

They disappeared down the hall far enough away that all I could detect was anger, not words. As I sat there waiting, my curiosity gene surged to the forefront, and I leaned across the desk. Picking up the prescription bottle, I read the label. One of those brands advertised on TV to help insomniacs.

"Ugh," said Vivian as I jerked back into my chair. "I'd rather have a root canal than talk to that guy, but I suppose I have no choice."

I laughed. "What's with the sandals in this weather?"

"Marv never wears shoes. The reason he wants to talk is that he just got canned, and I'm the one he blames." She sighed heavily. "Maybe if we get it over with now, he won't go postal on us later." She leaned back in her chair. "I gather you ran into Neal Patterson at the Washington soirée. Is he a friend of yours?"

"Sort of. He handles legal affairs for my uncle's business."

"Quite a dish, isn't he?"

"His girlfriend seems to think so. She was plastered all over him practically the whole evening."

Vivian raised an eyebrow and smiled. "Not envious, are you?"

None of your beeswax, especially since you nailed it. As soon as I could unclench my jaw, I changed the subject. "Here's my report. I wish I had more to say about the coat, but at least you know your board member has it." I handed her a manila envelope with her name typed on the front, followed by CONFIDENTIAL.

Vivian opened the envelope and read the one-pager. With a tiny scowl, she slipped it back into its envelope and dropped it on her desk. "You're new at this, aren't you."

"Yes. Just starting out. That's why my rates are so low."

"That may be, but I asked for documentation. Other than this" (she tapped a finger on the report), "you've got nothing. And this" (another hard tap) "is useless. You think the Feds would act on the basis of some piece of paper produced by a novice private eye?"

"They wouldn't let me photograph her," I explained. "What was I going to do?" Maybe I could persuade Alicia to turn over her videotape. Surely that would measure up as documentary evidence.

"Okay. Fine. But I didn't pay you to give up after one failed attempt."

I swallowed. "Okay. I did manage to get Senator Sutherland interested in having me photograph her, so I guess I could follow up . . . oh, yes. And she left with that guy who was in the *Post*'s gossip column. I saw him goose her."

"Juan Carlos Francisco?"

"Yeah. The big-time sugar daddy. He must be the senator's dear friend 'cause she didn't seem to mind."

"He ought to be her friend. She's cast many votes in his favor—although none, so far, on the Everglades. Anything else?"

"Nope." Except why was Sutherland on the Alliance board?

"I'd like you to get her to pose for you wearing the fur coat," said Vivian, a crease between her brows.

"Wouldn't she be suspicious, knowing that she stole it?"

"Perhaps. Although maybe it would be better to leave her out of it, just get a picture of the coat in her closet or draped across the bed."

"Look, Vivian. Short of going to Florida, I don't see how—"

"Marguerite is still in D.C.," said Vivian. "Her family owns a co-op in Woodley Park that she uses for a Washington pied-à-terre. She won't be heading back to Florida for a while, so you need to think up some way to gain access."

We stared at one another while I silently begged her, *please, please don't make me break in,* and she just as silently telegraphed, *do whatever it takes.*

Shit. "Even if I got a picture of the coat, what would it prove? Sutherland could claim it was a family heirloom, couldn't she? Or say a dear friend gave it to her."

"Yeah, I guess." Vivian swiveled her chair around and stared out the window.

"Supposing that friend happened to be Juan Carlos Francisco? He'd probably go along with it—if they're as close as the *Post* suggests. You need some way to prove the coat belongs to the government."

She swung back around and smiled ruefully. "I know. But I took the tag off. It was scratching my neck. I meant to put it back, and then . . ." The phone rang, and she picked it up. "Vivian Remington."

There was a pause before she said, "Hi, Gareth. Wait a sec. I've got somebody with me." She put her hand over the receiver. "What was I saying?"

"If you can't prove it's the coat the Feds lent you, you're just wasting your time and money."

"Wait." Vivian rummaged around in the drawer beneath her desk, finally emerging with a crumpled paper tag, which she handed to me. "Put it back on the coat, and we're still in business."

I looked down at the little white rectangle she'd given me. On it there was an official-looking seal and the words "PROPERTY OF U.S. FISH AND WILDLIFE SERVICE." There was a row of tiny holes where the tag had apparently been stitched into the lining.

On my way out of the building, I ran into Tony Marrero in the lobby. He was decked out in western garb, complete with buckskin jacket and cowboy boots. "Hey, Tony," I said, "thanks for fixing my typewriter."

"Okay. Yeah, sure," he said absently, peering at the directory of building residents. "You still oughta get a computer." He turned away from the directory, jammed a hand in his pants pocket, and pulled it out empty. "Damn. This broa—lady called me, and now I can't remember her name or where she works. Some kinda alliance, I think." He looked back at the directory.

"The Wetland Protectors Alliance?"

"Yeah. That's it."

"Fourth floor. Turn right when you get off the elevator."

"I owe you one," he said, making a dash for an elevator whose doors were closing. I stood there for a moment thinking that only in fiction would he be going to see Vivian Remington.

After getting as far as I could on tracing skips back at MoneySource, I treated myself to a cup of coffee and a slice of apple pie to get my daily ration of fruit and headed to the Banner Building where I'd promised I would shove the carbon copy of the unread report in front of the camera so that it could be read.

Halfway there, I ran into Leteisha Jackson, Samuel Lewis's latest conquest.

"Hey, Leteisha. P.J. Smythe. Remember me?"

She squinched her eyes into slits and then scowled. "You that repo lady?"

"I don't do repos," I reminded her. "I just wondered if you've seen Sam lately. I need to talk to him."

"Ev'body wanna talk to that man." She rolled her eyes. "I'll tell him you're aksing."

"How about giving me his phone number?"

"He don't have one." She laughed. "Nothin' but trouble, he tells me. People hounding him for all kindsa things he don't have and never did have."

Right. "Well, ask him to give me a call," I pulled out a Money-Source card from my pocket and pressed it into her hand. Leteisha ambled up the street where she dropped my card in the trash can at the corner. Oh well, plenty more where that came from.

Back in the Marlowe-era office, carefully restored to its pigsty conditions, I sat down at the scuffed wooden desk and pushed the button activating the hidden camera.

"Hi," I waved. "I'm P.J. Smythe. The 'P' stands for Private Investigator, and the 'J' stands for Jailbait. My client has just instructed me to break into the home of a Washington Mucky-Muck and photograph a spotted fur coat in her possession. Oh. After I reattach this label." I picked up the label and held it out in front of me. "Can't read it? It says 'PROPERTY OF THE U.S. FISH AND WILDLIFE SERVICE.' Now, if I do what the client asks, I will be breaking the law. You think I'm nuts?"

January 19, 2003

The hands of the clock move past six, provoking an impatient sigh. It seems these days all she does is hang around waiting for him. There must be someone else, and he's too chicken to 'fess up. Pain shrivels her heart as she fights back tears of self-pity.

Pulling her ponytail tighter, she takes another tiny sip of beer, trying to make it last until he shows up.

"Yo, P.J."

She looks up and waves to Johnny. Maybe when Gareth sees her with his to-die-for teammate, he'll feel a tiny bit jealous.

The redhead hauls a chair away from the next table and drags it over, straddling the seat and resting his arms on the back. "You look kinda lonely. Waiting for GQ?"

She nods. "He's a little late."

Johnny snorts. "More like he had something else to do."

"You know something I don't?" She leans forward, all the better to read his expression.

"As a matter of fact I do. I thought I'd find him here, but I guess I could give you the message, and you can pass it on."

"If he ever shows up."

"Yeah, well, he's got until tomorrow evening."

She leans back, tapping her nails on the table's rough wooden surface.

Johnny's looking around the room like a cop casing the joint. He leans forward and whispers, "Tell him he's gotta clean the place out."

She laughs. "As if he'd listen to me. The last time I was there, I had to wade through two weeks of dirty clothes to reach the, uh—"

"That's not what I mean." He signals the waiter, holding up two fingers. "You just tell him what I said. He'll understand."

"He's got to clean house."

"No. Clean the place out. Got that?" Johnny stands up, spins the chair around, and plops back down, hands in his jean pockets. "You don't know him at all, do you?"

Her face reddens as she realizes the only thing she knows for sure is that the sex is—or, lately, more like *was*—terrific. "We're both history majors. That's how we met. He plays varsity lacrosse, as you know. He plans to go to law school some day. He's from Staunton, or is it Leesburg?"

Johnny sighs. "Ever notice how expensive his clothes are?"

"Well, sure. The nickname says it all. But isn't his father a doctor?"

This time Johnny groans. "His father manages an auto parts store in Leesburg. His mom waitresses at one of those franchise restaurants—Applebee's maybe? I doubt his brother is old enough to work full time. So . . ."

"Where does the money come from?" An icy trickle of fear runs down her spine as two memories—Gareth telling her not to touch his precious belongings and Gareth promising some stranger on the phone that he can get it pure—fuse together to form one conclusion: "Drugs?"

Johnny nods. "He's been dealin' ever since freshman year."

"So it's not mama paying a visit tomorrow night."

"You wish." He shakes his head, turning toward her and mouthing one word: "Cops."

CHAPTER TEN

"Ha. Ha. Very funny." The television in the background was playing that dumb ditty inviting viewers to call the cheap (but chic!) outfit that could restore their grotty, disgusting bathrooms to mint condition.

"I'm serious, Alicia. This gig is finished."

She sighed. "P.J. We've been over this before. I would never ask you to do something illegal."

"I'm already breaking the law. Or didn't you do your homework? Private eyes have to be licensed in this state."

"So what? Who's going to rat you out?"

"Well, Vivian Remington, for starters. She doesn't think I'm doing a very good job."

"Look. You don't have to break into Sutherland's place. Use your head. There are a million ways you can get in there—starting with getting yourself invited."

"Oh, sure. And then I talk her into wearing the coat—which she knows is stolen—so forget that. Or I somehow incapacitate the woman long enough for me to search her closets, stitch this stupid label back into the coat, and photograph it. What, you think I should bean her with the sap I always carry in my back pocket?"

"No need to be sarcastic." The television was now touting the virtues of being built "Ford tough." Too bad I couldn't make my remote work over the telephone lines. "And, really, I shouldn't be giving you pointers, anyway. This is supposed to be about learning on the job."

"But it isn't. It's about your blind ego and using your best friend to—"

"Oh, P.J. Don't go there. I'm not using you. I chose you. You're the best candidate because you're clever and you know a hell of a lot more about the seamier side of life than I do." She paused as if to reconsider what she'd just said. "I mean, not that you yourself live that kind of life, but your job, your uncle's experience back in Baltimore, it has to have rubbed off. And then, well—Don't take this wrong, but I like the irony of the whole thing, you know? Here's this cute little blonde playing tough guy . . . and doing a really good job too. It'll be an inspiration to others. Think you couldn't possibly be a private eye? Well, take a look at Alicia Todd Ritchie's award-winning film. If P.J. Smythe can do it, anybody—Well, you get my drift."

What a gal. I'd seen my uncle pass by the cubicle a couple of times (never a good omen), so I ended the conversation. What was there to say, anyway?

I turned my attention to the pile of skips in my in-box but found it difficult to focus with the hot breath of Vivian's impatience breathing down my neck. I revisited the Alliance write-up on Everglades restoration and found something I'd recalled seeing on my first visit to their Web site. Only then it hadn't seemed significant. According to the Alliance, water that used to flow through the Everglades and down to Florida Bay had, for years, been diverted to drain land for agriculture, mostly sugar cane. This, they claimed, was not good for Florida, wildlife inhabiting the Everglades, or the people living along the coast whose flood-prone cities were also protected by diverting water from the Everglades.

Like we shouldn't rid the world of mosquitoes? Like we should pity the poor alligators? Gimme a break. On the other hand . . . didn't Florida have some kind of large ocelot-type cat that was rumored to be extinct? I scrolled through the site and found a list of on-the-brink species that included the Florida panther and another cute critter called the Key deer. Who would want to kill Bambi's cousin from the Keys? The answer was sugar interests, said the Alliance, pooh-poohing the industry's claims that restoring the Everglades would spell the end of sugar cane farming in Florida.

Forget the damned ocelot coat. What I was looking at was far more interesting. One of the Wetland Protectors Alliance's board members seemed to be the girlfriend of what Vivian had called a "big sugar daddy." Had she never heard of pillow talk? Conflicts of interest? Or . . . yeah. Vivian—maybe her boss, too—did know, but they couldn't find any evidence of conflict, so they hired me to document something that would get the senator in enough hot water to kick her off the board. Shit. For all I knew, Vivian had planted the coat. Or maybe she'd seen Marguerite wearing it and dreamed up the idea of making it appear to be stolen from the government. The label could be easily produced on a computer. I looked up just as Gareth Swenson's head peered around the cubicle entry. "Hi, P.J. I was in the neighborhood, so I thought I'd stop by to see if you want to grab a bite."

My head said no, but my stomach had different ideas. I gathered up my purse and jacket, and we wandered over to the Acme Bar and Grill. Gareth was all decked out in a gray wool suit with a crisp white shirt and a blue and gray striped tie. I wasn't doing too bad myself, luckily. In deference to my meeting with Vivian Remington, I'd ditched my usual sweatshirt in favor of a long-sleeved pink t-shirt covered by a V-necked ruby red sweater.

"Nice jacket," said Gareth as we dug into our sandwiches.

"Thanks. Vivian's people nearly killed me when I walked through the door."

He nearly choked, coughing briefly into a napkin. "I could have warned you, I guess."

"Look, Gareth. I know what you're after, and I'm not going to give them to you."

"Hey." He raised his hands, fingers spread. "You made that pretty clear the other night. But a guy's still gotta try, right?" His cell phone chimed, and he flicked it open. "Yeah?" There was a long interlude as a thunderous cloud of Joe Btfsplk-like gloom settled over his brow. "Oh, God."

Was it his wife? Had something happened to her? Listening made me feel like the worst sort of voyeur. Gareth must have noticed, because he abruptly stood up, saying, "Back in a sec."

I couldn't help watching as he continued the conversation outside. His shoulders slumped forward as though he'd been kicked upside the head. Slipping the phone into his coat pocket, he brushed the back of his hand across the side of his face. Was he crying? His eyes were a little bloodshot when he resumed his seat.

To give him time to compose himself, I buried my face in my sandwich.

"That was Sarah."

I wiped the grease from my lips. "She okay?"

"No. They want to try another drug. It's only about eight times more expensive than the last."

I didn't know what to say. I couldn't help Gareth—financially, anyway. As for the photos, I couldn't remember where I'd stashed them, and I didn't want Gareth to offer to tear my place apart looking for them. Besides, those photos weren't going to do a thing to kill Sarah's cancer. "I'm sorry."

He gave me a long, sorrowful look. "Funny, I've never had to beg for anything before now. I'd give anything to get that DEA job. It's the only thing that's going to save Sarah."

Of course, he was distraught, not thinking clearly. I recalled what Neal Patterson had told me about Gareth getting fired from the Baltimore office of Meredith, Geitrich, and Smeal. But, numbers-wise at least, weren't law firms a plague of near biblical proportions? "I assume you've got other irons in the fire—just in case . . . ?"

His gaze swung to the left. "It's just that I'd been hoping I could, uh, you know, somehow atone for the past. A private law firm just doesn't—"

"But if you had to, surely you could find something—like in a nonprofit or public defender?"

The corners of his mouth turned down. "None of those would be nearly as remunerative or as secure as a government job."

"You'll tell Senator Sutherland, though, won't you? Surely, she can help."

"Maybe. I've been trying not to seem too desperate. That always puts people off."

The generous side of me was about to say, "If there's anything I can do . . ." when the unforgiving part made me bite my tongue. How did I know the guy wasn't just totally bullshitting me, like he'd done before? Maybe this was nothing more than a dramatic ploy to wheedle those blasted pictures out of my possession so that Gareth could sail into a job he should never be allowed to have. I compromised by buying our lunch.

"Something will come up," I said lamely, as we parted on the street.

The whole thing left me with a bad taste in my mouth. If Gareth was telling the truth, then I was a real shit—not that I could do much of anything concrete to help out, other than the obvious. I called the only person who might know the truth.

Vivian seemed rushed when she answered the phone. "Yes, his wife's name is Sarah. So?"

"Has Gareth shared any details of their personal life?"

"Good grief, P.J. You're not trying to drive a wedge be—"

"Are you serious? I can't stand the man. But I did hear something about his wife's health, and I was wondering if—"

"Well, you know more than I do. I do find it annoying as hell, however, that you don't seem to be working too hard on the job I hired you for." She slammed the phone down.

Out of spite, I spent the remainder of the afternoon laboring over the skips that could be resolved on the Internet with a few clicks of a mouse. Marguerite Sutherland could wait. And so could the impatient Ms. Vivian Remington.

As I clicked away, I couldn't help noticing how dark it was getting. Winter was not my favorite time of year, and since my skinflint uncle only put light bulbs in every other fixture, the hallways outside my cubicle were filled with gloom.

A quick peek at my watch told me it was after seven P.M. No one else would be around, so why did there seem to be a shadowy figure—large enough not to be a woman—lurking behind the frosted-glass door to the reception area? The ghost vanished and then returned, standing there patiently. When my phone rang, the figure jerked backward out of sight. "Congratulations! You have just won two tickets to Disney World. All you have to do—"

I cradled the receiver. What I wanted to do was crawl underneath the desk and curl up like a five-year-old, secure in the knowledge that if I couldn't see an intruder, he couldn't see me. Instead, I tiptoed across the room and peered through the frosted glass. I could yell, not that anyone would hear me. Of course, my .38 special was stashed in the drawer beside my bed, nor did my sneakers pose much of a threat as a possible alternative weapon.

After a small eternity of not hearing anything or seeing any motion, I decided I was spooking myself. It was probably somebody wanting to make a payment and not realizing the office was closed for the day. On the other hand . . . I locked the door, recalling as I did so how easy it would be for somebody to smash the glass.

Back at my desk, I stared at the telephone wondering if I should summon help. I could call my uncle. He would rescue me, or he'd send Jake and Rake in his place. And that would be embarrassing. If I was going to accede to Alicia's wishes and learn on the job, then I would have to walk the tough talk. Alone.

The shadow came back into view and rattled the doorknob.

"Go away," I yelled through the door. Then I picked up the telephone. "I'm calling the police."

As I cradled the receiver, I could hear the footsteps receding—but not far enough. An eternity passed while I waited breathlessly for the dinging of the elevator's bell or the creaking of hinges on the stairwell door.

Nothing. And maybe much ado about it. Whoever it was didn't seem inclined to break down the door, so maybe all I needed to do was outwait him. But waiting turned out not to be so easy as a sudden urgent need to use the facilities at the end of the hall swept through me. Gritting my teeth, I counted backward from a hundred. If I could distract myself, I would forget about it. At about sixty-three, I was in agony. At forty-two, I remembered the metal wastebasket with its plastic liner and the convenient supply of paper towels I had stashed in the filing cabinet to mop up coffee spills.

"Jeez, P.J. What's that awful smell?"

I awoke with a start. The lights were blazing, sun was shining outside the windows, the clock on the wall read 7:45, and Uncle Alex was standing right outside my cubicle, his fingers pinched against his nose. I jumped to my feet, picked up the wastebasket and pushed past him. "Back in a jiff," I said, heading for the bathroom.

When I returned, Uncle Alex had opened a couple of windows to let in some frigid fresh air along with the sound of pigeons pecking away at something in the alley below.

"You look like you spent the night here."

"I did."

He sighed, crossing his arms. "What dedication. I'm impressed. Get caught up?" Scowling, he sat down on the corner of my desk. He was wearing a gray flannel suit with a pale pink shirt and a black and gray striped tie. The pink shirt must have been a gift from somebody, because he would never pick that color for himself. Or maybe he was going through a mid-life crisis a little on the late side. "Anyway, if you're going to pull all-nighters, you could let somebody know."

"Sorry."

"I stopped by because Neal Patterson called me early this morning saying he had been trying to reach you all evening. After calling your apartment, I drove over there and didn't see your Bug, so I came down here."

I hadn't heard much of what he'd been saying past the mention of my fantasy lover. "What did Neal want?"

"How should I know? But really, P.J. I never asked you to pull an all-nighter. This can be a pretty spooky place after everyone's left for the day."

"I coulda been the victim of a mugger, right?" I tried a laugh, but it came out raspy. Only occasionally does my job scare me. Usually, it's so routine that even I find it tedious. But there had been footprints on my patio a couple of days ago, a crank call, and then last night . . . whatever that had been about. It had all started the day Vivian Remington walked into my life. But it would definitely not be wise to tell my uncle about her.

"Look, Uncle Alex. I thought maybe it would be a good idea

to clean up my files since things have kind of piled up here. I guess I just fell asleep."

He gave me a somewhat skeptical half smile and stood up. "C'mon, let's hit Chick and Ruth's. I'll buy you breakfast. You look like you could use it."

I make it a policy never to turn down a free meal, even though I knew Uncle Alex was going to pull the usual stunt. He'd probably start with suggesting that I would be smart to snare the luscious Neal Patterson. Then, he'd move on to my career ambition (or lack thereof) and wind up trashing my car. To fortify myself, I ordered a large glass of orange juice with my coffee, Belgian waffles topped with strawberries and whipped cream, and a side of link sausages.

My uncle poured milk over his oatmeal. "When you get back, be sure to call Patterson. I bet he wants to ask you on a date. Wouldn't that be great? He's a real nice fellah. Smart as a whip, too . . . although lately I get the impression he might be bothered by something."

I wanted to change the subject—maybe tease my uncle a little about the origins of the pink shirt, maybe even suggest that he get a haircut since what little hair he had left was spilling over his shirt collar. But I knew the drill, and it had never involved fussing over Uncle Alex. "Right," I said. "I'll call him soon as we're finished."

"Good. I like that young man. You will, too."

For once, I happened to agree with my uncle. "Neal has a girlfriend, you know. I saw her at the Washington shindig, and she looks very high maintenance to me."

"Hmmm." He scratched his chin. "Wonder if that's why he calls me the other day to ask what kind of interest we charge on a loan."

"Neal Patterson? Isn't he kind of well off? Why wouldn't he go to a bank?"

"Good question. I told him the same thing, and he sort of gives me this funny laugh like 'been there, done that.' "

"Alicia's sure he drives a luxury car and probably owns a boat. Maybe he wants to upgrade to something bigger, more luxurious—you know, to please the girlfriend."

"Which the bank can handle at much lower rates—not that I wouldn't be glad to lend him the money."

"Who knows? He may just want to give you his business. You know. Check you out to see how you handle things." I could tell Uncle Alex was skeptical.

He held his cup out for the waitress to refill and then sat back, crossing one leg over the other. He still wore white socks with his dress shoes. "You know you could move up to something more responsible—loan officer, maybe even credit manager."

"Not my cup of tea," I said, mopping up the remaining syrup with a piece of my uncle's toast. "I appreciate it, Uncle Alex. Really. But I don't want to spend the rest of my life in finance." Check off Topic B.

He sighed. "Rhoda would turn in her grave if she knew what little ambition you have."

My mother would turn in her grave if she knew what I'd let Alicia drag me into. "She'd be pleased I'm helping you," I delivered what had become my standard rebuttal.

"You could at least get a more reliable car."

Bingo. "Remember that Woody Allen movie? Beetles are indestructible and reliable."

Signing his name on the credit card slip, Uncle Alex slipped the copy into his wallet. "You should get something with air-bags," he said, as his reading glasses joined the wallet in the inside pocket of his suit coat. "Those tin cans are lethal."

"As soon as save up enough, I'll go looking for a newer car. Okay?" Sheesh. I hated to make promises I had no intention of keeping, but looking wasn't exactly the same thing as buying. Maybe Uncle Alex would forget I'd ever said it.

Did I mention that Annapolis is small? Why, of all the sidewalks in all the world's sailing capitals, did my ex have to be walking toward me on the one right outside of Chick and Ruth's? I turned back toward my uncle, but he'd already rounded the corner and was out of sight.

"Don't you ever read your e-mail?" said Bobby by way of greeting someone he hadn't seen in more than five years.

"The server's down." I looked down at my hands, which had suddenly become fists. I shoved them into my pockets.

He looked the picture of health with his sailor's sunburn and his sun-bleached hair. But the scuffed topsiders and frayed cuffs of his khakis, rimmed with grime, told a different story: He was down on his luck. And the tiny red veins around his nose and his bloodshot blue eyes signaled that Bobby was back on the booze. I couldn't help noticing the marked difference between him and the two crisply attired midshipmen walking toward us, in lock step with their hats at the same angle. They might look the part—and someday might actually even become sailors—but scruffy Bobby with his three-day beard and flaky attitude was the genuine article.

"Look, P.J., I need a place to crash for a couple of days. You can put me on your couch, can't you?"

"No." I brushed past him, but he grabbed my arm.

"Hey. Is that any way to treat an old friend?"

I jerked my arm, but he wouldn't let go. "Get real, Bobby. You haven't been a friend since you tried to steal from me."

He grinned. "You know that was just a misunderstanding. I was going to give you your half of the account, but I needed to wait till after the bank verified the balance so I could get maximum financing for my boat."

"Yeah, right."

"C'mon, babe," he pleaded, forcing a phony smile. "For old time's sake?"

"I don't think so."

"It's only for one night, for Chrissake."

"Hey, P.J.," came a familiar voice from behind me. It was Vivian Remington, looking for all the world like Shaquille O'Neal about to block a shot.

"Well, hellooo," said Bobby, giving her the once-over. "You going to introduce me, P.J.?"

"Vivian, Bobby Crane. We used to be married. Vivian is one of my cli—friends."

"Well, any friend of P.J.'s—what say we all go get a cup of coffee?"

"I just had one," I said.

"I bet you played college hoops," said Bobby, who might have weighed more than Vivian but was at least two inches shorter.

"Nope," she replied. "But everyone asks me that."

"Were you on your way to see me?" I asked Vivian.

"Meredith, Geitrich, and Smeal, actually. I've got a ten o'clock with Neal Patterson."

"I'm going in the same direction," said Bobby. As they walked off, Bobby stopped briefly to point a finger in my direction. "I'll be in touch."

It was too late, not to mention highly out of line, to ask Vivian about the nature of her appointment with Neal. None of my business. Only problem was, Vivian Remington was a very attractive woman—something I was betting Neal Patterson had also noticed. I watched her stride down the sidewalk, my cheating ex rolling along beside her as she parted the crowds on either side like the waters of the Red Sea.

Chapter Eleven

Whoever said traffic circles were a psychological as well as a physical barrier was right. It always seemed that my uncle's finance company was much farther away from Chick and Ruth's than ten or so blocks down West Street because I had to go around Church Circle to get there. By the same token, I felt less anxious having the circle between Bobby and me. I told myself that was why I would first put in some time tracing Samuel Lewis before revisiting the idea of continuing with Alicia's game. The truth was more complicated, however, for I was not one tiny step closer to figuring out how I was going to get an audience with Senator Marguerite Sutherland.

It was time to pull a Scarlett and nowhere more appropriate than within the faux Southern walls of MoneySource, which at one time had been a funeral home, replete with Ionic columns lining the length of a Colonial-style building with an old brick facade not at all unlike Tara.

The only concession my uncle had made to the more prosaic business he offered was a large garish sign at the corner of West and Lafayette with green letters on an aqua background:

MONEYSOURCE
NO COLLATERAL • NO INTEREST • NO FOOLIN'

For 90 days. Some Exceptions Apply.

www.moneysource.com

That's what made my job interesting. The no-collateral loans didn't give me much leverage except implied threats about ruined credit, but they also tended to be for amounts small enough to be written off without causing Uncle Alex a major coronary. The no-interest promise only applied to people with outstanding credit ratings, none of whom were likely to be needing money to tide them over till payday. I'd always assumed the no foolin' part had to do with me, followed up by Jake and Rake, making it real hard for deadbeats to forget about their obligations. As for the Web site, it was still under construction and likely to remain so since my uncle had never bothered to hire a webmaster, claiming he preferred to do business the old-fashioned way. "Most of our borrowers can't afford a postage stamp, let alone a computer," was the way he put it.

According to Leteisha's neighbors, she was spending far too much time with Samuel Lewis and not enough with her two boys, who needed somebody to keep them off the streets before they got caught 'jacking cars or running drugs. Leteisha drove a white 1997 Mitsubishi with a dent in the rear passenger-side door. The car belonged to Baltimore Trust, and she was regularly late on her payments. That meant if I didn't find Lewis before he bought Leteisha that diamond ring he'd promised her, she'd end up having to pawn the diamond to catch up on her car payments, and MoneySource would be stuck with a huge write-off for Lewis's Yamaha motorcycle.

After some careful work with the phone book and some other creditors who wanted to find Sam as much as I did, I learned that Leteisha worked at a burger joint in Eastport. It took some persuading to get the manager to let her come to the phone.

"You seen Sam lately?" I asked her when I finally succeeded.

"Sure, last night he come over."

"Well, next time he shows up, tell him to call me. I have a money-making proposition for him."

"No shit?"

She took down my numbers at both offices, a good sign. I hadn't misrepresented myself either. The money-making proposition I had in mind, however, was that MoneySource would make some money off the guy by the end of the week or my name wasn't P.J. Smythe.

I checked my e-mail and deleted several messages having to do with office administration—changes to the health plan, open season on the 401(k), yet another threat to cut off the free coffee if people didn't clean out the moldy stuff they'd abandoned in the fridge. I picked up some papers that had been blown off the desk onto the floor when my uncle had opened the windows (now, thankfully, closed). I played Solitaire until I won a game.

Okay, I was stalling. I'd promised to call Neal Patterson. I even wanted to call him, but I was afraid he would have something other than me on his mind. Meanwhile, I was trying to figure out how I could return the diamond clip to the senator in person, rather than just dropping it in the mail or handing it over to a staff person. Once I had Marguerite to myself, there was the problem of how I was going to photograph the suspect coat, let alone sew the label back onto it. Right then, the task looked daunting to the point of impossible. When the phone rang, I didn't know whether to jump for joy or scream.

"You like deep water?" came a vaguely familiar-sounding high-pitched non-child's voice.

"Who is this?" My heart skipped a couple of beats as I listened to the silence at the other end.

I was about to hang up when I heard a sigh and then "Fool."

"But I haven't done anything!" I said to the empty room.

The phone rang again, and I snatched it up. "Who is this?" I yelled.

"Holy Cow, P.J. It's Neal Patterson."

"Oh. Sorry."

"I was just calling to see when I can collect on that promise."

"Oh. I thought you were a crank caller."

"You get many of those?" The sound of concern in his voice started my icy blood thawing.

"No. Probably a nut case."

"Well, be sure and tell your uncle so he can change your number."

I knew that, and I also knew that, as nice as it sounded to have Neal Patterson concerned about me, I did not want him telling me what to do.

"So I was wondering if you'd like to have lunch." The words slid from his mouth as smooth as glass, like he'd said them on numerous occasions to lots of women.

Like a gawky adolescent caught totally off base, the only thing I could think to say was "Why?"

There was a brief silence. "Why not? I'm getting hungry. Aren't you?"

You bet, and for a whole lot more than food, too. But dining with the dapper Neal Patterson with me wearing a grungy sweatshirt and jeans was not the way I wanted it to happen. "Okay," I replied. "Can I meet you somewhere?"

We settled on 49 West at 12:30, which gave me forty-five minutes to dash home, change clothes, apply a modicum of makeup, fix my hair, and scoot back to West Street. I made it with five minutes to spare, just enough time to get my breath back under control.

"I've been wanting to do this for a while," said Neal as we perused the menus.

He was wearing a charcoal suit, yellow shirt, and an understated blue and red paisley tie. I hadn't noticed the tiny crow's feet at the corners of his eyes before. They made him look tired. "Yeah. This is a cool place."

"I meant take you to lunch," he said. "It's so hard to get

away from the office." He put his menu down and took a sip of water. "That's a nice color on you."

His compliment made my cheeks burn, and I mumbled a thank-you. Trust Alicia to know exactly what worked for me. It was a cobalt blue sweater that she'd given me for my birthday. She always gave me clothes since I hardly had time, or money, to shop for myself. "Do you come here often?" I asked, mentally kicking myself for not being able to think up anything more sophisticated.

"Sometimes." His gaze roamed around the room and settled on me. "What's this about Vivian Remington and a missing coat? Fur, was it?"

"Oh, just something she asked me to look into." I smiled. "Can't say more than that, I'm afraid."

He chuckled. "Let me guess. You're threatening to repossess it if she doesn't get up to date on her payments."

It was my turn to laugh. "Hardly." I took a sip of water. "Besides, I told you this was freelance."

He leaned forward, pinning me to my chair with an intense blue gaze. "I bet it's got something to do with Marguerite Suth-erland."

I couldn't hide my amazement. But then I remembered mentioning the senator when I'd talked to Neal before. "That's why it's confidential," I explained. "You know. Because she's a public figure and all?"

He sat back, arms crossed, as the waiter delivered our lunch. "Okay. You don't know me well enough to be spilling the beans on your, uh, freelance jobs. I'd sure like to change that, though." He hesitated. "The part about you not knowing me well, that is."

"What would that involve?" I asked, my heart slamming away like a sledge hammer, "considering you're probably chained to your desk, being a lawyer and all."

He grinned. "Dinner? A movie? Do you like to sail?"

"Yes, yes, and not really. Sailing is not my cup of tea." I could hardly breathe. Dinner and a movie with Neal Patterson? Be still, my heart.

"Good. I've got some travel coming up, so let me check my calendar and I'll get back to you." He paused to take a bite or two of his salad. "You know, they have medicine for seasick—"

"It's not that," I jumped in. "You might as well know that I'm divorced. I was married to a sailor—a boat racer, actually. It didn't last too long, but I've had enough of all that—"

"I understand." He patted my hand, sending shivers down my spine. "So dinner and a movie. I assume you don't like slashers."

"Depends," I said. "If they're really scary, it's great. Like *Alien*. I'm not big on gore, though."

"Comedy, then." He smiled.

"No slapstick. No bathroom humor or juvenile stuff like that."

"Damn, you're picky."

We both laughed.

"Now about your crank caller . . ." He leaned back, signaling for the check. "Have you told your uncle about it? It shouldn't be too hard to change your number."

Oh yeah? Try getting a human being at the phone company. "If it happens again, I'll do it, okay?"

Neal laughed. "Just like Alex." Then he looked up from signing the check. "Except much more attractive."

Again, I felt pinned to my chair by the intensity of his gaze. This time, I matched it with my own, all the while feeling my face heat up and my pulse race. Lord help me if we ever found ourselves alone somewhere. I'd be on him like a cat in heat.

As I wandered back to MoneySource, visions of a romantic waterfront dinner and all that might come after it darted around my inflamed brain. But visions of the kissy brunette in white organza and possibly even Vivian Remington intruded. Damn. I'd owned up to being a divorcee. Why hadn't Neal returned the favor? Well, early days yet. Maybe he was the kind of guy who had dinner and a movie with a different woman every day of the week.

When I walked in, the phone was ringing. "It's Vivian," came the voice of one of the women I'd just been visualizing in Neal's arms. "When are you seeing Sutherland?"

"I haven't figured out how to get an invite," I replied, "but since she's on your board, why don't you call her and tell her you hired me to photograph board members for the annual report or something?"

"What part of 'she hates my guts' don't you understand? She never takes calls from me."

Not my problem. Or was it? I could feel my temper flaring up. "You think she'd take a call from me? Practically a stranger?" Then I remembered the diamond hair clip. Of course, she'd take a call. I just had to be persistent and not let myself be fobbed off on some underling. "Well, I suppose I could give it a try . . ."

"Like right now, okay? I must have that coat. My Fish and Wildlife contact is throwing a fit, and things are coming apart at the seams."

"Isn't there a chance the coat is in Florida by now?"

"Nope. Not with temperatures down there hovering in the eighties year round." Vivian sighed as though she had serious reservations about my intelligence. "However, speaking of Florida, I have learned that the senator might be going down there soon. Her calendar is pretty full on Wednesday and Thursday, but you can probably work something out."

I didn't much care for iffy words like "probably," but what was I to do? "How'd you find out all this information?" I asked.

"Neal Patterson. Although that reminds me. I think you ought to know that—" She stopped talking abruptly, and I could hear a man's voice in the background, telling her to get off the phone. "Gotta go," she said and hung up.

I ground my teeth in frustration. What was it I needed to know? Trying to get a photo of that stupid coat was making my head ache big time.

I was still gritting my teeth at home in bed that night, as I listed all the reasons why I should bite the bullet and just get the job done. Number one was the chance to repay, with quadruple interest, all that I owed Alicia. Number two, however, was the inescapable fact that I'd gotten myself caught up in a fascinating situation that might involve blackmail and corruption—a situation that, if I played my cards right (I, being the "cute little blonde," that is), Alicia and my uncle (I'd figure out a way to explain it without really explaining it) and maybe even Neal Patterson would have new respect for me as a force to be reckoned with—as in: Don't mess with P.J. Smythe!

On the dark side, if I got caught breaking and entering—again—it would be impossible to hide the ugly facts from Uncle Alex. He would have a coronary. I would go to jail. And the man I very much wanted to get to know better would be really glad he hadn't tarnished his own reputation by associating with a criminal.

Soon after dawn, just as I was about to nod off, the telephone rang.

"I've got horrible news," said Alicia. "I just found out that Vivian Remington is dead."

CHAPTER TWELVE

I was not accustomed to the presence of the Grim Reaper—except for my mother's death, which had not been unexpected and which had provoked feelings of grief and guilt, mixed with relief, because it had meant an end to her horrible suffering. But Vivian Remington! I'd spoken to her only a few hours earlier. How could someone so vivid and alive suddenly be otherwise? "What happened?" I asked Alicia.

"It was on the late-night news. A neighbor who'd been walking Vivian's dog returned and found her body."

"Oh, my God." I sat there staring at the illuminated readout on my alarm clock. It was 6:30. And, yes, it was like a huge weight being lifted from my chest. The charade was over. Life could go back to normal.

"I doubt it was natural, someone her age. So there's probably going to be an investigation."

I felt the hairs on my arms stand up. "And they'll find out I was one of her visitors at the office and, oh shit."

"Yeah. And I was so close!"

"Is that all you can think of? Your precious goddamn film? What about me? The cops are going to ask me about my relationship to her, and I'll have to tell them about the film, and then they'll arrest me for impersonating a private investigator!"

"Calm down, P.J. First off, you think they'll believe a story like that? The more you tell them, the more likely it is they'll think you're covering up the real relationship."

"The real relationship was phony, Alicia." I could hear a fingernail tapping against the phone.

"Look. Just play dumb, okay? Say Vivian knew about your expertise tracing skips and asked you to do a personal favor and you never really got around to doing anyth—"

"—It won't work, Alicia. If they do a serious investigation, they'll find out she wrote me a check for five thousand. There's probably even a way they can trace the invitation she gave me for the reception in D.C. Why would she do that?"

"Let me think."

"Did you deposit the check?"

"No. I still have it. I wasn't going to do anything till the filming was finished. And so . . . how about this? Remington asked you to do a favor and wrote out the check. You never cashed it because you wouldn't agree to do whatever it was she wanted you to do."

"And leave Marguerite Sutherland out of it. Totally."

"Right. Think up some innocuous thing that you, excellent skip tracer that you are, could do but wouldn't do for ethical reasons. I'll give you the check. If there's any way you could get over to Vivian's office and put it in a drawer somewhere, it'll look even better."

"Oh, sure. Just when the police are starting their investigation. You know, Alicia, I always had a bad feeling about this caper. I should have trusted my instincts. But, unfortunately, you are right. They would never believe the truth. Uncle Alex wouldn't either. That said, if I do wind up in jail, you had better find me the slickest, meanest criminal lawyer you can afford. Deal?"

"Deal." Pause. More finger tapping. "And thanks, P.J."

"Oh. And one other thing: I assume you're planning to remove the hidden camera and shut down the Banner Building office."

"Yeah. I guess so."

"Well, don't. Shut the office, that is. I can't have the police showing up at MoneySource. So I'm going to try to be at the Banner Building office as much as I can until we get a better idea of how serious this is. You can afford it, can't you?"

"At those rates? You must be kidding."

Hands shaking, I put the phone down. Given the circumstances of my all-too-brief relationship with Vivian, it was probably understandable that I didn't feel broken up about her untimely demise. I wandered into the bathroom and looked myself in the eye. "What's wrong with this picture?" I said to the image staring back at me. The good and virtuous citizen would help the police with their inquiries, not stonewall them, let alone obstruct justice. But doing so would put me in the slammer. I didn't want that to happen. This mess wasn't my fault, after all. It was Alicia's. And yet ratting her out would be the height of disloyalty. She'd skate because there was nothing illegal about filming a documentary, no matter how whacko it was, and I'd still wind up in jail.

What if the police determined that Vivian Remington had been murdered? If Marguerite Sutherland had somehow learned that Vivian might be trying to nail her for stealing the ocelot coat (or embarrass her by creating the impression that she had stolen it), would she commit murder? If I were a detective, Sutherland would be my number one suspect. Only I had just agreed to keep Sutherland out of the picture. I splashed cold water on my face.

After a brief shower and a promise to myself that I would scrub the stall thoroughly before I again set foot inside it, I brewed myself a cup of instant. There was nothing in the *Capital* about Vivian's demise, but perhaps the paper had already gone to bed when her body was discovered.

The sky outside my bedroom window did not promise a

sunny day, but at least I didn't have to scrape ice off my windshield. It was time to clean up the so-called "office." I drove to the Banner Building, mentally willing the weather gods to think it might as well be spring, only I couldn't recall the lyrics.

Somebody had dropped the *Bay Weekly* on the lobby floor, and I found myself staring at a lurid headline: "Environmentalist OD's on Heroin." Now that was a stunner. Vivian, a drug addict? I scanned the short item to discover that not even her boss believed it. I tore the page out and dumped the paper in the trash. Grabbing a wad of paper towels, I wiped off the desk, restacked the notepads, covered the ancient office machines, and tore the one remaining copy of my "report" to Remington into tiny little pieces, flushing them down the toilet.

Oh, God. The original was on Vivian's desk. It mentioned Sutherland by name. I was up the creek—unless I could somehow retrieve the damned thing before the police came calling.

The woman answering the phone at the Wetland Alliance had a frog in her voice as though she had been crying a lot. After introducing myself as an investigator whom Vivian had hired, I asked to speak to the person who would be taking over her work.

"I don't think that's been decided yet," she said with such palpable hostility that my hand involuntarily brushed my chest to see if I'd worn fur. "Let me put you through to the executive director."

Before I could ask for a name, the line clicked and a deep voice said, "James Morton." I recalled hearing similarly basso tones in the background telling Vivian to get off the phone when she'd called me yesterday.

"This is Paula Jones," I said. "First of all, let me say how sorry I am about your recent loss."

"We are devastated." I heard a slight catch in his voice. "Which paper are you with?"

"Oh. Sorry. I'm not a reporter. Vivian Remington hired me recently to look into a matter, and I wanted to talk to the person who'll be taking over her work."

"Look into what?" Clearly Morton did not believe his ears. And that meant Vivian had never got around to telling him about the missing coat.

"Illegal wildlife trade," I blurted out.

"You must be mistaken. This is the Wetland Protectors Alliance. We do wetlands conservation."

"But you do, uh, did employ Vivian Remington, right?"

"She was an expert in ecosystem water flow, yes. But we don't have anything to do with wildlife trade issues."

"And there's no connection between the two?" I was stalling, trying to figure out how I was going to get from Vivian's clueless boss to a person who actually might be able to help.

"I don't have time for a lesson in ecology," he said, and the phone clicked to silence.

Ouch. Now what was I going to do? What I wanted was to just forget the whole thing. Let the police figure out what Vivian was up to. Let the Feds try to get that stupid fur coat back from Senator Marguerite Sutherland. I wondered if there could be a connection between what happened to Vivian and the unbelievably bad run of luck that I had encountered ever since I'd agreed to star in Alicia's film. In addition to the crank calls, the break-ins, the lurker in the hallway, and my "client" dying, my ex had showed up, trying to take advantage of my hospitality. Talk about bad karma piling up.

While trying to sort it all out, I used my cell to log onto the Wetland Protectors Alliance Web site, mental fingers crossed that they didn't update their staff directory too often. With any luck, there would be only one Marv.

"Could I speak to Mr. Ross?" I asked when the receptionist answered the phone.

"He no longer works here."

"Oh. Well, I have a cashier's check from the comptroller's office that I need to mail to him. Could you give me a phone number where I could reach him?"

"No." I heard a click as though she'd hung up on me, but then a more mature-sounding female voice said, "Human Resources."

"Ah, yes. I was just trying to get in touch with Marvin Ross. I'm with the comptroller."

"I'm sorry. We don't give out telephone numbers or addresses of former staff."

"Oh, dear," I said trying to sound terribly concerned. "I don't know what I'm going to do. I've got a cashier's check here for him, and the only contact information is his telephone number there at work."

"Maybe he'll call you," she said helpfully.

"But he doesn't know we have money for him. It's part of a settlement from a class action suit." Praying that Ms. Human Resources was as ignorant as I was about payouts from class action suits, I pressed on. "I realize you must respect the privacy of your current and former employees, but couldn't you at least give me the name of his current employer?"

"I don't have that information, but perhaps James Morton, our executive director, might know. Hold on a minute."

Uh-oh. Since I'd just spoken to James Morton, he might recognize my voice. I was just about to hang up when a man with a Spanish accent said, "Allo?"

"I'm trying to get in touch with Marvin Ross."

"Jes," said the man. "He ees my fren. You give me your number. I give to heem, and if he wan', he call you."

I had no choice. I really wanted to talk to Marv, and I was

betting he definitely wanted to talk to me since the purpose of my call seemed to involve a large sum of money. "And you are . . . ?"

"Jesús. Marv, he going with my seester."

From what I recalled of the sandal-shod, overall-clad visitor to Vivian's office, Marv was not exactly an eyeful. He'd struck me as an angry loser. Definitely not my type, but maybe Jesús's sister was near-sighted.

I could hear sleet pinging against the windows, and the sky lightened from slate to white. With any luck, the sleet would turn to rain and send the icy stuff westward toward Washington. I pulled a deck of cards out of the drawer and laid out a hand of solitaire. Playing cards (physically or online) sometimes helped me get my thoughts in order. I had to think of a plausible, though unethical, reason for Vivian's willingness to pay me five thousand, and I had to figure out how to get somebody at the Wetland Protectors Alliance to send that incriminating report back to me.

When it rang, I almost didn't answer the phone, fearing it might be the crank caller, but this time the gods of luck were smiling. Leaning back in my chair, I propped my feet on the corner of the desk. "Mr. Ross," I said, trying to inject a weary sigh into my voice, "This is P.J. Smythe. Did your employer tell you the nature of my call?"

"Something about money you got for me?"

I could barely hear him over the thumpa-thumpa din of a reggae number being played at stadium-level decibels. "That's only partially correct," I held the phone away from my ear.

"I could sure use it. What happened? I overpay my taxes last year?"

"No, nothing like that. This is a bit more complicated. Before I can give you the money, I need something in return: an envelope that's on the desk of one of your colleagues at the Wetland Protectors Alliance."

"I don't work there anymore. The bi—They downsized my job."

"Oh, that is really too bad. You see, the envelope contains a report that could be potentially damning to one of your scientists."

"Who?"

"Vivian Remington."

I could almost hear the smile in his reply. "No shit? What do you want it for? I mean, supposing I could get it for you—say, I still have contacts there who'd do it for me—what would you do with it?"

"I'm sorry, Mr. Ross. I'm not at liberty to reveal that kind of information. Indeed, I myself don't really know what my superiors intend to do with it. All I know is they are willing to pay quite a handsome sum of money to retrieve the document."

"What's it look like?"

Shoving a fist in the air, I described the envelope. "You'll be able to spot it from any other items on the desk because, strangely, her name was typed on the envelope. It wasn't computer-generated, if you get my drift."

"Typed, huh? Like with one a those clunky old manuals?"

"That is correct."

"Weird, man."

"I couldn't agree more. It's the sort of people we're dealing with. They just don't . . . well, enough said. Do you think you could do this for me?"

"How much money are we talking about?"

"Let's just say it's quite generous. You'll be pleased. Oh. And, I must caution you not to open the envelope. In fact, you—or your friend there—should wear protective gloves, just to be safe. It's nothing that can be inhaled, but contact with the skin could be . . . well, I've probably said more than I should."

"It's not anthrax, is it? No way am I gonna—"

"No, I can assure you it's not anthrax. However, it has been known to cause dreadful skin lesions—and leave scars."

"Holy shit. Was she a spy?"

"Again, I'm not at liberty . . ." I paused. "Oh. One other thing: I'll need to pick up the envelope from you and get you to sign a receipt, Mr. Ross," I said in my most bureaucratic tone of voice. "If you'll give me your address, we'll make the exchange tomorrow." I had to cradle the phone against my shoulder so I could write down the answer, and by the time I'd confirmed the location somewhere in Eastport, permanent deafness seemed likely.

Why I made the next call can only be explained by the fact that I was on a roll. Or, more accurately, I was really into my role as P.J. Smythe, private eye. Having snookered Marvin Ross into retrieving the report, I was riding a wave of supreme confidence. If I could unravel the mystery of Vivian's real motive in hiring me or her true intentions regarding Senator Marguerite Sutherland, I would win a gold star. The police would readily forgive my failure to possess a real license in exchange for the chance to go after much bigger fish.

Using the staff directory, I dialed the Wetland Protectors Alliance one more time and got the voicemail of Sandy Jones, program assistant for Everglades Restoration. I gave the perky-sounding Sandy my number at MoneySource, figuring the Banner Building office would be shut down as soon as Alicia showed up with the check.

Then I went to lunch, greatly cheered by the sight of dry streets, even though the sun was glaring right in my eyes. I stopped at the Deli Depot and got a turkey Reuben to go, side of redskin potato salad, and a fudge brownie.

When I got back to the Banner Building, there were two strangers loitering in the lobby.

"P.J. Smythe?"

I nodded, swallowing a lump. I knew they weren't prospective clients. The five-foot-nine stunning redhead with light blue eyes was wearing a camel-colored cashmere blazer and jeans. Her name, according to the ID she showed me, was Rowena Fitzhugh. Her thin, short, wiry partner had cropped gray hair and the clenched-teeth jaw that one often sees in jockeys. I wondered if this was his second career. His name was George Peabody.

"What can I do for you?" I asked as we reached the fourth-floor office. I held a hand out offering the sole client chair to Ms. Fitzhugh. She stood while the jockey perched one hip on the chair's arm. Both of them eyed the *Bay Weekly* in the trash can with a big hole in the page where I'd ripped out the item about Vivian Remington's death.

"Vivian Remington," he said. "You know her?"

"Briefly. She asked me to help find, uh, somebody."

"You a licensed private eye?" His gaze roamed around the office's stained walls where it landed on an Edward Hopper print of a Depression-era cafeteria.

"Oh, no. No. No." I replied, my hands out. "I'm a skip tracer. I guess she thought I could help."

"Why?" said the redhead. "I mean, why you?"

Good question. "She said she'd heard about me and thought I might be able to help her locate a younger sister who used to live over in Eastport but who doesn't seem to be there now."

"Did you?" Peabody had pulled out a notebook and was taking notes. "Find the sister, that is."

"No. I told her I couldn't do it. My unc—Uh, my boss doesn't like us to freelance."

"So that was it? She asked. You said no. End of relationship?"

I nodded. "More or less."

"You her pusher?"

Fitzhugh's question made my heart freeze. "Her *what?*"

Peabody flipped some pages back. "Our records indicate you were involved in the drug scene in Charlottesville seven years ago."

Where's that lawyer? "I was arrested for breaking into my boyfriend's apartment and trashing it. He didn't press charges."

"He, meaning Gareth Swenson?" Redhead was giving me the you-might-as-well-confess-all stare, which at least got my heart thudding again.

I nodded. "I have never done drugs. Period."

The jockey's eyes turned cold and flat. "Okay. Just dealt them, huh? Otherwise, how can you explain why your fingerprints were found on a bottle of prescription pills in the victim's apartment?"

My hand flew up to my mouth. "There must be some mistake!"

"Maybe you didn't understand when I asked if you were Ms. Remington's pusher," said Fitzhugh. "Nowadays, that includes prescription medications, not just dope."

As she spoke, my frozen brain unstuck itself, presenting for my rueful examination a tiny memory of my visit to Vivian's office when I'd taken advantage of her absence from the room to peek at the label on her prescription. "I think I need a lawyer."

Peabody snapped his notebook shut. "Normally, we'd be taking you in for further questioning, but there are other things we need to check out first. It would be helpful, however, if you'd cooperate."

"It wasn't sleeping pills?"

Neither of them bothered to answer me.

"Okay. I was in Vivian's office on Tuesday, and she pulled this bottle out of her backpack and set it down on the desk and then she got up and left the office momentarily and so I, uh—I guess I was just too curious for my own good, huh?—anyway, I picked it up so I could read the label."

"She catch you doing that?" asked Fitzhugh.

I shrugged. "Hard to say. She didn't mention it. Went right back to what we'd been talking about earlier."

"Sure." Peabody gave Fitzhugh a quick nod. Even though he never unclenched his jaw, I could swear I heard him say, "We'll be back" as they headed out the door. I plopped into the chair, wondering how bad things could get.

I phoned Neal Patterson to tell him about the visit from the police and asked if he'd seen the item in the *Bay Weekly*.

"No. What does it say?"

I read it to him, waiting breathlessly for a reaction.

"No way. Not Vivian. Not possible. She did not do drugs. Ask anyone who knows her. She was Nature Girl personified."

"They seem to think somebody might have given her an overdose."

"Like you, for example?" He gave a short laugh. "How'd they reach that stupid conclusion?"

Okay. Nobody but Alicia (and Gareth) knew about my Charlottesville adventures. "My fingerprints are on Vivian's medicine bottle. I explained that, but I don't think they bought it."

"You should never volunteer information to the police, P.J. It can end up biting you on the—anyway, I think you should get a lawyer. I'll ask around here. See who they recommend in the criminal area."

The thought of Neal Patterson coming to my rescue made me feel warm in a way I hadn't when Alicia had made the same offer. Still, if I was in as much trouble as seemed to be the case, maybe more than one lawyer would be a good idea, although, dammit, I was innocent!

"I appreciate your concern, Neal, but no way can I afford—"

"Don't worry about it. We'll see if we can find somebody to

do it pro bono."

"And in the meantime, I just hold my breath, waiting to get arrested?"

"That would be my advice. But don't worry. The police are just shaking the bushes to see what jumps out."

"So far that's been yours truly. I better see what I can find out before—"

"Bad idea, P.J. You don't want to get into anything you can't—"

"It's my neck, dammit."

"You still need a lawyer."

"Okay. Okay. But I'm not going to sit here, twiddling my thumbs."

I could hear fingers drumming on a desk. "You're not thinking this has something to do with that favor Vivian asked you to do?"

I wonder if events would have taken a different course if I'd blurted out the complete story of the film project and the stolen fur coat and Marguerite Sutherland and the report that was still lying on Vivian's desk, just waiting for the police to find it. I didn't, partly because it was important that Neal Patterson think of me as a normal, squared-away sort of woman, not a craze-o wannabe private eye, but mostly because truth-telling wasn't in my nature. Instead, I said, "I don't know. All I need to do is prove she wasn't into the drug scene, right?"

"Proving a negative can be really hard, P.J."

"Going to jail is harder."

"Fine. Do what you can. But remember, the police are not your friends—and they will get really mad if you meddle in their affairs."

"I understand."

"Man, this sucks. I bet your uncle is furious."

"He doesn't know, and I want to keep it that way, *capisce?*"

Neal chuckled. "At least you've got the vocabulary mastered."

"Look," I jumped in. "No need to get Uncle Alex worried, okay? This whole thing will be cleared up in no time."

CHAPTER THIRTEEN

With the blinds shut against the sun's glare, I put my feet up on the desk. What would a real private eye do in such circumstances? He—she—would talk to the victim's friends and family. Then she'd search Vivian's home and office (after the police were finished, of course), looking for any indication of a drug habit—the problem being the police would take with them all the pertinent evidence. But maybe not. Maybe they were so convinced of a drug overdose, their search would be mostly focused on finding Vivian's supplier. I suppressed a shudder. And then sat up, dropping my feet to the floor.

Gareth Swenson. Back to his old tricks? Maybe his so-called friendship with Vivian in grad school had a drug component to it. And how would I find that out? I could ask him, of course. But he would deny it. I could also rat him out to the police, show them the evidence I had of Gareth's prior dealings—if, that is, I could find the damned pictures—and then I would forever wonder if he had, indeed, changed. People do, after all. Plus, his wife would be in real trouble if her husband ended up in jail.

Pulling a yellow pad out of the drawer, I started making a list of suspects and possible motives. It looked like this:

Gareth Swenson: Sold Vivian an impure dose or murdered her because she knew about his C'ville past?

Marguerite Sutherland: Had Gareth (or some other minion)

kill Vivian? Possible motive: Revenge for earlier job termination? Vanquish Everglades foe? Cover up theft of coat? Cover up illegal trade in spotted fur coats?

Marvin Ross: Revenge for getting fired?

Juan Carlos Francisco: Vanquish Everglades foe? Cover up illegal trade in fur?

unknown home invader: robbery?

other unknown individuals: ???????

Vivian herself took too many sleeping pills?

Notice all the question marks? Neal was right. This was not going to be easy. Of course, I'd strayed way beyond proving Vivian didn't do drugs. Somehow, I'd convinced myself that she'd been murdered by any of the possible suspects on my list. At that point, I developed a sudden need for popcorn and headed off to the Seven-Eleven.

When I walked back to the office, Bobby Crane was sitting at the desk, his scuffed topsiders propped on the corner, hands clasped behind his head. I'd only figured to be gone a minute or so, so why lock up? "What are you doing here?" I asked him.

"What's with the office décor? Looks like something out of a film noir movie."

I tapped my foot and sighed.

"Do you have any idea how cold it gets on a sailboat in the winter?"

"And your point?"

Bobby's bloodshot eyes peered past my shoulder as though he hoped to see Vivian lurking in the hallway behind me. "Where's the Warrior Princess?"

"Dead."

"Whoa. You're kidding."

"Nope."

"Well, that's a bummer." He dropped his feet to the floor,

stood up, and offered me my own chair. "I have a favor to ask," he said.

"Why am I not surprised?"

"Look, P.J., all I want is a bed. For one night. Is that too much to ask?"

"Go to a shelter."

"That's cold, P.J. Really cold."

"The shelters are warm."

"C'mon, P.J. Gimme a break." His smile reminded me of how charmed I'd once been to be its recipient. "How about I repay you? Maybe watch your back now that Xena's—"

"Vivian. Her name is—was Vivian."

"Whatever. Couldn't I help somehow? Earn my keep?" He sat down in the chair in front of my desk.

I rolled my eyes heavenward, praying the skies would open and send an alien UFO straight down through the ceiling to whisk Bobby off to the inky depths of intergalactic space.

"It might snow," said Bobby. "I heard it on NOAA."

"You really want to help?" I eyed him suspiciously.

"Sure."

"Then start by telling me how long you've been in town."

"Only a coupla days," he said. "But it's really frigid on the boat, and I figured—"

"You figured out how to find this place."

"Vivian pointed it out the other day. You're practically the only tenant, you know."

He had a point. I leaned against the doorjamb and crossed one ankle over the other. "Where were you Tuesday night?"

"At Davis's over in Eastport, having a few." He dropped his feet to the floor and leaned forward. "Jason Pilcher was there. You remember him? We were talkin' about what happened to his pal Max at last year's tug."

Every fall in the Slaughter Across the Water "International"

Tug of War, a rope is stretched across Annapolis Harbor from the City Dock to Eastport, and volunteer teams from each side battle each other to tug the rope across one of two equally distant floats to raise money for local charities. The losing team must send one of its members into the water to atone for the loss.

"Let me guess. He was the designated dunkee."

"Man, he was so wasted, he nearly drowned."

Wonderful. I made a mental note to write down the name of Bobby's drinking pal. "Where were you last Saturday?"

He scratched his head a moment. "Somewhere between Cape May and Baltimore. I didn't make it into port here until Tuesday morning. Now, what's this all about?"

"None of your business, Bobby. It's just that some strange things have been happening—"

"Which is why you need me watching your back."

Like he'd be any good at it, being boozed up most of the time. If Bobby had not been the intruder who'd visited my apartment on Saturday and if he had an alibi for Tuesday when I'd had to lock myself in my office overnight, then maybe it would be okay to let him crash in my place. He'd drink all my beer, maybe even find the wine in my cupboard, but it *was* frightfully cold outside. If he wound up dying of hypothermia, I'd only have my hard-hearted self to blame. Okay, it was crazy, but I reached into my purse anyway. Twisting off the key to my apartment, I tossed it to Bobby. "Go ahead and stay there tonight. But that's it, you understand?"

He caught the key one-handed and pocketed it, giving me another razzle-dazzle smile. "Want pizza? I could order in."

"Don't even think about it," I said. "I'm offering you a place to sleep. Nothing more. In fact, I'm not going to be there at all."

His face fell and then rearranged itself into a leer. "Got a hot date?"

"Yes," I said, enjoying the brief flash of green that I glimpsed in those pale blue eyes. If only he knew the truth.

After Bobby left, I called Alicia and invited myself over to spend the night.

"Sure. We need to talk anyway, and I'll give you the check."

"Actually, I need it before then." I explained the ploy I'd used to retrieve the report off of Vivian's desk. By the time I'd got to the anthrax part, she was giggling like a teenager.

"He fell for this?"

"Like a stone."

"Hmmm. And you said the amount he'd get would be what?"

"Generous. I didn't know how much you'd be willing to fork over, but, frankly, that report in the hands of the police would put Senator Sutherland straight into the picture, not to mention making them even more suspicious of me." I then told her about their visit. "So this isn't funny anymore—if it ever was. It was your idea to launch the caper, so—"

"Okay. Okay. I hear ya. How about three hundred?"

"Way too low."

"Five? Six?"

"Look, a super-secret spy agency wouldn't be paying chicken feed for valuable intelligence. I'm afraid you should be thinking thousands, not hundreds."

We settled on thirty-five hundred, not a bad price for a one-pager. Cash, not check, and therefore untraceable, to be delivered to me at the Banner Building later in the afternoon.

As the day stretched on, I kept revisiting the implications of Neal Patterson getting me a lawyer. For starters, I'd have to tell the guy why I'd become implicated in the death of Vivian Remington. I could stick to the story Alicia and I concocted, but then I'd be lying to the one person who needed to know the truth. It complicated things, especially because Neal had asked me to let him know what my plans were over lunch tomorrow. (Oh, happy day.)

I Googled Vivian, only to find a couple of sites reporting her murder and tons of stuff about her work, including some articles in scientific journals. What I wanted was much more personal, so I wound up having to thumb through the battered telephone book Alicia had provided to go with the vintage telephone. It had only an address and phone number. No other Remingtons. Of course, what did I know about the dame? She might be divorced or widowed, keeping her husband's name. Her family might live in Florida or some other watery place that would capture the imagination of a budding hydrologist.

As for her doing drugs, I wished I knew more about Vivian Marchman Remington than what Google could tell me or from what I'd managed to glean from our all-too-brief "business" relationship. Sure, she'd been harsh enough to try to force me into breaking and entering Sutherland's home, but that didn't really equate with a drug habit, to my way of thinking. Unless that fur coat wasn't really U.S. government property. Unless Vivian herself stole the coat and Marguerite Sutherland found out about it and was going to blackmail her! Damn.

Okay, it was way past time to return the missing diamond clip. In fact, if I'd been listening to that little voice in my head, I would have heard it tell me to suck it up and make the phone call I'd been avoiding because of the barriers that are always erected between public figures and the person trying to reach them.

"I'd like to speak to Senator Sutherland, please," I lowered my voice a couple of octaves to make it sound older and more professional.

"And the nature of your call?" came the polite southern-accented reply.

"I found something at a Washington reception that I believe might belong to her."

"If you'll give me a description and your telephone number, I'll ask her about it."

"Sorry. I need to have the senator describe it to me just to be sure it's hers."

"Hmmmmph." Soon I was listening to the Musak version of "Hey Jude." I checked my watch. It was 3:50 P.M.

At 4:10, I had managed to uncover all but one ace in my game of solitaire and was trying to figure out if I had a chance of winning. "Patience," I kept whispering to myself. "Patience is a—"

"You imbecile!" The voice at the other end of the line was so shrill, it nearly shattered my eardrum. I yanked the phone away as the pitch sheared up another octave. "Those notes were critically important. If you don't find them in the next five minutes, you're outta here. Got that?"

"Uh, hello?" I said. "Is this Senator Marguerite Sutherland?"

There was a slight cough, and the voice dropped back down to normal pitch. "What can I do for you?"

Okay. I'd have to take it on faith. The accent was certainly not as southern as the person who'd answered the phone. "Hi. I'm P.J. Smythe." I smiled pleasantly so she could hear my good intentions. "The photographer? We met at the reception for the Florida Legislature in Washington last Saturday?"

"Yes?"

I could tell she didn't remember me at all. "I was just calling to see when you might want to schedule a photo session. I've got some time available in the next week or so, and I know you'll be really happy to have some mementos of your illustrious career."

"Did I tell you I was interested?" She didn't sound so much hostile as puzzled.

"Oh, yes," I lied. "You said you couldn't wait to get started."

"I'm really booked right now, but maybe I could fit you in sometime next week."

"Great. And one other thing, Senator. We really must get a shot of you in that gorgeous fur coat I saw you carrying at the D.C. reception."

"Oh. Were you thinking of photographing the gown too? Because I won't be able to do that and change in time for—"

"Oh, no problem. We'll skip the dress, but that coat is just too lovely for wor—"

"Fine. Whatever."

"And, oh, I almost forgot! Weren't you wearing a beautiful diamond clip in your hair the night we met?"

"Mm-hmm. I do remember losing it sometime around then. Did you find it?"

"Perhaps. If you could just describe it to me, so I can be sure it's yours and not somebody else's?"

"It was oval-shaped with about twenty or so diamond chips in it and a platinum setting."

Yep. "I found it in the ladies' room at the Cosmos Club, and I wondered if it didn't belong to you. Tell you what. I'll return it when we get together next week."

There was a sigh at the other end of the line and the sound of rustling papers. "I have a theater engagement Tuesday evening. You could come by at four-thirty. That should give us an hour or two for whatever you had in mind."

Pumping my fist in the air, I collected the directions to her posh Woodley Park address.

Darkness had fallen by the time I crossed Spa Creek into Eastport. In January 1998, a few denizens of the area staged a mock secession from Annapolis, declaring their neighborhood the "Maritime Republic of Eastport." Decking themselves out in

Revolutionary War costumes and firing Brussels sprouts from mock muskets, they'd protested the hegemony of snooty Annapolis across the harbor. They even had their own flag, featuring a boat and two Labradors and sporting a motto dear to my heart: "We Like It This Way."

No sentry stood guard on the Eastport side, waiting to arrest invading Annapolitans, so I reached Marvin Ross's apartment right on time. I knew it was the right place from the noise pulsing through the walls.

"Hi, I'm P.J. Smythe," I announced to the overall-clad, shirtless, and barefoot punk who opened the door. "I'm the one who called this afternoon?"

"Oh, right. The envelope." Ross stood back from the doorway and motioned me inside. "Say, didn't I see you in there the other day, talking to Viv?"

I gave him a secretive smile. "We always try to go straight to the source, but if that doesn't work . . ." I shrugged, gazing at the surroundings. I'd been expecting a hovel strewn with dirty clothes and dried pizza crusts, but the room I entered was immaculate. The gray wall-to-wall carpeting had only a few signs of wear and tear. A serious stereo system was stacked in the corner, surrounded by neatly filed compact disks. A laptop was open on the coffee table in front of the room's only piece of furniture—a fifties-style divan covered in herringbone tweed. The scent of cloves permeated the place, making me wonder if Marv smoked pot.

"Nice place," I yelled, plopping down on the sofa.

Marv lowered himself into a Yoga-like pretzel position on the floor beside his open laptop.

"Could you, uh—?" I gestured toward the stereo.

He grabbed the remote and clicked us into blissful silence. "So. I got the envelope. How much money we talking about?"

"First, the envelope, please?" I held my hand out and then

pulled it back. "Oops." I pulled my glove on. "There, that's better."

Ross jumped and went into the kitchen where I heard some
drawers slamming. Reappearing with one hand inside a plastic
glove, he handed me a familiar-looking manila envelope.

I opened the flap. "Your, uh, colleague took precautions as
well?"

He nodded, shoulders tense, as I read the document.

"Good. Excellent. I pulled a wad of cash out of my purse and
counted out the thirty-five hundred.

"Wow. This is more than I—Although, considering the
risk . . ." He shoved the wad into his pocket. "Anything else you
need along these lines, you just let me know. Okay?"

"Actually, there is. We're aware that Vivian Remington was
responsible for firing you from the Wetland Protectors Alliance."

His eyes narrowed. "So?"

"We need to know why."

"None of your business."

"Too bad," I replied. "I'm not sure what we'd pay for it
anyway, but it might be substant—"

"—The bitch accused me of being a spy."

"Really. How ironic. What did you do?"

"Nothing wrong. One of the board members wanted copies
of some memos on stuff they were doing. I did what she asked."

"Oh, dear. You got fired for doing your job?"

"Sucks, doesn't it? That bitch deserves—well, I guess dying's
kinda harsh . . ."

"Of a drug overdose. Did you know that?"

His eyes widened. "You're shitting me."

"That's what I read in the paper. You get the *Bay Weekly*?"

"Naw. I'm not into that scene. But it's just the kinda story
you'd find in a rag like that. If Vivian did drugs, then I'm

dumber than I thought. That gal—uh, woman—was so into living green, she made the rest of us look like oil company executives."

"Well." I stood up. "Let me get back to you, Marv. I'm not sure what you've told me will impress my superiors, but you never know."

"So what else can I tell you? Like, did she have any friends? Not that I know of—except, she did have a visitor the other day. Not part of the environmental scene, either. The guy was wearing snakeskin boots."

Tony Marrero. "A friend, you think?"

"Naw. Didn't know where her office was. I'm thinkin' if she did drugs, maybe he was her supplier."

"But you just said—"

"Yeah. Yeah." He shrugged. "But sometimes you never know. I've seen him before, too. Can't think of where."

"Well, maybe it'll come to you later. If you do remember, please give me a call. Pulling my other glove on, I opened the door. "Nice talking to you, Marv. Oh. That board member you were helping? What's her name?"

He opened his mouth to tell me and then shut it. "No way, lady. You're just trying to set me up for—"

"For what?"

"I dunno. Slandering an important politici—" He stopped. "I've said enough—money or not."

Clearly, our meeting was over.

"Nice car," he said as I opened the door to my VW. I drove away, the reggae music beating against my eardrums as clearly as though I'd tuned it into my car radio.

February 4, 2003

She needs to use the toilet so bad, her eyes are watering, but the swarthy detective sitting across the table from her has his head down while he goes over his notes.

"You knew him for about six months, you say?"

"About that, I think." She squirms in the chair. "Is there a ladies' room here?"

The detective looks up, a knowing, I-knew-you-were-a-sissy smirk on his face. "Down the hall. First door on the left."

Back in the interview room, she notices for the first time that it is very warm. The detective's tie is loosened, and he's rolled up the sleeves of his blue cotton shirt.

She pulls her sweater over her head and gets another "you wimp" smirk. Or maybe her t-shirt is a bit too clingy.

"You never suspected him of being involved with drugs?"

"No."

The detective scratches what passes for hair on his head. "Funny. We had it on very solid authority that Swenson was dealing heroin."

She can't help suppressing a shudder at the thought of all the messed-up lives those little baggies had been destined to destroy.

"Cold?" He reaches across the table and hands her the sweater she's just removed.

She puts the sweater in her lap. They have nothing on her. She's never done drugs herself, even marijuana. She didn't know what Gareth was up to—until . . . And since he's dropped the vandalism charges, the least she can do is save him from his own recklessness.

"So this was all nothing more than a lover's spat?" The detective tilts his chair back and balances on the two back legs. "And when you heard that message on his answering machine, you just lost it?"

Now would be the time to produce a blush, but she's never been able to do it on demand. She settles for lowering her eyes and then raising them. "I thought he loved me."

The detective yawns and scratches the stubble on his face.

"So you trashed his kitchen and broke a mirror in the living room."

She nods.

The chair slams down and he slaps his hands on the table. "Bullshit. You were in on the whole thing."

"I was not." Her heart begins to thud.

"Hah. He tells you to get rid of the stuff and then throw a little pretend tantrum to explain why you're there."

"I wouldn't have to explain it," she says, blushing this time. "I sometimes spent, uh, slept over."

"Then how come you didn't have a key?"

Duh. Because she wasn't his one and only? She crosses her arms, determined not to say another word.

"Okay, having you break into the place does make it look more spontaneous. Guy's clever that way. But let me tell you something, girl. I ever see the two of you together, it'll be all the proof I need that you destroyed the evidence of his crime."

CHAPTER FOURTEEN

It was shortly after nine when I left Eastport, my head spinning round and round with thoughts of the damage Marvin Ross could have caused by giving Marguerite Sutherland copies of the Alliance's memos—especially if they had been about the Everglades. I still couldn't understand why Vivian hadn't told her boss about the danger they were in with Sutherland on their board. Okay. Vivian couldn't tell him. But the only reason that made sense was that Morton was in on it—that he was, in effect, undermining the outfit he headed.

Back at the Banner Building, I dashed up the stairs, unlocked the door to Marlowe's office, and pulled open the middle drawer of the filing cabinet where I'd stashed the phone book. That's when I discovered what the peeling day-glo label meant. The C - NTENTS did indeed - IP. I'd been balancing one hand on the open drawer while thumbing through the directory, and the damned cabinet nearly fell over.

I dialed the offices of the Wetland Protectors Alliance and got a recorded message about their office hours. No real proof that the place was empty, but it would have to do.

My snooping life began at age seven. I could read pretty well by then, and I was determined to find out what my mother was hiding from me concerning my father's name and his where-abouts—or fate. She was downstairs ironing. I was upstairs, standing on my tiptoes on a chair beneath the shelf in her closet. There were scrapbooks full of family photos, including a few of

Uncle Alex when he was my age with his ears sticking out and a goofy, gap-toothed grin on his face. But I couldn't find one single picture of my father (although there were some suspicious gaps on a few pages), not one letter to or from him, nothing to indicate he had ever been a presence in my mother's life. I was too young to realize that the total absence of anything about him itself spoke volumes. And by the time I was old enough to demand some answers, my mother was dead.

All in all, it was not a successful beginning for my snooping career, but it did turn out to be addictive. The only time I deliberately didn't try to discover everything I could about a friend-roommate-boyfriend-husband was six years ago, when I should have defied Gareth Swenson and unearthed his dirty business before I was so far gone on him I would have crawled across cut glass to be by his side.

Knowledge is power, I told myself. And the visit from the police gave me a powerful incentive to do whatever it took to prove Vivian Remington wasn't into drugs. Maybe I'd get lucky and also find out who might have killed her. Was I nuts? The word that works better is desperate. I needed to clear my name before Uncle Alex had to be put into the picture—not to mention Neal Patterson, whose opinion of me would hit the sewers. Marvin Ross had been my only link to the Wetland Protectors Alliance, and I wasn't likely to get much information out of any of the other folks there who probably still held grudges against me for crossing their threshold wearing environmentally incorrect fur.

The lock on the door to the Wetland Protectors Alliance office suite was the kind you can jimmy with a credit card. I used one that was already maxed to the limit. The emergency exit lights gave the hallway a sinister pink glow. After shutting the door, I paused to listen and adjust my eyes to the semidarkness. I could hear the measured *clack clack* of the minute hand on the battery clock over the reception desk. The place felt empty. In fact, it was a fairly safe bet no one would be working in the dark. I flicked on the lights.

Leaning across the police tape, I could see that Vivian's office seemed to be as cluttered as when I'd last been there. I crawled under the flimsy barrier. (Surely the cops had finished. They'd probably forgotten to remove the tape.)

A quick shuffle through the papers on Vivian's desk showed that they were mostly about water distribution in the Everglades, water quality in Florida Bay, and studies of wetlands. Her desk calendar was gone. I could tell because at the top of her desk there was an empty space about the size of a desk calendar. I didn't boot up her computer, figuring the cops had most likely removed the hard drive. Besides, I didn't know the password.

A search of the middle drawer in the desk yielded a safety pin, a mound of rubber bands, and a sampler bottle of Shalimar, which didn't smell woodsy at all. I dabbed some on my wrists before dropping the check into the drawer. No. That would be dumb. The police would know it hadn't been there when they searched. I picked it up and pawed through the contents of the other drawers where I found a comb with three teeth missing, three packets of catsup, one each of salt and pepper, an empty picture frame big enough for a four by six snapshot, and a business card with the name "Gareth Windsor Swenson" engraved on the expensive-looking card stock. Funny, I seemed to recall that his middle name was Wayne. Of course, Windsor would look a whole lot better for a federal office-seeker.

A blank legal pad bore impressions that might have been made by a ballpoint pen on the top sheet, which was missing. I took the sheet with the impressions, folded it carefully, and slipped it into my pocket. As an afterthought, I added Gareth Swenson's card.

Taped to the computer monitor was a ruled index card on

which someone had written in large block letters, "YOUR TOAST." Did it mean "you're toast"? All I knew was Vivian had not written that message. Her handwriting, evidence of which was strewn all over the desk, was so small and cramped that I wished I'd brought my uncle's bifocals with me. The threatening card joined the stuff in my jacket pocket.

There was a memo from James Morton to Vivian sitting at the top of the pile that probably constituted Vivian's in-box. Scanning the first page, I gathered that he was asking her what she thought about a recent study suggesting that more research needed to be done into proposed Everglades restoration efforts because they might have negative effects on Florida Bay to the south. "Dramatically increased freshwater pulses could trigger and lengthen algal blooms and kill grasses in the bay," I read. After much squinting and peering at Vivian's cramped writing, I caught the gist of her note in the margin: "We've known that for years. Got to try something." I pawed through the pile of papers looking for anything that didn't fit the professional hydrologist persona and found zip.

I'd been in Vivian's office for about fifteen minutes, and the bookshelves looked like a three-hour job at least. Would there be anything helpful—like a clue pointing to a killer—in all that mess? Maybe, but who had time to find out? The filing cabinet seemed less daunting. The top drawer held an empty three-ring binder and a three-hole punch. The middle drawer held pay stubs and other office administration trivia like the policy and procedures manual and a training booklet titled, "Negotiation Tactics Workshop." The bottom drawer was dented, as though someone had kicked it, and I had to yank hard before it came flying open. Oh, Vivian. What would your mama say?

It must be the joke photo Vivian had mentioned last time I saw her, but ooh-la-la, what a weird sense of humor her co-workers had! There she was in a full-length ocelot fur coat, open in the front to reveal an expanse of flesh from head to foot, interrupted only by a triangle of dark hair where pelvis met legs. Other than the fur coat, Vivian was wearing a pouty come-hither smile on her face and bright red nail polish on her toes. One hand was shoved in the pocket of the coat. The other dangled a coiled whip in front of the camera. She stood with one foot on the back of a nude man who was lying face down at her feet. His head and feet had been cropped out of the photo, and he had a thin pelt of dark hair running across his shoulders.

I slid the photo into my pocket, jammed the drawer shut, and was headed for the door when I thought, what the hell? I dashed toward the reception desk in search of a floor plan. Halfway there, I figured an office this small wouldn't have one, so I began looking for the largest office, the one in the corner, probably. James Morton's suite was indeed larger, but it was located at the end of a windowless hall at the very back of the office suite as though visitors desiring an audience with Morton were routinely obliged to see everyone else on the staff first.

There were two identical desk calendars on Morton's desk. One was sitting in the middle, and one was at the front of the desk where most people put their calendars. I started flipping backward through the one that had surely belonged to Vivian when I found what Morton and the police had probably discovered earlier: The pages were blank. That's when I remembered the palm-sized electronic toy that she'd been fiddling with the day we first met. No paper records for this hi-tech gal. I slipped the check into the page dated February 6, the date of our second—and last—meeting.

A quick glance at the other calendar showed me that James played squash every Wednesday at one P. M. and that his wife's birthday was tomorrow.

The credenza behind Morton's desk held a gallery of framed photos, one of which showed him shaking hands with Senator

Marguerite Sutherland. Probably when she joined the board. But wait. The woman in the photo looked about ten years younger than the one I'd met at the Cosmos Club. So Morton and Sutherland went back a ways, which might just lend credence to my suspicions that he was in on the whole thing. It would certainly explain why Vivian had been reluctant to tell her boss about Sutherland's reputation for sticky fingers.

The longer I stayed there, however, the more nervous I became. Leaving Vivian's calendar where I had found it, I made my exit. Whoever got there first in the morning might figure someone had forgotten to lock up last evening but would find that nothing had been stolen. I patted the treasures in my pockets, scampered down the stairs to the parking garage, walked under the exit barrier and up the ramp to the street where my uncle's car was parked at the curb.

I shrank into the shadows. Had Uncle Alex been following me? I wouldn't put it past him. He took his parental responsibilities seriously. My stomach grumbled so loudly that I was surprised my uncle didn't turn his head. Except he wasn't sitting in the car. Was he just now letting himself into the offices of the Wetland Protectors Alliance? Was I paranoid? Yep. But wait. I hadn't told him a thing about my current difficulties, so he couldn't possibly know which office suite I had been visiting, could he?

I stood there in the shadows, quietly starving. Surely even Uncle Alex knew that an unattended luxury sedan could not be left that way for too long in this neighborhood before some adventurous teenagers let the air out of the tires. I heard a woman laughing and the click of approaching high heels and stepped further into the shadows as I watched my uncle, sixty-four years of age, holding the car door for a buxom blonde in a skin-tight red dress and four-inch "fuck me" heels. I could smell the perfume she was wearing, but I could not see her face as she slid into the car. Uncle Alex shut the door and, jingling the keys, stepped jauntily around to the driver's side and drove off.

I didn't know whether to be relieved or outraged, so I settled on a mixture of both as I headed up the street toward a pizza parlor where I encountered a swarm of Johnnies so deep into a discussion of the meaning of Plato's cave that it took me twenty minutes to get a medium sausage and pepperoni with extra cheese and a bottle of Bud. I found a table in the corner where I wouldn't have to listen to discussions of metaphysical dialectics and other riveting topics.

Uncle Alex was a bachelor. What he did on his own time was none of my business. Judging from her appearance, chances were that his lady friend didn't earn her living legally. Did I care? Yes. Was it any of my business? I ordered another beer to go with the rest of my pizza.

I sure didn't need this little distraction, but maybe the next time I visited Uncle Alex's office I would look a little further than his in-box. Of course, the better thing to do would be to ask him outright. "Say, Uncle Alex, who's the hooker I saw you with the other night on Clay Street?" Right. Like that wouldn't get me in a bunch of trouble, as in: "What were you doing in that neighborhood?" Better to take the devious route. Same result, fewer negative consequences. Which reminded me that my next destination—only not tonight—should be Vivian Remington's apartment. Once the police were finished with it, of course.

Halfway home, I remembered that Bobby was sleeping over. I detoured to the Banner Building office and spent a few minutes making a record of my interview with Marvin Ross while it was still fresh in my mind. Alicia was expecting me, so I shoved the notes into the filing cabinet and headed over to the Severn River estate that was home to Alicia, her mother, and a staff of servants too numerous to count.

"I don't want to discuss Vivian Remington," I said as Alicia plopped herself onto the cushioned window seat near the bed she'd given me in one of the Ritchies' lavishly furnished guest rooms. I would be sleeping in a four-poster extravaganza so high that it came with a little footstool to help guests reach their destination. Fortunately, the gauzy canopy covering the bed would shield my eyes from exposure to the room's overly ornate red and blue floral wallpaper. A fire that had been burning in the grate had reduced itself to embers, and someone had placed a vase of roses on the dresser. Ah, luxury.

Garbed like a film noir femme fatale, Alicia was wearing turquoise satin pajamas with white piping at the sleeves and neck. "Okay. But mission accomplished, right? You left the check on her desk?"

"Not exactly. The police have already searched her office. The tape's still across the door. If they come back and find the check, they'll know somebody's been messing with the crime scene."

"Damn." She paused, examining one of her nails. "But you did get the report back?"

"It's in a million pieces scattered over three different trash cans."

"And Marv was happy?"

"Words cannot describe. He even offered to tell—make that sell—me more."

"Which you agreed to."

"Without indicating he'd get anything much for it. It actually only confirms some things I already suspected."

Her face brightened. "If you're not careful, P.J., you'll wind up being an excellent private investigator!"

I could feel my face heating up. If only she knew where I planned to go next. "I'm just trying to clear my name," I reminded her.

"Right." She paced the floor, tapping a fingernail against her teeth. "I wish I'd been able to catch it on film."

I groaned. "Give it up, Alicia."

She shrugged. "Okay. Change subject. Did Neal Patterson send you a valentine?"

"I don't want to talk about him either." My head ached, and the aspirin I'd taken didn't seem to be working.

"Well, be a grouch then." She got to her feet, but I waved her back into the chair.

"I have not been home to check my mail. But I'm one hundred percent sure I did not get a valentine or roses or a box of candy from anybody, which I am sure is not the case with you."

"And here I thought the two of you were—"

"Maybe, Alicia. Maybe. I think he already has at least one girlfriend, so give it up. I wasn't expecting anything, and I wasn't disappointed. Although Neal did offer to find me a lawyer. Pro bono. He says I shouldn't say another word to the cops."

Alicia tapped a polished pink nail against her thigh. "Probably good advice. I'm not sure the pro bono thing's a good idea, though. Usually, those guys do civil stuff. They might not be the best thing for a criminal—"

"Do you mind?" I couldn't help how loud my voice sounded. Taking a breath, I lowered it. "I really do not need to be reminded of the mess you put me in."

"Sorry," she said. "I promise I'll make things right. Lawyer, money, metal file, whatever it takes." She spread her arms, palms out.

"Thanks." What else could I say? She knew what I thought of the whole thing. No point in rubbing it in. "My biggest concern right now is my uncle. I think he's seeing a prostitute."

"No!"

"I saw her getting into his car earlier this evening."

"You sure, P.J.? He doesn't strike me as the type who would—"

"Is there a type? I saw them, Alicia. And she was no respectable matron by any means."

"So what are you going to do about it? Confront him?"

"I can't. What would I say? And is it really any of my business?"

"Nope, but it sure is strange."

"What would you do, Alicia? I have always thought of Uncle Alex as such a straight shooter—well, except for his background in East Baltimore."

"He didn't live there, P.J. That's where he worked."

"But the work involved pimps and prostitutes and all sorts of lowlifes."

"And you think it rubbed off?" A pink-tipped index finger moved just beneath her eye and pulled downward.

"What else could it be? I know he hooked up with some pretty shady friends. Still has them too. And he knows how to pick locks . . . Holy cow!"

"What?" Alicia leaned forward.

"The office at the Banner Building. Remember how somebody broke into it last weekend and straightened everything up?"

"Yeah, but that would imply your uncle knows what we've—what you've been up to."

"Oh, God." I put both hands to my head. "Say it isn't so."

"Sounds like your uncle, all right."

"Stop laughing. It was probably him. He knows all kinds of ways to keep tabs on me. Only you'd think he'd be screaming at me by now, I'm so far behind at MoneySource."

"Maybe he's getting a kick out of the whole thing. Like he's just discovered you're a chip off the old block? Shit, next thing you know he's going to be offering you tips."

"Get *off!*"

"And you should take them."

I ran my fingers through my hair. "Dammit, Alicia, he was snooping on me."

She burst out laughing. "Clearly it runs in the family. So what are you going to do?"

"Turnabout's fair play, huh? He starts in on me about playing hooky from MoneySource, and I'll bring up the prostitute."

Stifling a yawn, Alicia stood up and headed for the door. "Maybe he's also the one who broke into your house. You did change the locks, didn't you?"

Like that would stop Uncle Alex.

June 22, 2003

There's a rush forward, and suddenly the black caps and gowns are swallowed up by mothers and fathers and sisters and brothers and she's right in there with them, throwing her arms around her uncle's neck.

"I made it."

"I never thought otherwise," he says. His eyes are watery, and he blinks rapidly. "Rhoda would be so proud."

And now she's tearful, too. Her mother must have longed desperately to see this day, knowing that it was not in God's plan, and God never disappoints.

"I'm so glad you came," she says, patting his damp cheek. "Mama would be so pleased if she knew."

"She knows."

"You two commune regularly, huh?" She's laughing as she looks up at him, but he is not amused.

"One of these days, P.J., you'll get over being so contrary about faith."

"Sure I will." She turns slowly, scanning the crowd. "Didn't you and Alicia sit together?"

He looks around him at the swirling mob. "She was here a minute ago."

A tall, well-dressed man with a ponytail is striding toward them across the grass, and her uncle smiles. "You say hello to that feller while I go find Alicia."

No! She has no intention of talking to that feller. But the crowd pushes them together, and he grabs both of her arms.

"How about giving me those pictures, P.J. Then we can put all this behind us."

"Congratulations to you, too," she says, jerking out of his grasp.

"I'm serious, P.J. You've had your fun, and now I want to know I'm in the clear."

"Tough."

He steps back, but the sun glinting off his glasses masks his expression. "Bitch." He says it softly, regretfully almost.

"Let's just call it insurance," she replies. "Against you ever doing something that stupid again."

"You're not my conscience." He's snarling now, and she steps to the side as Alicia and Uncle Alex emerge from the mob of celebrants. And that's when she spies the swarthy detective. He's standing at the edge of the crowd, watching her and Gareth Swenson. Even at this distance, she can see one eyebrow go up and a slight just-as-I-suspected nod of his head.

CHAPTER FIFTEEN

"So Cecil shows up carrying a dozen long-stemmed American Beauty roses, and what does he find right there in the foyer but two other bouquets that my mother had already put in vases."

I poured myself another cup of watery coffee. I'm one of those people who find it difficult to engage in chit-chat while feeling envious. In fact, I was afraid to make eye contact with Alicia for fear that she would notice that my eyes were crossed. Despite what I'd said the night before, where was the equity in Alicia getting three bouquets of roses for Valentine's Day? "Your mother must not care for Cecil," I said.

We were finishing off a breakfast of bagels and strawberries. The bagels were hard as diamonds and just about as tasty. The strawberries tasted like cardboard—proof of the wisdom that if it doesn't come with hash browns or grits, it ain't breakfast.

"I hadn't thought of that," mused Alicia. "She does think he's too stuck on himself. But imagine the dilemma I was in. Here we were, on our way to the yacht club dance, and Cecil wants to know who my other two admirers are, and one of them is his cousin Luke."

"What did you tell him?"

"I lied. I batted my little ol' eyes and said they were for my mother."

No doubt some of the roses had ended up in a vase on the dresser in the room I'd slept in. I carried my cup to the sink and rinsed it off. "Did you have fun at the dance?"

"No. Cecil was a bore, and my feet were killing me. We left early. Why can't they make comfortable evening shoes for women?"

"Beats me." Stifling a yawn, I peeked at my watch.

Alicia brought her plate and cup to the sink. "Luke is much more interesting. Too bad he's in Bermuda right now."

"Um-hmmmm."

"On the other hand, Neal Patterson . . ."

"Is not your type. He's a lawyer, remember?"

Alicia gave an exaggerated sigh. "Maybe I should reconsider . . ." Then she laughed. "But not while he still has the hots for you."

"What are the signs?"

"He's taking you to lunch today, isn't he?" Alicia twirled a strand of hair around one finger, a characteristic habit when she's goading me.

"I'm afraid that's strictly business. He's going to give me the name of the lawyer he found."

"Well, remember what I said. Of course, you don't want to turn down an offer of help from your soon-to-be boyfriend. So. Let's hit the mall. They're already having their President's Day sales."

I groaned. "What's that got to do with anything? You know I hate shopping."

"Who said anything about shopping?"

"It *is* your middle name."

"Well, since your middle name seems to be Snoop, I thought you might want to look at fur coats and see if somebody there can help you tell the difference between fake and real."

I jumped to my feet. "Will you quit it? Your filming is *over*. The issue of the fur coat is dead—as dead as . . . well. Anyway . . ."

"What if it would help clear your name? You *do* want to do

that, don't you?"

"We agreed to leave Marguerite Sutherland out of it!"

"No need to yell. But, think about it. Marguerite Sutherland stole that coat—maybe to embarrass Vivian Remington, which won't work now—or maybe because she has a thing for over-the-top, tacky-looking furs. Either way, if she knew Vivian was on to her, what better way to solve the problem than to have the threat, as they say, neutralized?"

"Brilliant, Alicia. Absolutely brilliant. I have already thought of it, and I think it's really far-fetched. The only person who says that coat is stolen is—was—Vivian Remington. So it doesn't matter if it turns out to be fake or real or whether I can" (I made little quote marks with my fingers) " 'prove' it's the coat that belongs to the Fish and Wildlife Service. Besides, the mall wouldn't have anything in real spotted fur coats. They're illegal."

Alicia crossed her arms and tapped her foot. "But a furrier would probably know how to tell, wouldn't he? All you need to do is ask."

She was right, of course. What better place to check out the difference between real and fake than in the coat departments at Lord & Taylor or Nordstrom? And I was, after all, going to have a chance to see the damned ocelot coat again. Real soon.

To avoid making the security types nervous, which was what usually happened when I entered upscale stores, Alicia lent me a glittery charcoal sweater beaded in sequins and jet. It fell practically to my knees, and I had to push up the sleeves, but it would do, especially with jeans and running shoes.

While Alicia was trying on designer gowns at Lord & Taylor, I decided to look elsewhere in the mall, provided I could get past a gantlet of willowy model types armed with perfume testers. One of them, an emaciated, overly made-up woman with shoulder-length dark hair, snared me right near the entrance to the store. She was surrounded by a scent so cloying, I sneezed violently, accidentally knocking the bottle out of her hand.

"Oops," I said. "Sorry, but that's almost industrial grade—"

"Go ahead. Take it." She picked the spray bottle off the floor and handed it to me. "I can get more."

"But I don't—" Oh well. Maybe I did. It was probably very expensive. I spritzed some on my wrists, sneezed again, and shoved the tester into my purse.

One level up, I found what I was looking for. The gold-plated sign over the door read "Martin de Jongh, Furrier" and the windows on either side sported mannequins decked out in a variety of luscious-looking coats. A very well-dressed sales clerk approached as I walked into the store.

"Could I show you something in mink or sable?" She had a lovely faux British accent and the attitude to go with it.

"What about something in leopard—or ocelot?"

The saleswoman lifted her nose slightly, probably because I smelled like a whorehouse. "We sell mink, fox, sable, beaver, lynx, or chinchilla."

I decided on sable, mostly because I remembered how lush it looked in the movie *Gorky Park*. Snuggling into the coat, I did a few rounds of the Paula Jo/Paris Hilton strut in front of the full-length mirror. Problem was, I looked more like a kid swaddled in a fur snowsuit than the elegant models one usually sees strolling through newspaper ads. Claiming to be cowed by the steep price, I asked the saleswoman, "Is there a furrier on the premises?"

She raised an eyebrow. "He's in Baltimore today."

Shit. "Let me try something in fake fur, then."

She narrowed her eyes, and looked down her nose. "Not in this store."

"Do you think Nordstrom might have fake furs?"

This got a heavy sigh, as though she couldn't possibly imagine why one would seek out the competition. "Naturally, I can't speak for others," she said with a sniff. "You'd have to ask them. But if you want a de Jongh genuine fur coat and nothing we have in the store appeals to you, I could certainly place an order." She handed me her card, and I immediately gave it to the only person I knew who might have occasion to wear fur—not to mention the money required to buy it.

Now all I had to do was help Alicia carry six shopping bags to her Boxer, which was parked at an angle in the designated slot so that careless people opening the doors of cars parked on either side could not damage the paint job. Fortunately for Alicia, the mall's parking lot wasn't full, and once again she'd escaped a key job.

"We should've taken my Bug," I muttered.

Fortunately, lunch was better. It was more than a treat having Mr. Hottie all to myself at a corner table at Café Normandie where the waiters hovered discreetly out of earshot and the mussels appetizer that I'd ordered was making my stomach smile. Neal was wearing a dark pinstripe suit with a light gray shirt and a navy paisley tie shot through with yellow and green. He looked overdressed, compared to the three men at a nearby table who were decked out in sport coats and open-necked shirts. Definitely not lawyers, but at least they wore dark socks with their loafers. With words like "solipsistic" and "semiotic" wafting our way, I figured they were St. Johns faculty.

"Any more visits from the police?" he asked as the waiter brought our entrees. We'd both ordered the linguine with a basil cream sauce.

"No, thank God." I wasn't about to tell Neal about my visit to Vivian's office, let alone how I'd tampered with a crime scene. As a lawyer, he would need deniability. "But I did find out from one of Vivian's co-workers—a former colleague, actually—that nobody at the Alliance believes she died of an overdose."

Neal lifted his wine glass and tilted it toward me. "I like that suit, P.J. You look good in red."

I could feel a flush creeping up my neck as we clinked glasses. Alicia had made me buy the red knit suit while we'd been shopping earlier. She'd even fixed my droopy hair so that I'd be presentable. Lord, his eyes were beautiful. I found myself leaning forward, my lips parted. So what if there were about thirty witnesses to us kissing?

Neal must have read my mind. He put his glass down and leaned back in his chair. "I've been in touch with Vivian's parents in Oklahoma. They told me she has a sister who's in drug rehab. Because of that, Vivian wouldn't touch the stuff. I know—uh, knew Vivian well enough to agree. She would no more do drugs than . . . than you would."

Right. Better not mention the Charlottesville detective who once nearly had me peeing my pants. "The problem is, it doesn't matter what you or her colleagues at work believe. They're not the police."

He sighed. "Yeah . . ." His gaze roamed around the room before returning to mine. "Unless there'd be a way to persuade them to change their focus. It wouldn't be a good idea for me to get involved, but maybe you could take a look through Vivian's apartment."

Moi? "Don't the police have it closed off?"

"When they've finished, then." He ran his fingers through his hair, and I felt my fingers tingle at the possibility that I might get a chance to do the same thing someday soon.

I wrapped some linguine around my fork. "Surely you're not suggesting that I break and enter."

"Good grief, no. But since the police are convinced Vivian OD'd, they probably didn't do a thorough search of the place— you know, to find anything that might indicate she was murdered." Reaching into his trousers pocket, he pulled out a key and handed it to me.

Ah yes. As I had suspected all along. Still, my heart sank to my stomach. I pushed the barely touched pasta aside, took a long swallow of water, and excused myself to go to the ladies' room.

Of all the rotten luck. But it did explain a few things. It wasn't for my sake that Neal was pumping me for information about Vivian. Only my romantic, foolish nature had convinced me he cared about my predicament. I snatched a piece of toilet paper off the roll and blew my nose. Cold water would have to hide the evidence of tears, or Neal would notice. He'd leap to the not-so-far-fetched conclusion that I cared. And that would be awkward, especially given how closely attached he must have been to the recently departed hydrologist. I blotted my eyes one last time and tried out a smile. It needed work.

By the time I got back to the table, I was pissed off. Oh sure, I had no one to blame but myself for thinking Neal Patterson cared about me, but I couldn't help thinking it was at least partly his fault for leading me on. I grabbed a tissue, and wiped the corners of my eyes.

Neal stood up, holding my chair for me. "Are your contacts bothering you?"

I shook my head. "Allergies." Yeah. Allergic to heartless men.

"I haven't forgotten about dinner," he said as we left the restaurant and headed down the street to where I had parked. "Maybe after all this is over, we can take up where we—"

"My car!" I shrieked.

The VW that I had owned since 1999—the car that had liberated me from high school and carried me to and from UVA, even round trip to Florida back when Bobby was trying to cheat me out of my share of the divorce settlement—had been vandalized beyond redemption. Someone had slashed the tires, smashed the glass, and dented the body to the point that it resembled a giant yellow golf ball.

CHAPTER SIXTEEN

"You have to ask yourself why anyone would wreck that piece of junk," said my uncle when I buzzed him from my cubicle at MoneySource. I had my suspicions, but I didn't want to sound paranoid. Somebody was definitely trying to mess with me. Could Bobby do such a thing? Would he? Or had Gareth Swenson gone berserk after the cops paid him a visit? It would be just like the man to blame me for his past transgressions. "I'll find another one just like it," I said defiantly.

Uncle Alex groaned. "Get a used 2000," he said. "At least they have air bags." He must have heard me pouting. "Tell you what. You'll need a ride home anyway, so let's go looking for a new set of wheels, say, six o'clock?"

I whimpered, which I knew Uncle Alex would interpret as a yes.

Two seconds after I'd hung up the phone, it rang again.

"This is Sandy Jones at the Wetland Protectors Alliance," came a high-pitched voice with a slight lisp, "returning your call."

Oh yeah. The other person who knew Vivian. This time, I tried another angle of attack. "I'm a friend of Vivian Remington's," I told her. "And I wonder if we could get together and talk about her and what she was doing for you there at the Alliance."

"You're a personal friend?"

"From high school," I crossed my fingers in hopes that Sandy was not a local Annapolitan. "I read about her death, and I just can't believe she'd—"

"She would never take drugs! The police are crazy if they think that."

"My feelings exactly. Jesús told me that you worked with Vivian and knew her pretty well."

"I should hope so. I was her program assistant."

Oh, lucky day. "Could we have lunch tomorrow? My treat?"

"I guess so. I never get out of the office."

After making arrangements to meet Sandy at 49 West, I spent the remainder of the afternoon and early evening with Uncle Alex, driving around in cute, colorful modern VW bugs with air conditioning and air bags and even CD players. I kicked a tire or two to look serious, but all the while out of the corner of my eye I kept searching for the real thing.

By 7:30, I was so frustrated, I found myself on the verge of crying "uncle." Then my luck turned. The car was low on gas. "I'll find something used," I said as we left Fitzgerald Auto Mall. "I don't want you to waste another tank of gas, not to mention your time."

"I got time for you, doll," said Uncle Alex in his best Fells Point tough-guy imitation. "And I definitely got time for Cantler's. Whaddaya say?"

I didn't have to answer. My uncle knew I wasn't about to pass up as many crabs as you can eat, plus the coleslaw and beer that go with them—especially on his dime.

"Gotta make one stop on our way," said Uncle Alex as we headed back to center city.

"No problem, but could we listen to something other than Pat Boone?" Not waiting for a reply, I reached forward and punched the "search" button, stopping when I heard Mary Chapin Carpenter belting out "I Feel Lucky." Maybe some would rub off on me . . . especially in the neighborhood we had just entered. Pulling up next to a rundown apartment house on a pothole-riddled side street just off of Clay, Uncle Alex put the car in "park" and asked me to wait.

When I'd first started out skip-tracing, my uncle had put his foot down about me visiting scruffy neighborhoods like the one he had just taken me to. The front of the building was covered in gang graffiti. The windows had bars on them, and the entry telephone was apparently broken, because my uncle had to bang on the metal door until somebody came to open it. And holey-baloney. There she was again. The woman in the skin-tight red dress who'd gone for a ride with my uncle last night.

Today, she was wearing form-fitting yellow cropped low-rider pants and a midriff-baring fuchsia tank top that might have been enticing on Britney Spears, but not this lady. I tried not to stare, but the thought of Uncle Alex involved with a hooker was making me wonder if he might be suffering from an as yet undisclosed to me—or maybe still unknown to him—medical condition that had impaired his judgment.

Mary Chapin Carpenter had yielded the stage to Kenny Chesney by the time my uncle had finished talking to his lady friend. He had a big smile on his face when he got back to the car.

"Who was that?" I asked.

"A friend." He pulled away from the curb. "I'm starving. Aren't you?"

"Do you—uh—see her often?"

"Not much, really. Not as much as some of the others, anyway."

Lordy, lordy. Where was this heading? And did I really want to know?

I was halfway through my second Bud at Cantler's when Uncle Alex said, "Neal Patterson came in this morning. Signed a note for twelve thousand."

161

For some reason, that reminded me that I hadn't asked about the pro bono lawyer, nor had Neal offered up a name. "It has to be something he doesn't want his bank to know about." Holy shit. Was he borrowing the money to pay for a lawyer? To represent *me?*

"Got overextended on his credit cards, I figure."

"That's a huge amount of money, Unc—especially at Money-Source rates."

"Yeah, but he's golden. It's only a six-month term, anyway."

"What's the collateral?"

"I said it was a note, didn't I? Neal's good." He signaled the waitress for refills on the beer. "You got a new boyfriend, P.J?"

My mind raced. It would be weird, bordering on Twilight Zone, if Uncle Alex had seen me talking to Bobby on Tuesday. I decided to go on the offensive. "You got a new girlfriend?" I pointed at the blue and yellow madras plaid shirt he was wearing. What was with all this color? His usual wardrobe consisted of dark trousers and white or conservatively striped shirts.

"I asked you first." He tilted his chair, balancing on its two back legs.

"The answer is no."

The chair came forward with a thunk. "Then who answered the phone at your place last night? It wasn't Neal Patterson."

Oh boy. "Bobby Crane. I let him stay there."

"You're not gonna get back with that ass—"

"I slept at Alicia's. He just wanted a place to crash for one night."

"Yeah, right." My uncle signaled for the check. "Now I'm gonna have to bring in Jake and Rake to get him outta there. Don't you have better sense?"

I swallowed the last of my beer, wishing I could order another. But that would just prove the truth of what my uncle had just said. "Don't worry, Uncle Alex. I can handle Bobby."

"Sure."

"He'll be gone when you drop me off."

"He'd better be, or I'll drop him off the pier!" He slammed his credit card down on top of the bill. "Don't you ever learn anything? You let that man back in your life, and he'll be just as much trouble as he was before."

"I am not letting him back!" I shouted. A couple at the table nearby turned and stared. I glared at them and then decided to change the subject. "So who's the girlfriend?"

"None of your business."

"Well Bobby isn't your business either unless . . ."

"Unless what?"

I'd been about to suggest that Bobby might have been the one to vandalize my VW, but it would only make Uncle Alex so angry he'd probably put Bobby in cement shoes before dropping him off the pier. "Nothing," I said. "Bobby's just a bum, you know. He can't stand to be on dry land for more than a week. He's probably already under sail."

"Let's just test that theory." My uncle pushed his chair away from the table. "We'll have coffee at your place."

The moment we walked in the door, Uncle Alex said, "Make sure he didn't steal anything."

I folded up the blanket that Bobby had thrown onto the floor and picked up yesterday's newspaper, which had food stains from the pizza he'd had eaten the night before. He'd tossed the box and three perfectly good pieces into the trash, but it was about twelve hours too late to rescue them. I opened the refrigerator to confirm that Bobby had indeed finished off all of my beer. A peek in the cabinet where I stored the occasional bottle of wine showed that it too had been discovered and consumed. But the key I'd lent him was sitting right there on the kitchen counter, exactly where I'd asked him to leave it.

"Let me get you some coffee first," I emptied the stale

grounds and rinsed out the dregs from the pot.

My uncle grabbed a dish towel. "I'll do that, P.J. You go check your belongings."

I sighed. Bobby was a money-grubbing, cheapskate, alcoholic sailing bum, not a thief. But it wouldn't hurt to see if the only valuable that I currently possessed, which didn't even belong to me, was still where I'd hidden it at the bottom of my bedroom drawer amid my underwear.

I know I didn't look right when I returned to the kitchen because my uncle said, "Uh-oh. What'd he do this time?"

"A, uh, Bobby might've taken something Alicia let me borrow. A diamond hair clip. What am I going to *do?*"

CHAPTER SEVENTEEN

Uncle Alex reached for the phone. "I'm calling the police."

"No! I don't want Bobby to get arrested—and it's not because I care, either."

My uncle snorted, his hand still on the receiver. "What'd you say he took?"

"A diamond hair clip. Alicia lent it to me." I shoved my fists into my eyes and rubbed hard. "That dirty rat."

"Maybe he's still in port. We could catch him."

"And, supposing that's so, he'll admit right off that he just happens to have it?"

"We could try. Then, if he denies taking it, we'll call the police." And I would be in such deep shit, unless Alicia covered for me. That bastard. Well, it was my own damned fault, letting him spend the night. Shit. Shit. Shit.

"Where's he docked?" said my uncle, pulling on his jacket.

"I don't know." It could have been any one of nine or so marinas in and around Annapolis. But somebody he'd mentioned the other day might know . . . What was the guy's name? Phil? Paul? Max? No. Max was the drunken designated dunkee. Pilcher! Jack or Jim Pilcher. I grabbed the phone book and pawed through the P's. Fifteen minutes later, we headed for the Eastport Marina where Jason Pilcher told me we'd find what we were looking for.

"I can't believe you didn't even know the name of Bobby's boat," said my uncle as we dashed down the pier, looking for the *Persephone J.* "Thank goodness that guy you called has a good memory."

"How was I to know he'd name the thing after me?" We came to a skidding stop in front of a thirty-foot sloop with its motor running. In the fitful light cast by a moon shyly peeking between the clouds, I spotted Bobby coming aft and grabbed hold of a dockline that was looped over the piling beside me before he could jerk it off.

"Hey," he said, "thanks for the cast-off."

"We're coming aboard," said my uncle. He swung one leg onto the deck and clutched Bobby as though to keep himself from falling.

I leaped onboard and grabbed Bobby's shirttail, but he jerked away from us both and yanked the dockline off its piling. We began to move slowly away from the pier.

"Stop!" I yelled. "Go back!"

"Unh-uh," said Bobby, grabbing the tiller. "It's time to get out on the water."

Uncle Alex made a beeline for the companionway ladder.

"Where's he going?" said Bobby as the engine dropped back to idle. "Well, shit!"

"Just give me the diamond clip," I said as my uncle's head emerged into view. "Then you can drop us off on the pier and be on your way."

"I don't have anything of yours."

"You're lying," said Uncle Alex. "Hand it over, buster." He stepped onto the deck and held out his hand.

"Go ahead and search the boat," said Bobby with a shrug. "You won't find anything."

"Watch him," I said to my uncle, and headed below.

As I searched the berths and galley, head, and various lockers, I could hear scuffling on the deck above me. I figured my uncle could take care of himself, so I focused on seeking out all the small nooks and crannies where a piece of jewelry could be stashed out of sight.

After about ten minutes, I emerged empty-handed to find Bobby lying face down on the deck and my uncle twisting one of his arms up between his shoulder blades.

"Stop!" Bobby yelled. "You're breaking my arm."

"That's not all I'm gonna break if you don't turn over the loot."

"Look," said Bobby. "We're still drifting. Somebody's gotta steer the boat, or we'll hit something!"

"Too bad," said my uncle, shoving Bobby's arm further upward.

"My pocket!" he screamed. "It's in my pocket." I stepped over my ex-husband and knelt on the deck. Shoving my hand into the pocket of his jeans, I felt nothing but a bony pelvis.

"The other one," he croaked, cocking his other hip in the air. As I reached over him, there was a loud crunching sound like giant fingernails on a blackboard, and the boat lurched to a stop, throwing Uncle Alex and me onto the deck.

A look forward showed me that we'd crossed the marina's inlet and run smack into a monstrous fiberglass sportfisher, the kind that takes wannabe sportsmen out to sea to wrestle with marlin or swordfish.

Bobby had slid across the deck to the starboard side of the boat and was staring at the damage. With his good arm, he plunged his hand into his jeans pocket, pulling out something that twinkled like a little star. "Good thing you gave me this, P.J. Because now I'm really gonna need it."

"It's not mine," I said. "Please, Bobby, give it back." I snatched at the hand holding the clip. As he jerked out of my reach, Bobby slipped and grabbed the rail. I watched in horror as Senator Sutherland's diamond hair clip fell overboard.

"Oh, man," groaned Bobby. "Look what you've done!"

"What we've done?" said my uncle. "You fuckhead!" He grabbed my hand and hauled me across the deck. "C'mon, P.J., let's get outta here before we get arrested along with dickhead here."

"I sure hope you have insurance," I yelled at Bobby, as we climbed onto the fiberglass wreck.

"Over here, P.J." My uncle moved forward along the boat's crumpled deck. He jumped onto the pier and then onto a nearby houseboat where we took refuge on the port side behind the cabin. "Let's hunker down for awhile till the cops are finished."

My instinct would have been to run, but then I hadn't spent ten or more years skulking through Baltimore's rougher neighborhoods in search of cars whose owners could no longer afford the monthly payments. So instead of heading right into the arms of the yard manager and his buddies, who were sprinting down the pier, we watched them jump aboard the wrecked boat and confront Bobby with his dastardly deed.

I could hear Bobby begging them to "get the other two—they did it." The manager laughed while his buddy gripped Bobby's elbow and dragged him off the boat.

"Geez, that was close," said my uncle. "Times like this, I really crave a cigarette." He patted his chest as though he could find a pack waiting there for just such an occasion.

"I could use a stiff shot of brandy," I replied, wondering which would be more expensive: hiring a diver to search the murky and most likely toxic muck below us or buying another diamond clip. As if I could afford either.

Peeking around the side of the cabin, I saw the red and blue blinking lights of an arriving patrol car. "They're going to arrest him?"

"I did smell booze on his breath."

"Oh, God. He'll be furious if he has to spend a night in jail."

My uncle's knees popped as he got to his feet. "You got a

worse problem, P.J. What're you gonna tell Alicia?"

"Why does she?—oh." I'd forgotten my lie earlier that evening. "I'll just have to tell her the truth." Which would have been easy if my uncle hadn't insisted on coming along.

"You'll need me to witness that Bobby stole it," he said as he drove me to her house.

What I really needed was a story that wouldn't upset Uncle Alex. He hadn't raised me to steal diamond hair clips from Florida senators.

Alicia herself answered the doorbell. She was wearing a floor-length turquoise satin robe that matched the pajamas she'd been wearing the night before. Her face was stripped of makeup, not that anyone else would have noticed.

"That jewelry you lent me the other night?" I said, wiggling my raised eyebrows as a signal for her not to mess up.

"Yeah?" She motioned for the two of us to come in. "Coffee anyone?"

"Love it," I gestured for Uncle Alex to take a seat in Alicia's cozy library where the fire was roaring in the grate and a soothing piece of classical music was setting the stage for sleepy time down South. As he lowered himself to the leather chair in front of the hearth, I nudged Alicia toward the kitchen. Stiffening her back in resistance to my hand, she stopped near the stereo system, lowered the volume, and gave a discreet tug on a velvet rope near the drapes to summon a servant. Rats.

"Cold out, isn't it?" said Alicia when the woman who'd brought us our coffee and brandy had closed the library doors.

"Frigid," I rubbed my hands together. Chit-chat was definitely the order of the evening.

"Care for a cigar, Mr. Smythe?" said Alicia, always the attentive hostess.

While Uncle Alex busied himself cutting off the end and commencing the elaborate ceremony of lighting up, I saw my opening. "That diamond hair clip you lent me the other night, Alicia?"

"Diamond what?"

"You know. For the Washington reception?"

"But I—"

"I've got terrible news, and I don't know how to tell you this," I rushed on. "Bobby—You remember that's why I stayed here last night—'cause I let him sleep over at my place? So when I went back home this evening, I discovered the clip was missing."

"He stole it," said Uncle Alex, puffing away with great contentment.

"No!" said Alicia. "That sleaze."

"And anyway," I jumped in, "I don't know what I can say except I hope it was insured because there's no way . . ."

"Well, whatever." She sent me a puzzled look. "Did you call the police?"

"The yard manager did." I caught my uncle shaking his head.

"That was for an unrelated matter," he said. "But it appears unlikely that the piece of jewelry will ever be recovered."

"Oh." Alicia sipped her coffee. "Well, maybe the insurance will—now what did you say he stole?"

"Your diamond hair clip." I gave her the nine-yard stare. "I meant to return it with the bracelet and earrings, but I forgot. Oh, Alicia, I'm so sorry!" I jumped to my feet and threw my arms around her. Leaning close to her ear, I whispered, "I'll explain later."

Later turned out to be another barely palatable breakfast the next morning with Alicia tapping her foot impatiently while we both pretended there was nothing we'd rather do than listen to Martha Todd Ritchie tell Alicia's Aunt Cecelia all about their plans for the family's annual skiing trip to Gstaad. When she finally got off the phone, Alicia's mother patted me on the head.

"Gotta run, girls," she said. "Do have another bagel, P.J., you're so skinny."

And guaranteed to stay that way if I had too many more breakfasts *chez* Ritchie. "Okay," I said as the doors to the breakfast room stopped swinging. "When I noticed the clip missing, I told my uncle it belonged to you. He doesn't know that it really belongs to Marguerite Sutherland."

"Huh?"

"When I was at the D.C. reception, the senator lost a diamond hair clip, and I retrieved it."

"Why?" Alicia had her arms folded across her chest. Not a good sign.

"Because it fell into the toilet, and by the time I picked it out and cleaned it up, she was gone."

"That reception was ages ago."

"I was going to return it, only—"

"You didn't, and now Bobby stole it."

I nodded. "I have an appointment in Washington next Tuesday afternoon to give it back to the senator. Now what do I do?"

Alicia ran her butter knife around the outside of her plate and dropped it onto the placemat. "There's no way you can make Bobby give it back?"

"Not unless he knows how to scuba dive. It's at the bottom of Back Creek."

"Oh, shit." Alicia leaned back. "You're sure in one big puking pickle, aren't you, girl? On the other hand . . ." She paused, a slow grin lighting her face, "What Marguerite doesn't know won't hurt her. Or us."

CHAPTER EIGHTEEN

"Everybody thought Vivian was a straight arrow," said Sandy Jones, stirring two packets of sugar into her iced tea, "but that wasn't the whole story."

Like her name, the woman sitting opposite me had wiry, sand-colored hair, a freckled face, and hazel eyes framed by rimless oval glasses. She was about my height but twenty pounds heavier. In another century, she would have been thought lush, but "porker" was probably closer to what she'd be called today. Something about Sandy's flower print high-collared dress and prissy demeanor hinted of spinster, but she wore a thin gold band on her left ring finger.

We had both ordered the blackened tuna salad, and my mouth was already watering in anticipation. With the sun streaming in the windows of 49 West, it felt more like May than February. I found myself wishing that I had nothing better to do than to sit there like a cat, soaking up the rays all afternoon.

"You know how it is with a small office," she continued. "Except for Mr. Morton, we're all around the same age, so we socialize a lot."

"Um-hmm." I was the only one under forty in my office.

"And sometimes, when we party, things get a little wild."

Really? Visions of toga-clad, beer-chugging, frat-house antics flitted through my mind. "How wild might that be?"

"Well, nothing illegal, actually. And certainly no drugs. It's just that some folks would have a bit too much to drink. We'd be coming down off a campaign high, celebrating a victory—and, mind you, that doesn't happen very often in this line of work—and the guys would make up stupid lyrics to songs, some of them pretty raunchy, or one of the girls would get up on a table and dance. You know what I mean."

Not since college. "I can't picture Vivian dancing on tables."

Sandy laughed. "Me neither. Vivian dancing would be like an elephant trying to tiptoe." She put her hand up to her mouth as if she regretted having made a derogatory comment about the recently deceased.

But I was laughing too, and then I remembered that I was supposed to have gone to high school with Vivian. "Ms. Figueroa, our modern dance teacher, thought Vivian was so hopeless that she should go out for basketball where the sound of her feet hitting the floor wouldn't be quite so embarrassing."

"Oh, wow. She told me that she loved basketball!"

"Well, she was a star." I hoped I wasn't pushing my luck too far. "All City, I seem to remember."

"Wouldn't surprise me." Sandy paused as the waiter refilled our iced teas. "But, just to show you what she was like underneath the professional hydrologist exterior, I remember one time when we were partying at the office on a Friday night and it turned out to be Vivian's birthday. A couple of the guys—computer geeks—had somehow found this out, and they put together a really funny birthday card for her.

"You see, she had a poster behind her desk of a model wearing an ocelot coat and—"

"I saw it the last time I was there."

"Well," Sandy giggled. "Marv and Jesús downloaded the original off the Customs Web site one day and doctored it so that the picture they printed out had Vivian's head on the model. But, instead of wearing a dress, she was stark naked!"

Oh, yes. I had seen that picture too. In the bottom drawer of

173

Vivian's file cabinet.

"And they made it look real kinky. Like Vivian was into some weird sex. She was holding a coiled whip and standing with her foot on some guy's back."

"You're kidding. So here's this serious scientist, wearing nothing but a fur coat and holding a coiled whip? How embarrassing."

"She loved it. She thought it was the funniest thing she'd ever seen. Showed it to Mr. Morton the next day, she told me. Practically scared him to death, she said, when she told him she was thinking about changing careers and becoming a dominatrix." By now Sandy's sandy face was pink, and her eyes had teared up from laughing.

"Speaking of careers, Sandy. Maybe you could tell me what the connection is between hydrology and illegal wildlife trade."

"Huh?" She squinted her eyes like she couldn't read the answer too clearly.

"There isn't one?" This was getting spooky.

"Not that I know of. Of course, I'm just a program assistant." She pursed her lips and put her napkin on the table like she'd decided lunch was over.

"Let's have dessert," I said. "My treat, remember."

"I don't think so." Now the splotches on Sandy's face were fed by anger. She was glaring at me. "I'm not going to say another word till you tell me who you really are."

"Okay." Opting, for once, for the (sort of) truth, I patted the table in an invitation for her to sit back and relax. "I lied. I'm not an old school pal. Vivian hired me to retrieve a fur coat, just like the one in the poster. She told me the Fish and Wildlife Service had lent it to her for a demo she was going to do on illegal wildlife trade. She claimed that one of the Alliance's board members stole it."

"You are *lying*," Sandy jumped to her feet. "Vivian had nothing to do with wildlife trade issues. Nothing."

I reached over and grabbed her elbow as she turned to go. "Please, Sandy. I'm not lying. That's what Vivian told me. And I think, for her sake, we need to get to the bottom of this."

I guess curiosity overcame distaste, because Sandy sat down and put her napkin back into her lap. "One thing for sure, as Vivian's assistant, I do all the administrative work. So if she hired you, where's your contract?"

Oops. I shrugged. "She gave me a check. On her personal account, actually. I gather it was something she didn't want anybody to know about."

"This is bullshit." Sandy shoved her chair back from the table.

"No it's not. Please stay and hear my story. Then you can forget you ever met me, if that's what you want." I motioned for the waiter and asked him to bring us both some bread pudding. "They don't have this too often, but I know you'll love it," I assured her.

With a sigh, Sandy unfolded her napkin again. "So talk."

"An ocelot fur coat Vivian borrowed for what she said was a demo on illegal trade has been stolen. By one of your board members."

Picking at a ragged cuticle, she gazed across the room as though the solution to the mystery I'd just presented her with lay somewhere in the paintings decorating the restaurant's walls or maybe at the table full of men in polyester suits who were trying to one-up each other telling off-color jokes. "It can't possibly be true. We're about wetlands conservation, not wildlife. Vivian was a hydrologist, not a biologist or whatever. So, what you're telling me is just plain cockamamie. It makes no sense."

"I swear I am not making this up, Sandy. How could I? I don't know diddly about wetlands. I majored in history. I wouldn't know an ocelot from—from a tiger or a panther. But I have seen the board member in question with a spotted fur coat—just as Vivian claimed."

Sandy continued to pick at her cuticle. "Vivian has never lied to me. But I can't believe any of this could be true."

"How well do you know the board members?" I pressed on.

"I don't know them at all," she said. "I mean, I know who's on the board, of course. But putting a name to a face? Couldn't do it."

I reached into my handbag and dragged out the crumpled *Post* gossip item about Marguerite Sutherland and Juan Carlos Francisco at the Washington reception.

As she read the item, Sandy's lips pursed in disapproval. "So that's Marguerite Sutherland."

"Ever see her in Vivian's office?"

"No, but then I'm not there all the time, you know. She could've come in to see Vivian when I was at lunch or maybe on a day when I was out sick. But I do know that this is the lady who got Mr. Morton his job way back when the Alliance was formed."

Really.

While the waiter delivered our desserts, Sandy paused and reread the item. "You know, judging from what they're saying here, Marguerite Sutherland isn't exactly on our side. Which makes me wonder why she's on our board."

Because Morton owed her his job. And possibly, if I could believe what Vivian had told me, because Sutherland would be in an ideal position to exact vengeance on the woman who had been the instrument of her involuntary termination.

"You seem pretty convinced that Vivian didn't do drugs, so let's assume somebody killed her and made it look like an overdose."

Sandy's eyes grew wide, but she nodded. Then she frowned. "I used to think Vivian had no enemies. But now, I'm not so sure. This lady here . . ." She tapped the column. ". . . certainly is no friend. And then there's—"

"Marvin Ross?"

Her brows shot upward. "How'd you know about him?"

"Vivian told me that she had fired him. True?"

"She found out that the opposition had somehow obtained working drafts of Alliance reports and campaign strategies. It was all done electronically and Marv works—uh, worked in IT, so . . ."

"So she fired him? Wow. That doesn't seem much to go on."

Sandy rolled her eyes. "She had some strong suspicions that he was the one—mainly because he's so weird, I guess—and Morton backed her up. But Marv threatened to go to EEOC—discrimination based on alternative lifestyle kind of thing—so she hired some computer geek to trace the source of the leaks on our server, and it turns out Marv was guilty."

"Could the opposition be someone like Juan Carlos Francisco, perhaps?"

"Absolutely. So there is a connection."

"Clever deduction. Can we further deduce that, considering her relationship with Francisco, your board member Sutherland probably shares that information with him?"

"Ohmigod. He's our biggest enemy. He claims that Everglades restoration will put him and other sugar cane growers out of business. And he says if that happens, America will have to import all of its sugar. Which is nonsense."

As was the idea that the guy would kill Vivian over a policy disagreement, even if he believed it threatened his business. "Vivian's death isn't going to stop the whole Alliance, is it?"

"Not on your life. I know she would've wanted us to continue the struggle if something happened—" Sandy's voice croaked upward as she fought to keep tears from sliding down her face.

I handed her my last tissue and sat there, fiddling with my

teaspoon. "Okay. Maybe Marvin Ross just lost it after she fired him. Is he the murdering kind?"

"How should I know!" wailed Sandy. "He certainly is weird. He's such a stickler for neatness except for the way he dresses—but all techies are weird, aren't they? He'd show up at work some days with his hair dyed purple and all in spikes, like he was into the rave scene. I guess they can get kinda crazy." She shuddered as though Marvin had just crept up behind her and was about to plunge a knife between her shoulder blades.

Instead of owning up to my illegal search of Vivian's office, I made up a story about finding the index card with its possibly misspelled threat in a package of materials that Vivian had given to me. When I showed it to Sandy, she agreed that the handwriting was not Vivian's and said she would try to find something Marvin Ross had written so that I could make a comparison.

"Oh. And one other thing," I said as we collected our coats. "You wouldn't happen to have a copy of Vivian's resumé, would you?"

"Of course. I'll e-mail it to you."

All I wanted to do when I got back to my office that afternoon was curl up in my comfy leather chair and take a nice nap. Of course, there weren't any leather chairs anywhere in the cubicle farm that was MoneySource—except perhaps for my uncle's office. Now, wouldn't that be smart?

The practical side of my brain kept suggesting that I should be car-shopping on a Friday, especially since all the President's Day sales had been extended. The less disciplined part had me daydreaming about Neal Patterson. After a suitable (but very short) interval of mourning for Vivian, he would realize that I was much more fascinating. No. Make that alluring. I wasn't a scientist, for one thing. And I did enjoy an occasional beer, a fast car, and slasher movies, provided they were really scary. When I uncovered the true nature of Vivian Remington's death and unmasked her killer, Neal Patterson might laugh, saying wasn't I just like my uncle, but, underneath the kidding, he would be truly impressed. There would be an awards ceremony. I'd be on television, lapping up my five minutes of fame, and that, in turn, would lead to—My fantasy was interrupted by the phone.

"Smythe here," I said in my best imitation of a crisp, alert, and very busy professional.

"But not for long," came the eerie-sounding voice of the crank caller.

"Who *are* you?" I stared at the phone, but the line went dead. Somebody was doing a very good job at trying to scare me out of my wits. If it hadn't been for the unfortunate accident with Bobby's boat, maybe I would have been better off with Bobby watching my back, as he'd once offered. Now, it was too late, for I was certain he'd aligned himself with all the other dark forces that seemed to be against me.

When the phone rang again, I let the answering machine kick in. It was Alicia.

"Did you learn anything useful from your lunch with Sandy Jones?"

Yes, but I didn't feel like talking to Alicia. I didn't feel like doing anything but taking a nap. My head fell forward onto the desk. Maybe just five minutes . . .

Not. My eyes were level with the voicemail readout indicating I had three messages. Okay. Skip Alicia. The one previous to that was a hang-up. The crank caller, perhaps? The third was from Samuel Lewis.

"Sam," I said when he came to the phone. "How-ya doin'?"

"Leteisha said you got some money for me." His voice was very high pitched, as though coming from a midget. But I knew he was nearly six feet tall and weighed close to two hundred and fifty pounds.

"Not exactly. What I told her was I have a money-making proposition, Sam. So why don't you stop by, and we can discuss it?"

"You're gonna have to come here, lady. I got a bum ankle."

"Did you trip and fall or something?" I asked in my most caring tone.

"Bike tipped over on me."

"Ouch. That must've hurt real bad. I hope your motorcycle's okay."

"Just a few little scratches. Nothin' I can't fix."

I pumped my fist in the air. "So, tell me, where can we meet?"

As they'd often done for me before, the tracking gods were smiling. I took down Sam's address, called Jake and Rake, and sent them off to collect the Yamaha. That would go a long way toward restoring some sense of fiscal equity at MoneySource.

The virtuous feeling of having cleared at least one trace lasted till about six o'clock when three more agreements marked "Skipped" were dumped on my desk. Two of them were guardsmen deployed somewhere overseas fighting the War on Terror. Weren't they already in enough trouble?

I shoved the two folders into the bottom drawer of the filing cabinet where I kept the rest of the files for loan defaulters who couldn't ever be located. That left one legitimate deadbeat. I couldn't decide which would be more depressing: digging right in, or calling it a day and heading home to an apartment in desperate need of cleaning, a pile of dirty laundry, and a long weekend stretching ahead of me with no Neal Patterson in it to brighten the February gloom. Well, didn't the skips need a break too?

I devoted the rest of the evening to cleaning up the mess Bobby had left behind. He'd probably spent the night in jail and would be looking for me once they let him out. Before going to bed, I double-checked the locks on the windows and doors. To make myself feel even safer, I pulled open the drawer of the bedside table.

My .38 special was gone.

CHAPTER NINETEEN

"Why do you think your ex has it?"

"Because he took something else." I handed Neal a beer. He'd come over as soon as I'd called, and now he was sitting there on my Naugahyde sofa, making the apartment feel much smaller but me much safer. "A piece of jewelry that doesn't belong to me."

"And you think he's in jail?"

I explained about the incident on the boat, omitting the part where Uncle Alex and I had hidden from the yard manager. "Wouldn't they arrest him for ramming his boat into that sport-fisher?"

"Not if he has insurance. It'd be just like with a car accident, P.J. They'd put him in touch with the owner, they'd exchange the details, and he's free to go."

"Yeah, but Bobby had been drinking."

"Oh. Then they probably did lock him up overnight to dry out. They've most likely let him go by now."

"Now that certainly makes me feel a whole lot better, knowing Bobby's roaming the streets with my gun and mad as hell at me 'cause he probably blames me for the accident."

"You don't have to stand over there on the other side of the room. I promise I won't bite."

The problem was I wasn't so sure *I* wouldn't bite. A nice little nibble on Neal's earlobe, for instance, could be followed up by a nip at his lower lip . . . Heat flooded my face as I sat down at the other end of the sofa—a frustratingly safe distance away.

"Come here, babe." Neal reached out his arm and hauled me into the comfort of his chest where I felt the scratchy texture of his wool sweater against my cheek and inhaled the scent of an aftershave that turned my insides to jelly. "You've had a horrible week, haven't you? First Vivian, then your car, and now your ex is after you with a gun."

"It's not funny, Neal. You don't know Bobby. He can be very unpredictable—especially if he's smashed."

As Neal leaned down to kiss me, I blurted out, "Congrats on the loan, by the way."

I felt his body stiffen. "That was supposed to be confidential."

I looked up at him. "Hey, he's my uncle, remember?"

Neal tried a smile, not quite pulling it off. "It's only a short-term thing."

"So I hear. Let me guess: Your boat is suddenly too small for a partner at Meredith, Geitrich, and Smeal." No sooner had Smeal's name slipped from my lips when I remembered my earlier suspicions that Neal had borrowed from MoneySource because he didn't want his partners to know he was going to pay for a lawyer to defend me against a charge of providing the overdose that killed one of their clients.

". . . fine, actually. Any bigger and I'd need someone to help crew."

Clearly, he didn't want to tell me the real reason, so I pushed harder. "I know. You lost a bundle in Vegas."

Neal stood up and crossed the room. "Something like that. Nothing you need to worry about."

"I'm just curious. Why didn't you go to a bank? You know what kind of interest we charge."

Neal crossed his arms. "I just thought I'd try your uncle. Besides, I'll be paying this off early, so the interest isn't a biggie." He tipped the bottom of his bottle up and swallowed the dregs of his beer.

"Can I get you a refill?"

He followed me into the kitchen. "This is a really nice place, P.J. Real cozy."

"I like it," I said, handing him another beer.

He smiled as we clinked our bottles together. "You are really something, you know?"

I found myself leaning forward, and the next thing I knew Neal's lips touched mine. Both our beers hit the counter, and I threw my arms around his neck. He deepened the kiss, which had my insides melting.

His hands, which were at my waist, moved up my back beneath my sweater, stopping when they hit my bra.

I shuddered a little, and he pulled back, gazing down at me. "Are you sure?"

Yes. Yes. Yes. Or maybe not. Just as his lips settled on mine, the thought of just how much I'd been deceiving him penetrated the fog of desire. I jerked away, pulling his hands into mine. "We can't—I shouldn't—"

"Oh, baby," he groaned. "Tell me you don't mean it."

"I'm sorry, Neal. It's just I'm a little old-fashioned, I guess. I don't think I would want to share you with anybody—like that brunette at the D.C. reception, for example."

He stepped back, crossing his arms, the gold watch gleaming beneath the overhead light. "Amanda's our Washington liaison."

"Not your date?"

Neal shook his head. "I'm not seeing anyone—haven't been for a few months. It's pretty obvious I want to change that."

Lord, the guy moved fast. Vivian's body was hardly cold. I picked up my beer and tossed back a decidedly unladylike gulp. "Why are you so curious about Vivian Remington?"

His jaw dropped in astonishment. "Talk about changing the

subject. I guess I sure read you all wrong."

"I want to know, Neal. It's not just because I'm a suspect, is it?"

"Yes, it is—at least partly."

"And . . . ?"

Neal shoved his hands into his pockets. "She was my client. I liked her."

No kidding. "Fine, so why don't you use the key Vivian must have given you and search her apartment yourself?"

"Aren't you forgetting something, P.J.? I'm not the one who got you in this mess." He turned on his heel and stalked out. There was a soft click as he shut the door, but a whole lot of rubber got laid on the street as he drove off.

On Monday, my mood was as unforgiving as the weather. The dawn's fresh batch of snow flurries had turned into sleet with a threat of more snow later. People expected to show up at work would most likely call in sick. Uncle Alex had the car, which meant I had to walk.

The closer I got to the Banner Building, the icier the sidewalks became. I had to slow to a crawl and even then slipped and landed hard on my butt, right in front of the place. Biting back tears of self-pity, I brushed the ice pellets off my jacket, gathered up the items I'd been holding that were now strewn across the sidewalk, and limped into the lobby. The office was so cold, I could see my breath. I kicked the radiator, which only made my foot hurt.

Okay. So I'd blown the jealousy containment part of being an adult professional last Friday. It pissed me off that Neal Patterson thought he could just lead me casually into bed. The nerve of him, making it all too clear that the reason he had to borrow twelve thousand dollars from a finance company was none of my business. Fine. Even if it wasn't my concern, was it so hard for him to share? I knew enough about the finance business to know that nobody wealthy enough to get a bank line of credit would choose to do business with a place like Money-Source.

Clearly, I'd been right not to take things where they'd been headed. Because it appeared now that Neal might be using me to uncover information about his former "client" while, at the same time, covering his ass. Bastard. From now on, ours would be a strictly business relationship—provided I hadn't made him so angry he'd never speak to me again.

Wrapping my hands around my coffee mug, the only warm thing in the room, I decided there was nothing left to do but keep on trucking. I would carry on as though nothing had changed. Licensed or not, I would become the private eye Alicia had always said I could be. And I wouldn't say one damned thing about it to Neal Patterson.

Mentally reviewing my conversation with Marvin Ross, I wondered if he might have written the note on the index card I'd found in Vivian's office. And what about the visit from Tony Marrero? Other than him wearing the despised snakeskin boots, I knew zip. Ditto for Vivian's real relationship with Gareth Swenson. Was Marv telling the truth about Vivian being such a straight shooter? Considering how much he hated her, why make her out to be such a goody-good? But he probably hadn't been completely honest about "just following orders" when he gave the Alliance memos to Marguerite Sutherland. She probably offered money, just as I had—although it was also conceivable (barely) that he'd been a spy planted by the opposition from the get-go.

Vivian had no record of our meeting—except perhaps in her digital calendar. But, if Sandy Jones could be believed, the woman had lied to me big time about the ocelot coat. Or maybe she just didn't tell her program assistant everything she was up to. I bet the information on Vivian's electronic gizmo was chock full of fascinating leads, all of which were, no doubt, being followed up by the police.

I shouldn't have had that thought because when I looked up, I found Detective Rowena Fitzhugh standing in the doorway.

"Chilly in here," she said as she crossed the room. "You must have a cheapskate landlord."

I sat there, arms wrapped around myself, as she plopped into the client chair and opened her notebook. Her uniform was the same, except today's wool blazer was scarlet. Did that mean I was in even bigger trouble? "Where's your partner?"

"At Laurel."

"You mean he actually races?"

She laughed. "So many people have told Peabody he looks like a jockey that he spends a lot of time hanging around Pimlico and Laurel, just playing the part."

As I sat there waiting for the grilling to begin, it occurred to me that I still didn't have a lawyer. No way would Gareth Swenson tell the police anything that would let them connect the word drugs with me. He would claim what he'd always claimed, especially now that he was seeking a position with the DEA. So why were they still after me?

"Our records indicate that you were under suspicion for destroying some illegal drugs that were stashed in your boyfriend's apartment and that you staged having a fit of jealous rage to cover up your activities." She stopped reading and looked at me.

"Your *records?* I don't know how your records could show any such thing."

"Trust me." Fitzhugh brushed an imaginary piece of lint off the red jacket. "Were they your drugs?"

I caught myself on the verge of answering no. "Which drugs are you talking about? I'm kinda confused here."

"Mm-hmmmm." She scribbled something in the notebook. Probably "liar, liar, pants on fire."

There was a long pause as she tried the old psychological trick of making me want to fill the silence with talk.

"Were you aware that Gareth Swenson was on the short list for a high-level position at the Drug Enforcement Administration?"

I was, but I didn't want to own up to having heard it from the man himself. "Really?" I said, trying to sound just a tiny bit bored.

"If those drugs you destroyed belonged to him, he'd be toast."

"The only thing I destroyed six years ago was a mirror over the mantel in Gareth's apartment."

Fitzhugh nodded, making another note. "Of course, if the drugs were yours and you've been dealing ever since then, Vivian Remington being only one of your customers who OD'd using your product, you might be up on some serious charges."

"I have never used drugs. And I would never, ever, consider dealing."

"Really?" She let her gaze roam over the stained walls, grimy window, battered filing cabinet, and scuffed desk as though to suggest I could certainly use the money.

"And it's rather obvious that I don't deal, isn't it?" I said, throwing my arms out wide. "Otherwise, I wouldn't be freezing my butt off in this low-rent office."

Fitzhugh shrugged like she'd heard that one before, and then she grinned. "It does remind me of one of those old black and white 'B' movies."

Alicia would be thrilled. "Look, I'm kind of busy right now. Are we done here?"

Fitzhugh stood up. "One way or another, Ms. Smythe, we're going to find the person who supplied the drugs that killed Vivian Remington."

"I hope you do," I said as she snapped her notebook closed, promising that she and her colleague would be back with more questions. As her long legs headed down the hall to the elevator, a terrifying thought hit me. My fingerprints were all over Vivian Remington's office. It's hard to sift through papers wearing leather gloves, so I'd taken them off. If the police had not finished with her office—especially if they hadn't yet dusted it for fingerprints—my goose was cooked. But wait. I had been in her office legitimately earlier that week, so with any luck and if the police decided to dust the place, it wouldn't make things any worse than they already seemed to be. Except that I had taken some things out of there—things the police might consider relevant to the case. Especially Gareth's business card and the "your toast" threat. Tampering with a police investigation was pretty bad, but when you also happened to be a suspect, it was dreadful. Where was my lawyer?

The phone rang, and Neal Patterson said, "I thought you'd be working today."

"I suppose you're lawyering?" I tried to keep my voice as nonchalant as a racing pulse would permit.

"Nope. I just got back from walking my dog. But the reason I'm calling is to correct a misimpression you seem to have."

"Such as?"

"Such as me being somehow romantically involved with Vivian Remington."

Visions of the key he'd pulled out of his pocket crowded out more charitable thoughts, but I didn't want to fight. I reminded myself it didn't matter who Neal cared about anyway. "It doesn't matter," I said. "Sorry I flew off the handle."

"All is forgiven. Now, how about meeting me for a drink later on and we'll take up where we left off?"

Is it possible for a heart to rise and sink at the same time? Of course, I wanted to take up where we'd left off, but not under the present circumstances. "I'd like nothing more, Neal, honestly, but it's making me a little uncomfortable because I'm, uh, not quite sure you're shooting straight with me." *And I'm sure I've been lying through my teeth to you.*

There was a slight pause before he said, "Good grief. I only wanted to help. Surely, you don't—"

"I don't think ill of you at all. And I definitely want to see you again. But couldn't we sort of cool it until I get the police off my back?"

"Look, P.J., this could get dangerous. I wouldn't want anything to happen to you just because—"

"I'll be careful, okay? And if things get scary, I'll call you first."

He laughed. "No. Call nine-one-one first and *then* me. But, okay. I get the message. Speaking of which, a friend of mine from the police told me the autopsy report for Vivian Remington shows a lethal quantity of heroin and a larger than normal amount of sleeping pills."

Oh, God. "Could it be suicide?"

"No way would Vivian kill herself. Of course, somebody could have tried to make it look like that."

I stared at the threadbare carpet for a moment. "The cops just paid me another visit. Have you had any luck finding me a lawyer? It's my prints on Vivian's prescription medicine. No wonder they think I—"

"Don't worry, P.J. You didn't do it. You have nothing to worry about."

"Spoken like a true lawyer who knows he's not the one facing a murder charge."

Neal sighed. "I'm sorry. I didn't mean to sound so callous. I must confess that finding somebody to defend you got lost in the shuffle last week. I'll get right on it."

"I'd be grateful. You and I know I'm innocent, and I certainly

190

have my doubts about a couple of Vivian's acquaintances, but—"

"You have anybody specific in mind?"

What about Marguerite Sutherland? A mole on the board of the Wetland Protectors Alliance. A possible blackmailer. Quite possibly a thief. Most assuredly involved with Juan Carlos Francisco, Florida's sugar cane king.

"You still there, P.J.?" said Neal.

"Just thinking. Have the police wrapped up their investigation of Vivian's apartment?"

"Yeah, and her parents are flying in tomorrow to pack up the place. This might be a good time for you to check it out."

It was a tempting proposition, given my secret addiction to snooping, but seeing me there would be all any detective lingering at the scene would need to nail me as the prime suspect. And then there was the problem of what I might find, something as depressing as love letters from Neal, for example. However, self-imposed though it might have been, duty called . . .

And that's why, as soon as it got dark, I paid a visit to the former Ms. Vivian Remington's Shearwater digs. Cursing the vandals who'd just destroyed the perfect vehicle for conducting a surreptitious search, I parked Uncle Alex's car three blocks away near a Seven-Eleven and hoofed it back to Vivian's place. There were no suspicious-looking vans or cars parked on the street, so perhaps the police had indeed closed their investigation.

Vivian had lived on the third floor of a fairly new but lackluster apartment complex with a tiny marble-floored lobby and no concierge. The police tape was gone, and the key worked. Once inside, I pulled the blinds before turning on the lights. True to the deceased owner's reputation, Vivian's apartment reeked of Nature Girl, including traces of the woodsy scent I'd noticed the first time we met. In place of the usual living room suite, there was a dirty-white futon and two bean-bag chairs, one lime green, the other deep purple. The coffee table was a metal steamer trunk covered with a tie-died sheet. There was no dining room furniture, not that I had any myself.

If the police thought Vivian had overdosed, they would have searched for her stash. I wanted her address book and her palm-sized electronic calendar, both of which were also probably now in police custody. So what was I here for? Ah yes. Something that would prove a negative—that Vivian did not do drugs. Pulling on a pair of latex gloves, I set to work.

Although I tend to do my eating, which is mostly pizza, on the floor in the living room while reading the comics, it appeared that Vivian either dined out most of the time or ate her meals while standing at the kitchen counter. The cupboards were empty of either dishes or food, except for a box of dog treats. I wondered if someone had already been there and cleaned the place out. Either that, or Vivian didn't eat at all. But such a healthy woman would have needed to keep her strength up. There was a row of tiny, droopy potted plants on the window ledge. None of them looked like marijuana to my totally untrained eye. But no coffee! How did she get herself off to work in the mornings?

I opened the refrigerator a crack and saw a couple of furry lemons, a bottle of catsup, and a jar of what looked like salad dressing. Through the glass of the vegetable bins beneath the shelves, I could see lettuce, cabbage, half a tomato, half a cucumber, a box of sprouts, two wilted green onions, a squishy green pepper that was so rotten its stem had collapsed inward, and some cut-up pieces of celery and carrot. Clearly, Vivian had subsisted on salad.

On to the bathroom where the medicine cabinet held a box of baking soda and a toothbrush, half a bar of Ivory soap—the other rested in the bathtub's soap dish—and a box of Band-Aids. The drawer beneath the basin held a spare roll of toilet paper and a box of tampons. I moved into the bedroom, which had been furnished with a mattress on the floor, another bean-bag chair, this one black, and a battery-operated shortwave radio. Imagine not having television. No cable either and no alarm clock—not even the mechanical wind-up kind. In fact, the place was so Spartan, I could not picture anyone actually living there, Nature Girl or not. The upended wooden crate that seemed to have served as Vivian's bedside table held only a notepad and pencil. I flipped through the notepad searching for clues. Next to the cardboard backing, I ripped out a page with three notations in Vivian's cramped writing: "NP," followed by a very familiar phone number, and "AC" and "GQ" each with numbers that I didn't recognize. Just because she had Neal's home phone number didn't mean anything serious, did it? Naw. Just because Neal had the key to her place didn't prove they'd been lovers. In fact, there was absolutely no reason for me to have such a heavy stone lodged in my gut.

"GQ, GQ, GQ," I muttered to myself, trying to recall why those initials seemed familiar—other than on a magazine cover. In the closet I found another steamer trunk on the floor. It was full of woodsy-scented t-shirts and sweatshirts in colors ranging from white to gray to black, but no bundle of carefully preserved love letters. Color-coordinated white, black, and gray sweat-pants were draped over the hangers, along with a couple of cotton long-sleeved shirts and one tie-died wraparound skirt, shoved way in the back as if hardly ever worn.

I wandered back into the living room and looked around, mumbling "GQ" to myself. What was to search anyway? No drawers, no end tables or bedside tables, no bookshelves, cabinets, or sofa cushions. I lifted up the hooked rug on the floor and found some dust and dog hair beneath it. I looked in the tiny coat closet and saw a gray parka on a hanger and the dog's leash looped over a hook. Poor dog.

This was not fun. I tipped over the futon and found some more dust. Ditto when I moved the steamer trunk–coffee table aside. Moving back to the kitchen, I opened all the drawers, searched under the sink where I found a dried sponge and a bucket and what might have been the dog's dish. I opened the oven door, peeked in the dishwasher, and even ran my hand around the insides of the garbage disposal. Of course, the police had already done all of this, so what made me think I could do better?

Because I wasn't looking for drugs. And that reminded me: The last time I had been looking for them, I'd known very well who GQ was. But that was seven years ago, and now he was the newly reformed Gareth Windsor Swenson, aspirant to high political office. So what if Vivian had his business card in her desk and his phone number in her bedroom? She'd made it quite clear that they knew each other.

The whole thing made my stomach ache. What I needed was something to take the edge off my appetite. Like some of those carrots, which didn't look too limp. I reached into the fridge and slid open the veggie bin. Now Vivian was a hydrologist, an expert in water flow, so maybe she knew something about refrigerators that the rest of us didn't. Still, in all the years that I'd cleaned people's houses during summers when I was in high school, I'd never seen anyone use paper towels to line the refrigerator floor *beneath* the storage bins. I pulled the bin all the way out and picked up a corner of the paper towel. Folded inside was an envelope sealed into a zip-lock plastic bag.

I pocketed the envelope, killed the flashlight, reopened the blinds, and locked the door behind me as I left.

On the way home, I picked up a Whopper and fries at a drive-thru. After pulling a Bud from the fridge, I crouched, Indian-style, on the floor of my apartment and enjoyed a picnic on the newspaper that I hadn't yet bothered to read.

Once I'd wiped the catsup from my fingers, I slit open the zip-lock bag. Then I got a pair of latex gloves from the kitchen so that my fingerprints would not be found on any of the incriminating evidence I was sure to find. After all, no one hides an envelope at the bottom of their refrigerator unless it is very incriminating. I slit the envelope open with a knife, and some photographs fell out. The one on top I'd seen before. And the one beneath it seemed to be almost an exact copy, except for the woman's face.

CHAPTER TWENTY

Tuesday dawned as dark and gloomy as Monday, but minus the snow. My spirits were high as I combed my hair, brushed my teeth, and fixed a cup of coffee. Then I laid the two photos side by side on the kitchen table. Talk about weird. Apparently, someone had decided to play the same trick on Marguerite Sutherland that they'd done on Vivian Remington. That someone had to be Marvin Ross. But why?

As I headed off to MoneySource, I puzzled the thing over in my mind. Why would he single out just one of the Alliance board members—unless there was only one woman on the board, perhaps? And how did the photo end up hidden in Vivian's apartment? Better yet, why?

The only thing I could figure was, again, blackmail. Vivian must have decided that if I didn't come through with proof that Sutherland had stolen the fur coat, she'd have to threaten to send the Marguerite-as-environmentally-incorrect-dominatrix photo to the tabloids. So maybe that photo was simply Plan B. Still, I couldn't imagine why Vivian would enlist the help of someone she was about to fire. Surely she knew he would rat her out once the dirty deed was done. The whole thing made my head ache.

I'd been perusing skip documents for about an hour when the clanging of the fire alarm jolted me awake. I joined the stream of co-workers evacuating the building and, when we hit the street, learned that it had been a false alarm. Everybody groaned and headed back inside. Clearly, I needed a pick-me-up, so I detoured to a Wendy's and ordered a large cup of coffee and a danish. Normally I don't do breakfast, unless Uncle Alex is buying, but he was at a meeting with his bankers. In fact, since he was out, there was no real reason for me to go back and try to track down deadbeats while waiting for the next false alarm.

When I got to the Banner Building, there was an envelope lying on the floor outside my door. On it was a post-it note from Sandy Jones, the rounded letters informing me that "the resume you requested is enclosed." I read through it quickly. Vivian had been employed by the Wetland Protectors Alliance since 2000. Her title was policy director. Reading between the lines of technical and scientific jargon, I gathered that her job was to make sure the campaign to protect and restore the Everglades did not get derailed in any legislative arena, national or state.

It was the previous job that I'd really wanted to study. Vivian had worked for the Stoneman Douglas Society, headed by none other than Marguerite Sutherland. No duties were described, probably because the title had to have been a bit of an embarrassment for someone with a doctorate in hydrology: For six months, Vivian had been the coalition's office manager.

I knew if I phoned the society and asked for information about Vivian, I would get the usual "we only verify employment" runaround, so I took a different tack.

"I'm with the Seacoast Institute, and we're doing a study of administrative jobs in environmental nonprofits," I told Faith Cutter (imagine the jokes!), who was the society's director of human resources. "I wonder if you could tell me what the duties of your office manager are."

There was a moment of silence and then a small cough. "We don't have an office manager."

"Oh. Well, gosh. We've collected all these resumes over the

years and . . . let me see here . . . yes. This one here says the person was office manager for the Stoneman Douglas Society."

"The name?"

"Sorry. That's been blacked out," I said. "Privacy issues, you know?"

She sighed heavily, like she really needed to be bothered by some meddlesome outfit doing another useless survey. "When was this? Perhaps before my time."

"Ninety-nine, it says here. From May through October."

It was her turn to say "Oh," but I couldn't be sure if she meant "Oh, what a short time" or "Oh, I know who you're talking about." She took her time clarifying things too, but finally said, "That was an anomaly."

"An anomaly? You had an office manager then, but not now?"

"The position to which you refer was created to pun—for one particular employee who has since left the foundation. It wasn't really . . . We didn't . . ." She took a deep breath. "Look. One of our hy—our professional staff got crosswise with the director, so the director sidelined her in the job you're talking about. Six months later, the employee resigned."

I could almost hear Faith add "and for good reason." Dared I push things just a little bit farther? "Hmmm," I said. "I don't suppose you'd let me talk to your director—you know, to get her—or his—take on things?"

"She's no longer here. But let me give you my take on things since we're not dealing with actual names. We in Human Resources strongly advised against moving that particular employee into what was, in effect, a non job. We were overruled. There was a lot of controversy stemming from the director's actions, and she ended up having to resign her position."

"Before the employee left?"

"That is correct. And that is all I am going to tell you." The phone went dead, and I noticed my message light blinking. It was Alicia telling me show-and-tell time at her place would be one o'clock.

"So long as it doesn't cost me next year's salary," I said to the empty room.

"What's gonna cost ya?" came a man's voice from the doorway. I spun my chair around and saw Tony Marrero, the repair guy, standing there with his arms across his chest. He was wearing black dockers with knife-edge pleats in them and a black, form-fitting t-shirt, topped off by a charcoal sport coat—an impressive wardrobe upgrade since the last time he'd crossed my threshold. No snakeskin boots, though. Just black loafers.

"Let me guess," I said. "You've just come from church."

"On a Tuesday?" He looked at his watch as if he could barely spare the time. "You called me, so what's it all about?"

"Photographs. I understand you know everything about computers."

"That doesn't make me a photographer."

"No. That's not why I called you."

He unbuttoned the sport coat as he dropped into the chair opposite my desk. Drumming his fingers nervously on his knee, he gazed around the office, raising a judgmental eyebrow at its decidedly down-market ambience. I placed the two photographs in front of Tony.

"Whooee!" he exclaimed as he ogled the two semi-clad women. "Nice pu—ahem. Ahem." He cleared his throat as a flush crept up his cheeks as tiny beads of sweat popped up on his forehead.

"Notice they don't seem to be the same person?"

"Yeah." He put the photos down and got to his feet like it was time to head off for his next appointment.

"Does either of the women look familiar, Tony?"

He froze. "No. Why do you ask?"

"One of them is Vivian Remington of the Wetland Protectors Alliance. Remember visiting her office last week?"

"Uh, yeah. I guess so." His gaze shifted to my right as though he found the filing cabinet fascinating.

"Since they have computers and a fully staffed IT department, what was it you went there to fix?"

He shrugged. "Just checking the Internet traffic of a guy they'd fired. "Anyway, what do you care?"

"She's dead, you know."

He paled. "No."

"Yes. And that's why I find these photos so interesting. Wouldn't you agree?"

"I think they're kinda kinky." Tony's eyes shifted toward the door, and he shoved his hands into his pockets.

I sighed. "Don't you think it's odd to have two different women wearing the exact same coat and standing in the exact same pose with the same background and props?"

He scowled at the photographs but left them on the desk. "One of 'em's been digitally altered. Probably both."

What was it with him? Last time we'd talked, he'd been open and friendly. Now I was having to drag the information out like the defense on cross-examination. "I'm betting it would be a snap for someone with your talents to play around with a photo like this. Am I right?"

Another shrug, followed by a pointed look at his watch. "Look. I gotta be across town in five minutes."

"Which one of these is yours?"

His eyes narrowed. "Don't know what you're talking about."

"Look, Tony, I'm not a cop. I promise I'm not going to turn you in for just helping somebody have a bit of fun. All I'm asking is which one is yours?"

He pointed at the photo of Vivian. "She wanted me to do one just like this, only with the other lady's head."

"Did she say why?"

He got to his feet, scowling. "I think I've said enough." He pointed his finger at my chest. "You better keep your promise, girl."

"Sure."

As Tony's footsteps receded down the hallway, I leaned back, propped my feet on the desk, and closed my eyes. Yet again, the more mature side of my brain was telling me it was time to throw in the towel. Things were only getting more and more confusing. In the process of seeking greater clarity, I'd spread my fingerprints and who knew what other physical evidence all over the dead woman's office and home. If the police changed their thinking and decided she'd been murdered, then I would be in deep doo-doo.

What I needed right now was legal advice—somebody to tell me just how much of a problem I faced being charged with pretending to be a licensed private investigator. What? Six months in jail? A heavy fine? Both? Alicia could take care of the fine, but I *so* did not want to do the time—nor did I relish having to face my uncle's reaction when he learned the truth about our little filmmaking caper gone wrong.

I stared at the window, which was streaked with rain. Alicia was expecting me at her house for lunch, and I was car-less. I'd already arranged to borrow Uncle Alex's car for my trip to D.C. to visit Marguerite Sutherland. I didn't dare ask him to lend it to me now, especially because he tended to be awfully grumpy following meetings with his bankers. With a sigh, I picked up the phone and called a cab.

"Like it?" said Alicia. She'd put the diamond clip on a velvet throw pillow that now lay on the rosewood table in the Ritchies' cavernous dining room. When she switched on the hotel-sized crystal chandelier above us, the jewelry's facets sparkled like the Milky Way.

"It looks *exactly* the same," I whispered in awe.

"The jeweler did a good job with your sketch. Of course, these are cubic zirconium, you know."

"She'll never know the difference." Throwing my arms around Alicia, I planted a big wet one on her cheek. "I'll pay you back someday, babe. What's the damage?"

"Don't worry about it."

I shook my head. "Unh-unh. This was not your fault. You didn't even know I had the thing when Bobby stole it."

Alicia rolled her eyes. "And how did you wind up with it in the first place? Because *I* sent you to that stupid Washington reception."

She had a point. Plus, she had oodles more money than I could ever put my hands on. Still . . .

"Just don't lose it."

Putting the clip back into the jeweler's box, I shoved it into the pocket of my jeans where it stayed until Alicia dropped me at MoneySource where Uncle Alex was waiting outside.

"Where the hell have ya been, P.J.?" he asked as I headed toward my cubicle. "The skips are really piling up, and I'm not making any money."

"Yeah, yeah. I'll get caught up by later this afternoon, okay?"

"Don't ask me to hold my breath," he snarled, turning away. Then he turned back. "Oh, yeah. Jake and Rake saw your dirt-bag ex-husband over in Eastport yesterday, so you'd better be on the lookout."

"You've been having him followed?"

Uncle Alex tapped his foot while examining his fingernails.

"Bobby won't come here," I continued. "He knows what you think of him. Besides, he's probably halfway to Florida by now."

"Don't bet on it. He's got a grudge against you."

"Us."

"Whatever. He won't come after me though, not after what I did to his arm."

"So you've got Jake and Rake playing bodyguards?" I slapped both hands on my hips.

"Nope. I figure you're old enough to get yourself out of your own messes. Besides, they got real work to do."

Before I could think of an appropriately snippy retort, he headed back to his office. I sorted the files on my desk, dumping the impossibles into the bottom drawer of the filing cabinet and arranging the remainder in order of easy to hard. But I couldn't focus even on the easy ones. My thoughts kept returning to the idea of making a full confession—not until after I'd talked to a lawyer, of course—but what a relief it would be to have the whole thing settled. Coward that I was, I hadn't had the nerve to mention my thoughts to Alicia. But if the police decided I was Suspecto Numero Uno, they might also search the Banner Building office, where they would find my notes on the meeting with Marvin Ross, the possibly incriminating things I'd removed from Vivian's office, the two really weird photographs of Vivian Remington and Marguerite Sutherland, and Alicia's hidden television camera—unless she'd managed to remove it. I should have asked her. But talk about incriminating!

I jumped up from the desk, slithered down the hall, and peeked into my uncle's office. He was gone, along with the sport coat that he usually draped over the back of his chair. That meant he was out somewhere and, with any luck, wouldn't return until I'd taken care of business at the Banner Building.

Panting from the exertion of running twelve blocks, I closed the door to the seedy office, removed the jeweler's box from my pocket, and put it on the desk while I gathered all the items I needed to hide. Including Vivian's resumé. Then I phoned

Alicia, leaving a message that she needed to remove her camera right away, before the police discovered it.

After that, I called Sandy Jones to thank her for sending me the resumé and to ask just one other question: "Have you had any luck finding out who wrote that threatening note to Vivian?"

"I'm pretty sure it was Marvin Ross."

So was I. I thanked her, but before I could hang up, Sandy asked me if I was any closer to understanding what had really happened to Vivian. I mumbled a bunch of nonsense about promising indications and said I'd let her know when I learned anything concrete.

The minute I put the phone down, it rang again. I jerked it up in time to hear the high-pitched crank caller's latest message: "The awful thing about drowning, P.J., is you can't help swallowing the stuff that's killing you."

CHAPTER TWENTY-ONE

Okay. So the kooky caller with the childish voice knew my name. Did that make things any worse? I got up from the desk, crossed the room, and locked the door. Where was my gun when I needed it? I pulled out my checkbook to confirm that I did not have the funds to buy another weapon. Nor was there any credible way to persuade my uncle that I'd lost mine and needed a replacement.

It was hard to concentrate on anything but my own fear, so catching a shadow of movement out of the corner of my eye made me flinch. Through the frosted glass on the upper part of the door, I could see a man's silhouette.

He pounded on the glass, yelling "let me in!" I got a much clearer view when the door came crashing inward off its hinges with Bobby plunging after.

The first thing I thought of was the faux diamond clip lying on the desk. I grabbed it just as he came around the side of the desk and picked me up by my shirt collar.

"You bitch!" he yelled, beer-laden spit splattering all over my face. "You better have some money, or you're in big trouble."

"You know I don't have a dime," I managed to sound relatively calm as I stared into his enraged, bloodshot eyes.

"Then get it," he snarled, gesturing toward the phone. "Doesn't that rich bitch friend of yours, Allison or whatever, have loads of cash?"

"Alicia. And she's not here," I lied. "She's off skiing in Vail."

"Well too bad for you." Bobby shoved me back into the chair. "What's that you're holding?" He grabbed my hand, pried my fingers off the box, and opened it.

"I'll be goddamned." He stared at the diamond clip. "And here I thought it was at the bottom of Back Creek."

"C'mon, Bobby," I said, jumping to my feet. "Don't steal it again. If you like, I'll pawn it and—"

"Don't you move. After all the money you cost me to fix two goddamn boats, this belongs to me."

"No it doesn't." Driving my knee upward, I rammed it into his balls, something that I should have done years ago.

He doubled over and screamed as I'd hoped he would, but instead of dropping the box, he staggered toward the door. I grabbed a fistful of shirt and yanked him backward. He tripped and fell, still clutching the box, as I took shelter behind my chair.

"Give me the box, Bobby, or I'm calling the cops."

Still doubled over, he struggled to his feet and lunged at me. Ducking down, I shoved the chair into his stomach.

"Oof," he said, and staggered backward toward the window. The hand holding the box swung outward to break his fall and ended up going straight through the window pane, sending shards of glass flying. "I'm cut!" he screamed. "Call the medics."

"The box!" I yelled. "Where's the box?"

"It musta gone out the window." He stood there, cradling his bloody hand.

Oh, shit.

"What's the problem here?" I looked up, and there stood Alicia Todd Ritchie and the guy with the mustache who'd been doing the camera work at the D.C. reception.

"He might need medical attention," I said, gesturing toward Bobby.

In two strides, Alicia's sidekick crossed the room, grabbed Bobby's arm, and examined his bloody hand. "This isn't as bad as it looks," he said. "Why don't we get you cleaned up? If it's still bleeding a lot, we'll take you to the emergency room."

"You bitch!" yelled Bobby. "You told me she was in Colorado."

"I lied." Turning to Alicia, I said, "Don't let him go. He threw the diamond hair clip out the window."

Her eyes narrowed, and she fisted her hands on her hips. "You slimy weasel."

"I'll be back in a sec." Before Bobby had a chance to say anything, I was out the door in a flash and running down the hall to the stairs. I could hear him yelling "Let go of me!" but I figured Alicia and Mustache could take care of him.

No tiny jeweler's box was lying among the shards of glass that littered the alley beneath the office window. I was just about to collapse in frustration when I noticed the large dumpster sitting up against the building across the alley. I boosted myself up and peered over the side. Someone had thrown a dead rat onto the mound of rotting vegetable matter that had me holding my breath to keep from gagging. And there was the box. Right on top of the rat's tail.

Hoisting one leg over the lip of the dumpster, I pulled myself over and dropped onto the garbage pile. The rat shifted onto the top of my shoe, and the box sank further into the sludge. I wanted to scream but couldn't because of the retching. When that was exhausted, I pulled my shirttail out and used it to pick the rat up by its tail, flinging it over the side of the dumpster. Then I got down on my hands in the muck and began feeling around for the box. In what seemed like an eternity later, I got my filthy paws on the sucker and shoved it into my jeans pocket. When I rose to my feet, I discovered that I'd tamped the garbage down to a level where there was no way I could reach the top of the dumpster, even by jumping.

Visions of being crushed in a garbage truck compactor danced through my brain as I pondered the situation. I could yell, but what good would it do if no one was there to hear me? Piling the garbage up in a mound against one side of the dumpster, I hoped it would be high enough for me to climb to the top. Not.

I was just about to exercise my vocal chords when I heard footsteps in the alley. A policeman? Bobby? Somebody else? Could I chance calling for help? The internal debate ended when a dead rat came sailing over the side and hit me in the face.

"Whoa," said a voice deeper and scratchier than Bobby's. "What all that screechin'? What you doin' in there?"

"I'm stuck. I fell over, and I can't get out."

The dumpster lurched to one side and a dirt-streaked face peered over the side. "How'd you fall in?" said the man. A dark knit cap hid most of his filthy gray hair, and a snaggly beard hid his mouth.

"Please, can you get me out?"

"Dunno. What's it worth to ya?"

A million dollars that I didn't have? My eternal gratitude? A bottle of hooch? I had no idea how one bargained with the homeless. "Just get me out of here. I promise you won't be sorry."

The face disappeared, and I heard a scree-scree-scree sound. The man was mumbling under his breath. Something about "stop it up good," and then a loud "oof." The face reappeared, followed by a scrawny torso clad in a black wool, mostly moth-eaten sweater.

"Okay, lady." Leaning over the lip of the dumpster, he extended a pair of grimy hands with long yellow fingernails. "Grab on tight, and I'll pull you out."

I probably bruised my ribs as he dragged me over the side and dropped me into a large supermarket shopping cart that he'd shoved up against the dumpster. Looking down, I saw that he had indeed "stopped it up good" by shoving a couple of sticks of wood underneath the wheels.

Feet firmly on the ground, I brushed myself off as best I could and led my rescuer back into the Banner Building and up the stairs to the fourth floor where I found Alicia sitting in the chair opposite Marlowe's desk.

Considering the look on her face, I felt it was only fair for her to reward my rescuer, who snatched three twenties out of her hands, gave us both a big gap-toothed smile, and disappeared before Alicia's sides even stopped shaking.

"Hey, Ramón!" she called out. "Let's get some footage of P.J. before we dismantle the camera."

"Too late," he yelled from the room next door. Had she also been renting that room the whole time?

I dropped the filthy box on the desk and plopped into the chair. "What happened to Bobby?"

"We let him go. His cuts were only superficial, by the way. We had a nice chat while you were otherwise occupied." A dimple flashed as Alicia tried to suppress a grin.

"Wonderful. I suppose he turned on the charm."

She nodded. "It's amazing how much that guy knows about sailing. Weird, though, how someone who regularly shimmies up masts in ocean racers practically falls apart seeing his own blood."

I could barely conceal my irritation. "I guess he's only human. But you shouldn't have let him get away."

She shrugged. "I persuaded him to leave town and not bother you again."

"It was that easy?" I could barely conceal my disbelief.

"He's had enough run-ins with the law. When I told him your

lawyer, Neal Patterson—who happens to be an officer of the court, for what that's worth—would come after him if he ever tried anything like that again, Bobby decided to be very accommodating."

Why were things so simple for the Alicia Todd Ritchies of this world and so fraught with complications for folks like me? "I don't suppose you asked Bobby what he did with my gun?"

"No, but he seems to need money. He probably sold it."

"Or pawned it." I sighed. "Dammit, I could use some protection right now."

"How about me?" Ramón stood in the doorway, holding the camera with one hand and tweaking his mustache with the other.

"You're spoken for," said Alicia, as we both stepped aside to allow him access to the button under the desk. "Ramón's wife would slit my throat if she thought I gave him any time to fool around."

"Hang on a sec," I said to the two of them. "Let me get cleaned up a little." I scurried down to the restroom where I used up all the paper towels washing dead rat, wilted lettuce, and rancid tomato sauce off myself. Taking a peek in the mirror, I nearly fainted. My face and arms were streaked with soot, and instead of removing it, I'd only managed to spread it everywhere.

What I needed was a three-hour hot shower followed by an aromatherapy massage and a whole new wardrobe. Gritting my teeth, I marched back down the hall. Only Alicia and Ramón had already gone. She'd left a note, "Item of interest is in desk drawer. Don't forget to get the door fixed before you hit the shower. I'll call you this evening." On the desk blotter lay a blank check to cover the repairs.

As I waited for a human being to answer the phone at Doors n' More, I looked at my watch. It was three-thirty. How in heaven's name was I going to re-secure my office, transform myself from street urchin into a professional photographer-poseur, and get to Washington in time for my tête-à-tête with Senator Marguerite Sutherland?

CHAPTER TWENTY-TWO

Citizen Cope was rocking through the CD player, the traffic on Route 50 was light heading into Washington, and I was fantasizing about how grateful Neal Patterson would be when I solved the mystery of Vivian's untimely death. He'd be so delighted he'd take me to dinner at Treaty of Paris, after which we'd go down to the water and watch sailboats bobbing against the pier in the moonlight. He'd administer several mind-blowing kisses, and then he'd suggest coffee at his place. He'd dim the lights, and we'd slow dance to something jazzy and cool on the stereo, enjoying the feel of one another's—wait. He had a dog. Okay. He'd put the dog out, then he'd dim the lights. One thing would lead to another and oh-oh. There seemed to be flashing blue and red lights in my rearview mirror. I slowed down and pulled off onto the shoulder.

"You realize the speed limit on this road is sixty-five?" said the burly state trooper as I handed him my driver's license and registration.

"Was I speeding?"

"You were going forty. I thought you might have fallen asleep at the wheel."

"No, sir," I said, my face turning crimson.

The trooper handed me the license and registration and leaned down to see if he could detect alcohol on my breath. There were no beverages, suspect or otherwise, in the car, so he tipped his hat and told me to pay attention to the speed limit, or I might find myself the victim of an incident of road rage. Of course, that made me late. To begin with, I'd forgotten to allow extra time for rush-hour traffic. Then I got stuck in a tie-up caused by the perpetual roadwork on New York Avenue with two lanes of cars suddenly forced to squeeze into one. It was five-thirty when I finally breezed into the lobby and announced myself to the concierge.

The senator's sixth-floor apartment covered at least one whole side of the building. There was a long marble hallway leading into a spacious living room with windows overlooking Rock Creek Park. The wine-colored Oriental rug on the floor looked like silk, not wool, and the sofa and chairs were a fancy French style with brocade upholstery. Off the entry hallway to the right was another hall presumably leading to some bed-rooms. I could see a large bathroom through the first doorway to the right. To the left of the living room was an immense din-ing room with a mahogany table large enough to seat a banquet. The rug beneath the dining table was a light green version of the one in the living room. No wonder the woman didn't panic when she lost diamond jewelry.

Glancing at the tiny watch on her wrist, the senator offered me a glass of water. Her words made me realize how thirsty I was after my encounter with the Law, but I politely declined. She led me to a corner of the living room where there were two brocade-covered chairs facing each other across a low, flat glass table on which sat a pile of coffee-table art books, carefully ar-ranged in an angled stack, and a bowl-shaped crystal vase with silk flowers. I reached into the canvas bag I'd brought with me and pulled out a serious-looking camera that I'd borrowed from Jake and a digital I'd borrowed from Uncle Alex.

"Let's take a couple of establishing shots," I said, clicking rapidly. "Then we'll do the serious stuff."

"Don't you need those big spotlights?" said Sutherland as I

checked the digital's screen.

"Oh, no. I didn't want to mess things up, bringing in all that gear." Hah. "If you could just remove the lampshade . . . ?"

She stood up and pulled the shade off. "Better?"

Nope. Worse. "Hmmmm. Let's do this in softer light." I gestured for her to put the shade back over the lamp.

As Sutherland smoothed her skirt, I walked around, framing the shot from different angles. "This will be perfect," I said as I clicked off two shots while she bared her teeth in what she probably thought was a warm, inviting smile.

"Now, if you don't mind, I really think you'll look fabulous wearing that fur coat."

"Oh, yes. I forgot." The senator jumped up and disappeared into the hallway leading to the master bedroom. I could hear nothing. No drawers opening or shutting, no closet doors either.

"It doesn't seem to be here," she said as she emerged from the hallway. "That's so odd. I could swear I didn't take it down to Florida."

I looked around the room. "Do you think it might be in the coat closet?"

"I doubt it." She headed for the foyer, spent a few minutes pawing through the garments in the coat closet, and then emerged, peering at her watch. "I'm afraid I don't have any more time. Perhaps you can come back?"

"Of course." I stood up. Reaching into my jacket pocket, I pulled out the twice-jinxed diamond clip, and handed it over. "Don't let me forget."

"Thank you for returning this," she said in a cool, unappreciative voice as the phone rang. "Most people would just keep it or sell it." She disappeared around the corner to answer the phone. "I suppose you'll want a reward."

I sat back down and doubled over in agony.

"What on earth!" said the startled senator as she returned to the living room. "Are you ill?"

"May I use your bathroom?" I gritted out between clenched teeth.

"Of course," she said irritably, giving her watch another glance. "I have to leave, or I'll miss the curtain."

"I might be a while." I staggered down the hallway leading to the bathroom. "Sorry to inconvenience you." I shut the door to the bathroom, locked it, and sat down on the edge of the bathtub. "Ohhhhh," I moaned. Then I coughed several times, leaned over the toilet, and flushed it.

"Are you getting sick?" yelled Sutherland through the door. The barely disguised disgust in her voice made me smile.

"Ohhhh," I moaned again. "Just give me a few minutes."

"Look, uh, Ms. Smythe. I have to leave or I'll be late. The front door locks when you shut it, so why don't you just let yourself out when you're finished in there?"

Yes! "Thank you," I coughed some more and flushed the toilet another time. Then I heard footsteps on the marble floor and the sound of the door clicking shut. Oh, P.J., you sly one. Still, I waited about five more minutes just to be sure the senator didn't come barreling back through the door, having forgotten her tip money for the powder room.

Sutherland's apartment had three bedrooms. Unlike the Frenchified living and dining rooms, the large master bedroom and bath were done all in midnight blue from the tile in the bathroom to the thick pile wall-to-wall carpeting and the satin canopy over the four-poster bed. The floor-to-ceiling closets had blue mirrored doors, and the lampshades on the dresser and the lamp beside the bed were in the same midnight blue satin as the bedspread and canopy. Heavy velvet drapes were pulled across the windows. I peeked behind one to find it lined with blackout curtains, which effectively obliterated the stunning view of a bejeweled city skyline.

Donning the gloves I'd stashed in my handbag, I pulled open the drawer beside the bed and saw a packet of condoms, a small jar of Vaseline, a pack of tissues, some reading glasses, and an emery board. Did I need to search such a small space for such a large garment? Of course not. But, considering I'd never get another chance, it was best to be thorough.

Scattered across the dresser were about seven different bottles of perfume, a jar of face cream, a can of hair spray, a silver-backed mirror with matching brush and comb, and a picture of Juan Carlos Francisco standing at the railing of what appeared to be a boat. Both hands were resting on the rail, and he was laughing at the photographer.

In the second dresser drawer, I found a dark brown fur stole with a Neiman Marcus label. I searched the closet but found no sign of the fur coat. Drat. Time was running out, and my mouth was parched. What if the senator had mentioned my bathroom emergency to the concierge and he was on his way up to investigate? I didn't want to go to jail.

If he showed up, I'd just say I was her niece, staying over for the night. I was a blonde. Marguerite was a brunette. Still, it would have to do.

I turned my attention to the two smaller bedrooms. One of them had a queen-size bed and matching dresser but did not look lived-in. The other had been cleverly transformed into a mammoth walk-in closet that held row upon row of garment bags containing what was probably Marguerite's spring, summer, and fall wardrobes. Either that, or she had a sideline selling the clothing she stole from others. Retracing my steps, I noticed that the closet in the other bedroom was empty. How long would it take to examine each of the garment bags? They weren't even transparent, which meant I'd have to unzip each one to find out which ones might include a purloined fur coat. How much time did I have before the concierge got nervous and wondered what I was up to? It might be smarter to look for other clues to the woman's relationship with Vivian.

Moving quickly back to the writing desk in the living room, I booted up the laptop, got the password prompt, and shut it down. A quick search of the rest of the writing desk showed that its purpose was more style than function. One drawer held some stationery with the senator's D.C. address engraved on thick laid-finished bond, and the other had only dust bunnies. A large display of dried eucalyptus in a brass vase was the sole occupant of the credenza in the marble foyer, and (not that I doubted Marguerite's word or anything) there was no spotted fur coat hanging in the coat closet. The kitchen's gold-flecked black granite countertops were bare too, except for a food processor, an Espresso machine, and a microwave.

Back in the closet room, I unzipped the bags, moving quickly through cruise and summer wear to linen and rayon frocks to silk pantsuits, a whole bag full of silk blouses and shells, another bag full of casual slacks and crop pants, and finally one that held lightweight wool suits and pantsuits. The coat was not there.

The next bag held wool dresses of varying lengths. She might wear a fur coat with those, I thought, as I pawed through the clothes. Nope.

Finally. A bag holding silk, taffeta, and satin evening wear in bright colors—all more likely to be worn in spring or summer. I looked anyway, my heart sinking as I reached the back of the bag with no ocelot coat in sight. There was only one bag left. It was full of velvet and brocade evening gowns, most of which were in black or dark colors. The gold gown I'd seen the senator wearing at the Washington fete was not among them. Slapping my hand upside my head, I left the room. Of course, it wouldn't be there. Sutherland had sent the gown out to be dry-cleaned. And the coat? Didn't most people keep their furs in some kind of cold storage? How could I be so stupid? And what a wasted trip.

Back in the living room as I picked up my handbag, I noticed the diamond clip on the telephone table where Marguerite had left it when she'd answered the phone. The proceeds from the sale of the bauble that now lay at the bottom of Back Creek would probably feed a thousand starving Africans. This one was worth so much less that I'd be in deep shit if Marguerite Sutherland ever tried to pawn it. A light was glowing under "messages," and I figured what the heck. Pushing the button, I heard a familiar voice. "Hi Marguerite. Gareth Swenson here. Just checking to see if you've had a chance to call Senator Crane yet. Could you give me a buzz?" The message had come in at around three that afternoon, before my arrival. Poor thing. He was so desperate for that DEA job. It wasn't funny, but I couldn't help giggling at the thought, and the giggle ended up tickling my throat. I started coughing.

In the kitchen, I poured myself a large glass of water from the kitchen tap, and wrote the senator a note on the bottom of a grocery list that had been lying on the center island. "So sorry for the problem," I scribbled. "I cleaned up after myself. Many thanks for your kindness—P.J." I am nothing if not good-mannered.

I had my hand on the doorknob when I heard a key turning in the lock. Was it that late?

Chapter Twenty-Three

Removing my shoes, I made a slip-sliding dash down the hallway leading to the bedrooms and scooted into the guest room. A quick peek at my watch showed it was only nine o'clock. Either the senator had come home early, or the concierge was checking because he hadn't seen me leave. Either way, I was in big trouble. Cursing myself nine ways from Sunday, I sat down on the bed, the words *amateur hour* running circles through my panicked brain.

If it was the concierge, I had my story ready. But the voice I heard next was Sutherland's.

"What a disappointment," she said. "I guess you just never know . . ."

"I'm afraid I always put too much faith in the reviews." The man had a slight Spanish accent. "Too bad we can't get a refund on the tickets."

"Let me fix you a nightcap, Juanito. It's the least I can do."

"Just a small one, my dear," he replied. "I really can't stay."

I crossed my fingers, hoping desperately that they'd click glasses, down the stuff in a gulp, toss the empties onto the hearth, and kiss goodnight. Then all I had to do was wait until the senator fell asleep. Surely the nightcap would help on that score.

"Must you really dash off, darling?" said Marguerite. "I've been missing you."

The senator's guest laughed, followed by a period of silence.

"Will that help tide you over till the weekend?" came the man's soft question.

"Mmmmm, maybe." The senator laughed coquettishly.

Another period of silence was followed by the tiny clink that glasses would make if the lovers were toasting each other. "What's this?" he asked.

"That's a piece of jewelry I thought I'd misplaced. The arm candy that Neal Patterson had with him at the Washington reception somehow got her hands on it and decided to return it."

Arm candy? *Moi?*

Juan Carlos was laughing. "Pretty bauble. How'd you lose it?"

"Who knows. It goes in your hair. Like this. It must have slipped off somehow. You know, sometimes if you bend over . . ." (I heard a plunk) "See? It must have happened while I was in the ladies' room. Neal's date probably found it in one of the stalls. And, speaking of Patterson, I'm having second thoughts. He's getting rather expensive."

Of course, Neal was expensive. You don't expect to pay chicken feed for the services of the most prestigious law firm in Annapolis. But expensive compared to what? I bet Meredith, Geitrich, and Smeal weren't half as costly as one of those K Street firms in Washington.

". . . whatever you decide," Marguerite's companion was saying. "This piece looks like it could fetch *mucho dinero* in a pawn shop. You are lucky Patterson's girlfriend didn't just keep it."

"Well I wish she'd mailed it back, instead of delivering it in person. Did I tell you the girl got sick in my bathroom while she was here? Pretty disgusting."

The man's voice softened as though he were addressing a beloved pet. *"Pobrecita."*

"You could kiss me and make it better."

"I could do more than that, my lovely. But not tonight, I'm afraid. Perhaps tomorrow?"

There was a long pause probably while they smooched. Then the man said, "Strange, that girl didn't just FedEx the thing to you. You don't suppose . . . ?"

"Well, actually, she's some kind of photographer. She wanted to get some shots of me in the coat I wore to the D.C. reception."

"She's some kind of paparazzo?" I could picture spittle flying as he spat the word out.

"Oh, heavens no, Juan. You always think the worst. She's done some state representatives, people like that. I admit I was flattered."

"Marguerite. Darling." He had lowered his voice the way a father would when trying to reason with a silly child. "You really must keep a low profile. There's way too much at stake."

She laughed. "You think that skinny little thing has any savoir-faire, let alone entrée? She hardly knew what she was doing. She didn't bring any gear or photographer's lighting. For all I know, she's a—Oh. My God."

"What?"

"She got sick just as I was leaving, so I let her stay!"

"You left her here alone?"

"I was going to be late, Juanito." The senator's voice had risen to a defensive whine. "I told her she could let herself out after she'd finished tossing her lunch in my bathroom."

"What if she was faking?" he said. "Is there anything here in this apartment that would upset things?"

I heard Marguerite pick up the phone and ask the concierge the logical question, and I began to sweat. I had no plausible explanation for hiding in Marguerite Sutherland's guest bedroom.

"Rafiq never saw her leave!" said the senator.

I carefully peeled back the latex gloves and stuffed them between the mattress and box springs.

"You stay there. I'll take care of this," said the man.

"Oooohh," I moaned when I sensed his presence in the room where I'd been hiding. By then, I was curled into a protective ball, lying on the coverlet.

"What are you doing here?" The fingers I'd last seen pinching Senator Sutherland on the ass gripped my elbow and jerked me up to a sitting position.

"Ooohh." I pressed to my stomach. "I'm sick. It must be food poisoning." This time I wasn't lying. The terror of being caught, coupled no doubt with the nauseating vapors that I'd inhaled earlier during my incarceration in the dumpster, had made my head swim. My stomach fluttered upward toward my throat and refused to retreat.

"I saw the note you left in the kitchen," said Marguerite from the doorway. "Why are you still here?"

"I had another attack. In fact . . ." I shoved a hand against my mouth, jerked out of Juan Carlos's grasp, and ran into the bathroom. After locking the door, I collapsed onto the toilet and lowered my head between my knees. Trying to breathe deeply, I pondered my predicament.

A silly phrase that Uncle Alex had used often kept spinning around in my head. "When the going gets rough, the tough . . ." do what? I couldn't remember. My chances of escape did not look good, especially with me inside a windowless bathroom and the two of them buzzing around like angry hornets on the other side of the door.

I heard steps receding down the hallway and wondered if the senator or her friend were going to summon the police. That made hiding in the bathroom unwise. After splashing my face with water, I emerged to find them standing in the foyer.

"I'm *so* sorry," I said to the senator. "I don't know what's been making me so ill, but I do hope you'll forgive me for abusing your hospitality."

"You think we are *estupidos?*" snarled the woman's Latin lover. "You're no photographer. So what's this all about?" He turned to Sutherland. "I bet it has something to do with—"

I jerked away. "Have we met?"

"—Vivian Remington."

Marguerite gasped. "But she's dead."

"I was simply returning her jewelry." I pointed at Sutherland. "I can't help it if I—"

Juan Carlos scoffed. "Vivian Remington put you up to this, didn't she?"

Shaking my head, I edged backward, beyond reach of his now-fisted hands.

"Vivian Remington is dead," said Marguerite, needle stuck in the same groove.

Juan Carlos took a menacing step in my direction. "You're not leaving until you tell us what this is all about."

I backed up, but not far enough to escape the nearly bone-crushing slap of his hand across my cheek.

"I detest smart asses," he said, "especially silly blond bimbo smart asses. Now *talk.*"

"Juan Carlos, please!" Marguerite placed a restraining hand on his elbow. "Let's not let things get out of control."

I nodded in shaky agreement as I gingerly pressed my jaw to check if any teeth had been dislodged.

"Please, darling." Marguerite said, placing her hand on Francisco's arm. "Why don't you just go on home, and let me resolve this with Ms. Smythe."

"There's a lot at stake—"

"And enough said," came the firm rejoinder.

"You must at least search the woman. She might have stolen something."

Marguerite's lip curled, but her eyes lit up. "All right. If you think that's necessary." Rising up on her tiptoes, the senator planted a light kiss on Francisco's lips. "*Ciao*, dear."

Locking the door behind her departing lover, Marguerite grabbed my elbow and propelled me into the living room. "Sit," she commanded, motioning toward one of the chairs.

"I'm really not feeling well. I've got a bad chill, and my face hurts."

"This won't take long." She left the room.

I was still trying to figure the odds of making a successful run for the door when Marguerite returned with my jacket draped over her arm. It wasn't going to make me feel much warmer, though, because she had her cell phone in one latex-gloved hand and a tiny pistol in the other. "Now, you're going to do what I say, or I'm calling the police to report the attempted theft of my jewelry."

For a moment, I thought so what? Alicia would vouch for me. She'd tell them I'd driven to Washington for the purpose of returning the bauble, not stealing it. But then I realized nobody would ask Alicia a thing unless there was a trial, at which time somebody would have discovered that the hair clip was cubic zirconium, and both of us would be headed to prison.

Next thing I knew, Sutherland had me up against the wall, my legs spread wide as she ran her hands over nearly every square inch of my body including places that I considered off limits to anyone who hadn't been explicitly invited to explore them.

When she released me, I turned to see her smirking. "There's nothing incriminating, although I'm certainly satisfied." She motioned me to sit down at the writing desk and handed me the fountain pen. "I will dictate. You write."

When I finished, she had a handwritten, signed confession from Paula Jo Smythe, to wit: "I, Paula Jo Smythe, visited

Florida State Senator Marguerite Sutherland at her Washington residence on the night of February 21, 2010, under false pretenses with the intention of committing robbery. The senator caught me stealing a piece of jewelry, a diamond hair clip, and in her attempt to retrieve the item, caused me to trip and fall, hitting my head against a table. I assume full responsibility for any injury that I may have sustained. I make this confession freely and under no duress." Hah.

Grabbing my elbow, Sutherland marched me to the front door. "I don't know what you thought you were up to, but I suspect Vivian Remington put you up to it."

"Who is she? You keep saying she's dead. So why—?"

"Oh, shut up." Sutherland tapped an impatient foot. "I wasn't born yesterday. You're from Annapolis. So is Remington. It's a very small town. Her death must be all over whatever they call a newspaper there."

"Did you have anything to do with it?" I asked.

Her face turned blood red. "Are you serious?"

"I Googled you to get your phone number. Your bio says you're on the board of the Wetland Protectors Alliance. That's where Remington worked, according to the account in the local paper. And, like you just said, Annapolis is a small town."

"And you're some kind of self-appointed private investigator, bent on avenging her death? Is that why you pulled this stunt?" She waved the pistol in the direction of the bathroom.

The way she was waving that thing around, I should have been cowering, arms over my head, waiting for the gun to go off—accidentally or on purpose. Instead, it emboldened me, especially because I was still seething over the way Marguerite had violated my person and forced me to sign a false confession. "One thing you're right about, Senator Sutherland" (I sneered the two words to make her name sound like the slithery snake she was), "we Annapolitans may not have a real newspaper, but we do get the *Post*. Did you see the item in the Style Section the day after your Washington shindig? The one that connects you to Juan Carlos Francisco?"

She shrugged. "So?"

"I bet you and the late Ms. Remington are on opposite sides of Everglades issues, given who your boyfriend is, and that—"

"Where did you get such a cockamamie idea?" The pistol she was holding rotated in tiny circles. Luckily for me, it was pointed at the chandelier dangling above us. "Even if I did happen to disagree with Vivian on some aspects of Everglades restoration, I would raise the matter with the board, not resort to murder."

"Unless you've already raised the issue and got nowhere with them. Plus, didn't I just hear him" (I shrugged my shoulder in the direction of the hallway outside) "say there's a lot at stake?"

She stood there, staring at me. "You are so off the mark, but I don't have time to deal with it." Then she seemed to remember what she was holding and lowered the pistol to aim right at my heart. "You may be clever, but you're not very smart. Just remember that I am a more powerful person than you. I could do you grievous harm without ever having to resort to this." She waved the pistol again. "You'd be wise not to mess with me or Juan Carlos Francisco. If I ever hear one word attempting to connect me to Vivian Remington's death, you will wish I'd used this gun. Now get out of here. Just hightail it back to that quaint little burg you call home. I don't want to see your face or hear from—or about—you again. Got it?"

Lucky for me there were no state troopers patrolling Route 50 on my way back to Annapolis because I pushed the pedal to the floor until I reached Bowie. That lady was scary.

Bruised and famished, I cruised into the Double-T Diner, ordered a roast beef sandwich smothered in gravy and a cup of coffee, figuring that would give me enough energy to make it home.

"You don't have to put up with that, hon," said the waitress who served me.

"Huh?"

She patted her face and gave me a concerned look. "They got hotlines you can call, places where you can find shelter."

"Oh, this." I covered what must have become a hideous discoloration. "Ran into a door."

The corners of her mouth turned down. "That's what they all say."

CHAPTER TWENTY-FOUR

The next morning, my uncle barged into my cubicle at Money-Source. He was wearing a dark blue suit with a blue and white striped shirt and a chocolate tie with dancing pink pigs on it. Either his shady lady friends had no taste, or there was some radically new fashion trend afoot for men's office wear. I was about to suggest that brown didn't really go with blue when I noticed his sour expression, and that made me wonder if I might be a little too close to losing my job.

"I thought you'd be happy that I washed your car," I said.

"Least you could do." He waved a hand. "When are you gonna get a new one?"

"I'm sorry, Uncle Alex," I said as contritely as I could. "I haven't had time, what with—"

"Your suspicious side trips to Washington?" He looked around at the stacks of loan agreements gone bad that I had not yet managed to get to. "Place is a pigsty. Who knows how far behind you are these days? You may not know it, P.J., but we need to collect some of this debt, or we're outta business."

"I'm sorry. I'll spend the rest of the week doing skips."

"No. You'll spend however long it takes to get caught up."

I made a whimpering sound and reminded him that I couldn't car shop and skip trace at the same time. That only earned me another baleful look from my uncle.

"Don't you try guilt-tripping me, Missy. And don't think that makeup you're wearing hides the bruise you got on your cheek."

"I can explain . . ."

"Mr. Smythe?" The sweet young thing who interrupted my explanation handed my uncle a piece of paper. "Doreen wants you to call her about tonight."

I suppressed a groan because it wasn't exactly the right moment to quiz my uncle when he was quizzing me.

He folded the message and slipped it into his breast pocket. "You were saying?"

"That I just had an accident. I tripped and hit my head on something."

He rolled his eyes. "Spare me your fairy tale. You think I was born yesterday? I used to repossess cars in East Baltimore. Somebody smacked you hard. I doubt it was Neal Patterson, and it sure as hell better not be that fuckhead ex of yours."

"He's gone. Besides, nothing's broken. I still have all my teeth."

"Yeah. But not a lick of good sense. That crud ball better not show his face around this town ever again, or I'll even the score."

"Bobby didn't do it!"

"Well whoop-de-doo. I should be pleased? The only other explanation is you going on a chase call when I told you not to." He paused, running his fingers through his hair. "I can see you're not gonna confess, so gimme a break. My blood pressure's bad enough as it is." He stomped off.

Good. I had more important work to do. Setting aside a pile of "easys," I started calling furriers in Washington, one of whom did have the account for cold storage of Senator Marguerite Sutherland's garments. The only problem was, they wouldn't tell me which furs were currently under their care. Then I called Washington and played push-button games with the U.S. Fish and Wildlife Service's automated answering service until I finally reached a human being responsible for public outreach. They kept very careful tabs on those items they provided for public education, she assured me. Furthermore, ocelot coats were usually not part of the props they used for show-and-tell.

I sat there livid with rage. Why bother trying to find out who had killed Vivian Remington? If she were still alive, I'd do the deed myself. Which reminded me that I was still a suspect and, unless I continued my investigation, would remain so. Unfortunately, I was also being paid to care about people who couldn't or wouldn't pay their debts. I grabbed the skip paper at the top of the stack and started reading.

An hour later, I found what promised to be the current phone number of Jesús Camacho, who, two months ago, had borrowed two thousand on a personal note. Unsecured. What were the loan officers thinking? No wonder my uncle was losing money.

A woman with a thick Spanish accent answered the phone. When I asked to speak to Jesús, she said, *"Un momentito,"* and I heard the phone clunk as it hit a hard surface.

"Joo wan Jesús Ramón or Jesús Ignacio?"

"The Jesús who borrowed money from MoneySource."

"Thas me," said the man, whose voice sounded oddly familiar. "I no canna pay righ now. Maybe nex mont."

"Are you Jesús Ramón?"

"No. Ignacio. Jesús Ramón ees my son."

I made a little note. "Are you currently unemployed, Mr. Camacho? Is that why you can't pay?"

"No, I working. I working real hard righ now. Only my seester is no feeling well. I take her to the hospital, but she no have insurance."

Oh boy. I'd heard that one at least a zillion times before, but somehow I thought Camacho might be telling the truth. "I'm sorry to hear that, Mr. Camacho. But we need to work out something on this loan of yours. Maybe stretch out your payments so you don't have to pay so much each month."

"Hokay," he said. "How much I pay you then?"

"Actually, you have to come into the office and refinance the loan. Do you understand?"

"I can no be leaving my job," he said. "They already fire my fren and they no replace him yet."

"Where is it that you work, Mr. Camacho?" But I already knew the answer. How many Jesús's were there in Annapolis whose colleague had just been fired? And suddenly a whole other ethical issue reared its ugly head. I could probably persuade Jesús to do something for me, something his employers would not approve of, like letting me read Vivian's incoming and outgoing e-mail. In return, I could keep his skip file at the bottom of the pile. Yes, I could do that, but should I?

"You no be calling my boss?"

"No," I replied, still wrestling with my conscience. This time, the better side won—or the side that kept reminding me where my real income came from—and I made arrangements for Camacho to come in on a Saturday afternoon. Maybe he'd be so grateful to be let off the hook that he'd offer . . . Don't go there, P.J.

Instead, I went home early, put a package of frozen peas on my jaw, curled up on the sofa, and fell asleep feeling sorry for myself.

Then Neal Patterson called, saying he wanted to see me. My spirits lifted, even though I realized that a face-to-face with him would not be smart. He'd take one look at the bruise and go ballistic. He'd insist that he accompany me everywhere. No way could I handle that much temptation. Better to lie low for a while.

"I'm not feeling well," I'd said, trying to sound like I had a cold. "Nothing major, though. I'll be fine in a couple of days."

That part, at least, was true.

Later on, the doorbell rang, and I found Alicia standing there holding a covered dish, giving off a divine odor that had my stomach growling in response. She was wearing white wool slacks topped by a to-die-for deep blue cashmere sweater. "Your uncle tells me you need some TLC," she said, holding the dish out. "Tuna-noodle casserole."

Aw. Wasn't that sweet? "You didn't need to do that."

Alicia grinned. "What are friends for?"

I invited her in and gestured toward the kitchen. Shoving the dish in the microwave, she set the timer and turned toward me. "That's one ugly bruise you got, kiddo. But really P.J., telling your uncle you tripped and fell is really lame. If you're gonna lie, make it so incredible, he at least has to wonder."

"If I told him the truth, he'd lock me up and throw the key away!" Whether for incompetence or foolhardiness, I wasn't sure.

"That bad, huh?"

"Senator Sutherland gives new meaning to the word *bitch.*"

"Let me guess. She discovered the diamonds were fake."

"No. That part worked." I returned to my spot on the floor and settled the package of nearly thawed peas on my face.

Stretching out on the Naugahyde sofa, Alicia dropped her blue suede loafers on the floor and crossed her ankles. "Only if you tell all will you get fed."

When I'd finished, Alicia propped herself on an elbow and gave me a long, hard stare. "Paula Jo, huh? I wonder if that means what you signed isn't legally binding. You ought to ask Neal Patterson."

"That's the tricky part, Alicia. I haven't told him why Vivian hired me, so, aside from a couple of lame questions I asked him about Marguerite Sutherland, he doesn't know much." I stood up. My face was slightly numb from the cold, and the peas were total mush.

"He knows you're in trouble, so why not ask him to help?" Before I could answer, she went on, "Men love to rescue damsels in distress."

"Neal is also Sutherland's lawyer. So that means he'd have to take her side. Against me!"

Alicia crossed her arms. "Not if he has the hots for you."

"Oh, please. He's an officer of the courts, remember? He has to take her side." I went to retrieve the last remaining bag of frozen veggies, returning to find Alicia pacing the floor. Not a good sign. "The whole stolen coat thing was a bunch of baloney, anyway."

Startled, she turned. "You're kidding."

I told Alicia about my conversation with the Fish and Wildlife Service. "No coat, no crime, no case against Marguerite Sutherland. Ain't that a bitch?"

"Wait a sec." Alicia headed for the kitchen where I heard the refrigerator door close. Returning with a couple of beers, she handed one to me. "Don't forget the conflict of interest over the Everglades. Those two women hated each other. Maybe Vivian found out Sutherland was sharing all the Alliance's secrets with Lover Boy."

"Duh. I figure that's why she thought up that whole business about the coat—and, might I add, hired the world's lamest private eye."

"Well, I think things have gone far enough." What a brilliant deduction. "We'll just have to let the police do their thing."

"I'm the number one suspect!"

Alicia took a swallow of her beer. "I doubt it. They're just rattling your cage because of what happened at UVA."

"Easy for you to say."

"I still don't think we should involve that Florida bitch. People in a position of power like she is can really make your life miserable if they want to."

"Ya *think?* Even if Sutherland is helping ol' Lover Boy torpedo Everglades restoration efforts, that wouldn't be a reason to commit murder, would it?"

"Doubtful." Alicia pulled the casserole out of the microwave, and we sat down to eat. Sometimes, especially when you're nursing a badly bruised face, comfort food is absolutely what the doctor prescribed.

When I got back from seeing Alicia to her car, the message light was blinking on my phone. It was Neal Patterson, asking me to call him in the morning.

I fixed myself a cup of instant and sat down on the floor to read through the classifieds looking for a vintage Beetle. I knew my uncle was right about getting a newer car with airbags, but I was nothing if not stubborn. Besides, the newer VWs looked like bubble gum. I also couldn't afford a quality used car. One look around the place told me I needed to spend some of my precious money fixing it up. The hem on one of the window curtains needed to be resewn. A peek beneath the Naugahyde sofa showed a tear in the lining. Okay, I could probably fix those myself.

After rummaging through the kitchen drawer for a needle and thread, I noticed the packet of photos I'd found in Vivian's refrigerator. I'd never gotten past the surprise of seeing the same "joke" photo of Sutherland that was identical to the one Vivian had mentioned. There were two others. One showed Marguerite and "Juanito" on board a very handsome yacht. The decks were wood, the rail was brass. She could afford it. Shit, probably he could too. The other was a photograph of a gathering of people, many of whom had their backs to the camera. Marguerite and Juan Carlos were standing in the corner of a living room somewhere. The brocade drapes in the background looked vaguely familiar. Hadn't I seen them in her Washington apartment? I examined what could be seen of some of the other faces but didn't recognize anyone. I wondered if Neal could help me on that. He represented Marguerite. He'd know.

And there he was. I hadn't noticed him right off because his head was in profile. It was certainly conceivable that more than one tall, good-looking, dark-haired man could have a few streaks of gray at the temples, but this one was holding his glass up as though offering a toast, and I recognized the watch.

CHAPTER TWENTY-FIVE

I've always considered Thursday the most impatient of days. Usually, it means you're impatient for the weekend to arrive, but Thursdays can also be impatient in the sense that, if you've been waiting all week for something to happen or someone to show up, or just anything important—especially something that's been promised—by Thursday, you've run out of patience. I didn't even pause to fix myself a cup of coffee before calling Alicia and asking her to get me a lawyer, someone I could talk to immediately.

Two hours later, I sat there, nearly swallowed by an overstuffed, gold and white striped chintz-covered chair and surrounded by Williamsburg blue walls, complete with wainscoting. The woman seated beside me—not behind the glass-topped desk, thankfully—looked to be in her fifties with a salt-and-pepper, no-frills brush cut with gelled spikes. She had a long thin nose, a generous mouth, and light blue eyes under thick, straight brows. Her name was Olive Chatterton, and, boy, could she talk. I was wondering when I'd get a chance to explain my reason for wanting to see her, when she finally finished up telling me more than I really needed to know about her credentials—Bryn Mawr undergrad, Georgetown Law—and particular area of expertise: criminal defense.

According to Alicia, she had a reputation for knowing—and using—the narrowest, most precise interpretation of the law to confuse juries, confound prosecutors, and win acquittals. Just my cup of tea.

"So. What can I do for you?"

I started with the film project, the story of which consumed another thirty minutes of the time Alicia would be billed for. Then I described the two visits I'd had from detectives Fitzhugh and Peabody and the basis (in Charlottesville) for their suspicions that I might have supplied Vivian's overdose. Then I handed Chatterton Alicia's videotape, a couple of digital photos that she'd had taken after decorating the Banner Building office, the card and photo that I'd removed from Vivian Remington's office, and the photos I'd found in her refrigerator.

Chatterton set them aside. "I'll look at these later. But so far, you could be charged with practicing without a license, abetting murder, and tampering with a police investigation."

"I thought the police had already finished when—"

She held up her hand. "Oh, and breaking and entering— Remington's office, that is."

"I don't want to go to jail."

She laughed. "Who does?" She'd crossed her knees when we sat down, and now the foot that dangled began to jerk from side to side. "We might consider mitigating circumstances for the break-in, although that would be a hard sell. As for this stuff" (she gestured at the card and the photo), "we could claim that the police must not have thought they had any significance or they would have taken them when they did the search."

"But I'm still not off the hook."

"I wouldn't worry about the Charlottesville thing. They were just trying to pressure you."

"They seemed awfully serious to me!"

"That's their job." The foot-jiggling slowed and then stopped. "It really doesn't matter how Ms. Remington died, you know. At least from your standpoint."

"But if it *wasn't* drugs . . ."

"The autopsy says it was." She paused and made a note on her legal pad. "Of course, you heard that second, possibly third hand. I'll double-check."

"Somebody killed Vivian Remington. I'm convinced of it. Aren't you going to—wouldn't I be in better shape if we found the real killer?"

A corner of her mouth turned up. "Only in crime novels. To be frank, you'd be in better shape if you had never participated in Ms. Ritchie's so-called documentary film project. Now, it's true the police don't know about the phony license, nor do they know—yet—that you broke into the victim's office, crossing a police barrier to do so, and removed material from the crime scene—otherwise known as tampering."

I felt my shoulders relax, realizing the cops' ignorance would be my bliss.

"It doesn't change the fact that you broke the law."

I felt my stomach knot up. "I suppose you can't defend me if you know I'm guilty."

"*Au contraire,*" she smiled. "Everyone's entitled to a defense. And, lucky for you so far, you don't need one."

"But, just in case—I mean, I know I did some stupid things, but I was feeling kind of desperate."

"Impaired judgment might have worked back when you were in college. Hell, we all do crazy things when we're finally liberated from our parents. But I wouldn't try that tack now. If I were you, I'd keep a very low profile until this thing gets settled."

I leaned forward, resting my elbows on my knees. "That's why I did what I did. It will never be settled till we find out who killed Vivian Remington!"

She laid her index finger across her mouth. And, yes, my voice had become a bit strident. "That is not our job. More precisely, it is not *your* job."

"But I know who did it!" Where that came from, I'm not so

sure. But it made Chatterton's eyes focus a little more sharply as a tiny crease appeared between her brows.

"I'm not going to ask you to tell me because it really is not my business. But if you do know—not just sense or feel or suspect—who did it, you have a duty to inform the authorities."

I crimped the corners of my mouth. "So we're back to where I started." I stood up, extending my hand. "I appreciate your listening to my story, Ms. Chatterton, but I need something more than that."

She stood up and shook my hand. "A word of advice? Don't go out tilting at windmills. Investigating murder is what police do, and they're much more experienced at it than you. If you do have suspicions, especially if there's a shred of evidence to bolster them, you really must talk to the police."

I could feel a tear sneak out of the corner of my eye and make its way down the side of my face. "Don't you see my problem? If I go to the police, I'll have to tell them what I just told you, and then they'll charge me with impersonating a private investigator and B and E . . . and tampering and . . . and probably that I occasionally drive barefoot!"

Chatterton snorted. Reaching into the pocket of her gray pin-striped suit, she pulled out a crumpled tissue and handed it to me. "Don't worry. It's clean."

I wiped my eyes and then blew my nose. "Sorry. I am just so damn frustrated."

Of course, that was only the tip of my emotional volcano. I was filled with rage at the injustice of it all. This was America, for God's sake—a place where the bad guys always got their comeuppance. Only now a killer—not to mention a really nasty, conniving bitch (whether the same person or two different people, I wasn't sure)—was making a mockery of things, and an innocent person—yours truly—seemed to be headed for the hoosegow.

I declined to discuss the second item of business I'd wanted to go into with Olive Chatterton, but I did promise I would call if things heated up. Then I headed back to MoneySource, finally understanding what could turn an ordinarily calm, cheerful person into a raging seeker of vengeance. Discounting Bobby, of course.

All of that suppressed emotion—or residual effects of being slapped and my humiliation at the hands of Marguerite Sutherland—had given me a killer headache. It was getting worse, so I swallowed a couple of aspirin, leaned way back in my chair, and stared at the ceiling, which is where Uncle Alex found me an hour later when he came barging into my cubicle. "Why in hell aren't you tackling that skip backlog?"

I rubbed my eyes and dropped my feet to the floor. "Hi, Uncle Alex. What's up?"

"What's up is I found a car for you." He held out a set of keys sporting the famous blue and white BMW logo.

"Can't afford it."

"It's used—or certified pre-owned, like the high-end dealers say."

"I still can't afford it." And I didn't want to go on a test drive because I was afraid I would love it.

"C'mon, give it a whirl." My uncle was reading my mind again. "It's a stick like you seem to prefer."

True, I did prefer, but that was mostly because the Beetle had been a stick shift, and I'd formed the habit of pushing my left foot forward to engage the clutch. To keep myself from inadvertently slamming on the brakes when driving my uncle's sedan, which was an automatic, I'd had to curl my left foot underneath my right leg.

It was a 2004 three series, pale blue with beige leatherette seats. It was far more powerful than the old Beetle and so quiet I could hear myself breathing. It even had a CD player, air conditioning, and airbags. After forking over two dollars and fifty cents for tolls, I took the Bimmer over the Bay Bridge onto Kent Island and turned around and came back singing, "She's my little deuce coupe. You don't know what I got!"

"I can't afford it," I said to my uncle as I handed him the keys.

"Sure you can. Neal and I—"

"Neal Patterson?"

"We got a sweetheart deal on this one."

My normally low blood pressure was skyrocketing. "That loan you gave Neal was so he could buy a car for me?"

"Whoa, P.J. Where'd you get that idea?"

"What's Neal's involvement then?"

"Calm down, girl. Neal's secretary's cousin's wife wanted to get this year's model, so we persuaded her to sell us the oh-four rather than trade it in."

"Us? You and Neal bought this car?"

"You don't have to yell at me, P.J. I'm not hard of hearing yet."

"How much did you pay?" I asked in as menacing a whisper as I could produce with the blood roaring in my ears.

"Don't worry. It's all taken care of." He offered me the keys.

"I am *not* taking any more charity from you, and no way will I accept it from Neal Patterson." I shoved my hands into my pockets.

"Consider it a loan, then. No down payment, hardly any interest, you can pay whenever you're able to."

"How much did it cost?"

"I am not going to tell you, P.J. Now take the friggin' car and give me back my Lexus. I'm sick and tired of planning my driving life around your mysterious social life. I'm even sicker of worrying about you getting rear-ended by one of those sport utes that could carry six Beetles at one time in its cargo bay. I have a life too, you know? And I want to enjoy what's left of it without burying you the way I had to bury your mother."

Uh-oh. Mentioning my mother meant he was dead serious. And he did have a point—several points, in fact. I had been hogging his car, probably keeping him away from his mysterious social life. And of course it had never occurred to me that Uncle Alex would worry about me that much. I didn't want him to have to bury me either. "Okay," I said, holding out my hand. "I understand what you're saying. But it really bothers me that Neal Patterson is involved."

"All he did was put me in touch with the seller." Uncle Alex dropped the keys into my hand.

Whew. Now all I had to do was figure out where I could park the car for free and not have it stolen. I thanked my uncle by kissing him on both cheeks and told him I would give him as much as I could from the money I had been going to use for a down payment. To further demonstrate my gratitude for the car, I spent the remainder of the afternoon tracing skips, two of whom were about to get a visit from Jake and Rake—as soon as I could locate my uncle's goons.

When I returned after finding at least Rake, I spied Sandy Jones pacing the hallway outside my cubicle, her sturdy walking shoes wearing a hole in the carpet. "I've got something for you," she said as I motioned her inside.

The cubicle was too small for even a visitor's chair, so she remained standing in the doorway. "If Mr. Morton finds out what I've done, he'll fire me."

"Good heavens. I hope it's nothing illegal."

"I don't care. I want to find out who killed Vivian."

"So do I. You said you have something for me?"

"I've been playing detective," she said with a note of pride. Reaching into her commodious handbag, she pulled out a flash drive and handed it to me. "I had Jesús do it. He owes me one."

Imagine that. My wish had been granted without me having to stretch even a toenail across that ethical boundary line. "Let me guess. Vivian's e-mail?"

"Right. All of her incoming and outgoing messages from the first of the year till the day she—she got killed."

"Jesús won't rat you out to Morton, will he?"

"Oh." Sandy's face paled beneath the freckles. "I sure hope he doesn't. That would be so mean."

"Did you find messages that seemed suspicious or odd?"

"I didn't have time to look. As soon as Jesús gave it to me, I came over." Sandy looked at her watch. "Can I go now? People are going to wonder why I'm late."

After slogging my way through tons of incomprehensible gibberish about water flows in the Everglades and algal counts in Florida Bay, not to mention the usual office trivia, I struck pay dirt:

From: James Morton (JMorton@wetlandprotectors.org)
Sent: Tuesday, February 5, 2008 3:58 PM
To: Marguerite Sutherland
bcc: Vivian Remington
Subject: Heads Up

As a board member, you may know that it is our policy to review the e-mail accounts of any employee who is terminated for cause. In reviewing the account of Marvin Ross, we came across several messages that he had sent to you, attaching documents of a confidential nature. It is also our policy that any board member who wishes to be more fully informed of our work should request further information from me, in writing. As you did not do so, I can only conclude that your intention was to obtain the information without my knowledge. Given recent media stories about your purported relationship to Juan Carlos

Francisco, a major opponent of Everglades restoration, I felt compelled to convene a meeting of the executive committee to discuss whether it would be advisable to seek your resignation.

P.S. Marge, this is a very painful message for me to send you. However, it would be a breach of my fiduciary responsibilities were I not to do so. You have been my champion, and I will be forever in your debt.

Ouch. So the senator from Florida had been ousted from her favorite board—or was about to be, depending on when the executive committee met and how decisive it was. And Vivian Remington had visited me that very same day, although it appeared from the date on the message that she'd hired me before she'd learned of Sutherland's impending ouster. I wondered if the senator had informed her sweetheart.

But it was one of Vivian's sent messages that ruined my day. Why she did it, I'd never know. Maybe she was one of those know-it-alls who couldn't stand having anyone think she didn't know it all. In a message to Gareth Swenson, she'd assured him that she would keep secret the details of my first experience at B and E.

Gareth immediately moved to the top of the suspect list. If he thought I'd told Vivian, then he might very well have decided to silence her. The only person to whom I'd confessed all the details of the Charlottesville caper was Alicia. Even Annapolis's Finest had been obliged to get their information from their Charlottesville brethren. I had been careful to tell them only what I had done, not what they suspected—probably even knew for sure—that Gareth was up to. A chill went down my spine. What if he thought I'd ratted him out to Vivian and, later, the police?

I didn't have a chance to pursue the thought further because my uncle came barreling out of his office, jiggling his car keys.

As he passed by my cubicle, I picked up a stack of "impossibles" and shoved them into my desk drawer. I spent another thirty minutes perusing some "possibles" and then grabbed my coat. I was halfway down the hall when I heard a phone ringing. By the time I got back to my cubicle, the phone had stopped, and the message light was blinking. It was probably the crank caller back on the job or maybe Alicia calling to see how the thing with Chatterton had gone.

As I turned to leave, the phone rang again, making me feel like a puppet on a string. Only this time, the person jerking me around turned out to be my ex, calling from Tampa.

"What do you want?" I snapped.

"Money. I am flat broke, and the guy up there in Annapolis that you hit with my boat is threatening to come after me."

"I can't help you. I'm pretty broke too."

"Even two hundred would help. Maybe make him think there's more coming later."

"So pawn the gun you stole from me."

"The what?"

Yeah right. "How many ways can I say I don't have money, Bobby? Even if I did, I wouldn't give any of it to you."

"I'm begging, P.J. The guy's a bruiser. You don't want to be the cause of me ending up in the hospital, do you?"

"How could I be the cause?" I was yelling by then. "I am not responsible for you trying to escape with a piece of jewelry that you stole from me!"

"You got it back, didn't you?"

Only sort of. "That's beside the point," I said in exasperation. "If you hadn't been trying to run away, your boat wouldn't have hit that sportfisher."

There was a long silence during which I could almost hear the wheels turning in Bobby's pickled brain. "Okay, P.J. You had your chance."

"And what's that supposed to mean?"

"Oh nothing. Only I was just wondering . . . Does that cop your friend told me all about know what you used to do for a living?"

CHAPTER TWENTY-SIX

So Bobby thought Neal was a cop. Of course, to somebody like my ex, "officer of the court" meant the Law—as in justice and rectitude and honesty. Only the lawyer Bobby was referring to had lied.

Okay, to be fair, maybe Neal simply forgot he'd been entertained in Marguerite Sutherland's home. He probably considered it work, just as he had the D.C. reception. I would give him the benefit of the doubt, which reminded me I hadn't returned his call. I wondered how much time I'd have before Bobby made good on his threat to tell Neal what had turned out to be one of my more stupid career choices. We all make mistakes, don't we? But Neal struck me as a real straight arrow. He might think the college gig veered a little too close to the edge of propriety. And he'd be pretty much on target, except that I'd only worked there for four months. Then one of the regulars had started getting a little too personal. It went like this:

"Your singing turns me on so much, Paula Jo, I can hardly stand it. Why don't you and me—"

"No."

"Aw, c'mon, babe. I've been hanging around joints like this a helluva a long time, and I can tell that by that steamy look in your eye. You've got an itch only I can scratch."

"No."

"You sure? I can promise you it'll be better than anything

those college boys can deliver."

"No."

"Aw, babe. Don't be a tease. You know you want it bad . . ."

"No."

Two days later, I'd handed in my notice, moving on to the kind of job Uncle Alex would have approved of—typing graduate student theses.

I dialed Neal's number but hung up after the first ring. It would be better to confess in person where I could read his reactions more accurately. Besides, Bobby was a drunk. Maybe he'd forget he ever made the threat.

Naw. He needed money, and that would remind him of my cold-hearted refusal to provide the funds.

I rummaged through the refrigerator, debating the pros and cons of the McDonald's drive-thru versus a slab of stale bread with peanut butter on it. On the one hand, McDonald's would be more filling, and I had missed lunch. On the other hand . . .

The doorbell rang. Hoping it would be Alicia bearing another comfort food offering, I flung it open to find Gareth Swenson standing there. He was wearing brown corduroy trousers, a dark gold cashmere sweater, and a tweed jacket. "We need to talk, P.J."

"Sure." He'd come for the Charlottesville photos. Thank heavens I hadn't returned them. Gareth could have showed the police the photos as evidence that I'd been the drug dealer—or at least that's what the police would believe until I had a chance to explain myself—if I could even convince them I was the one telling the truth.

He sat down on the sofa. I chose the floor. "We could have handled this much sooner, but for some reason you've decided to be stubborn."

"I've been busy."

"I've had a visit from the Annapolis police, inquiring about my relationship with Vivian Remington. I told them I'd met her in grad school. I guess you told them I was the one who recommended that she hire you."

"I said nothing to them about you except to admit that I'd been arrested for trashing your place back in oh-three and that you'd dropped the charges."

Gareth crossed his arms. "So, of course, that brought up several more questions that the Charlottesville police still have about what I was up to back then. I'm not at all happy about this turn of events."

"I'm sorry, Gareth, really" (although he'd certainly brought it on himself by dealing in the first place), "but I didn't tell Fitzhugh and her pal anything that would connect you to Vivian."

He rolled his eyes. "Yeah, right. So how come they asked me about her?"

"Maybe they found something in her cell phone records or a note." Or your business card on her desk. I could see that he might have to agree with me. "Anyway, you did recommend me."

"Look, P.J., at the time it seemed a good idea. If I sent some business your way, you would owe me. Payback being returning those photos."

"Ah." I played dumb.

"Actually, that's only part of the reason. I think you'd be well advised to forget that Vivian ever hired you or why."

"You're the second person lately to warn me off."

"The first being Marguerite Sutherland."

"She told you?"

"No. Just a good guess. You're like a dog with a rag in its teeth. I've been hanging around Marguerite Sutherland long enough to discover that she has a pipeline to Vivian Remington's outfit. Until recently, somebody was giving her private internal policy documents on Everglades restoration. I suspect she passed them on to a friend of hers who isn't exactly pro-environment."

Nothing I hadn't already learned, but I played along. "It's not still happening, right?"

He shrugged. "Not since Vivian turned up dead. But that may be simply because Vivian was the policy wonk on Everglades stuff for the Alliance, and they don't have anyone to replace her yet." Gareth rested an argyle-clad ankle on his knee. "I'm guessing that when Vivian found out about the leaks, she decided to fight dirty. So she hired you to plant something incriminating in Marguerite Sutherland's apartment."

"Wrong. I went there to return a valuable piece of jewelry that belonged to Sutherland. She left it in the ladies' room at the Cosmos Club the night of the D.C. reception."

He rolled his eyes. "Like you couldn't just send it back registered mail."

"This may be hard for you to believe, Gareth, but Vivian Remington had already paid me a hefty advance, so I felt I owed it to her to—"

"What did she ask you to do?"

None of your business. "Just take some pictures."

"Of what, pray tell?"

"Vivian told me that Marguerite Sutherland had stolen an ocelot fur coat that really belongs to the U.S. Fish and Wildlife Service. Vivian was doing a demo of things you shouldn't try to bring back from trips abroad. According to Vivian, somebody at the Alliance saw Marguerite carrying the coat out to her car."

Gareth's foot was jiggling the whole time I talked, and it stopped when he said, "This is beyond incredible. Where do you get these wild ideas?"

"Vivian Remington. Only it turned out it was all a big fat lie. Believe me, I've checked it out thoroughly." His lip was curled.

"I honestly don't know what she really wanted—unless she was trying to embarrass Senator Sutherland."

Gareth crossed his arms. "I can't picture Vivian being that sneaky. Now you, on the other hand . . ." He stood up, pulling a gun from his jacket pocket. The weapon looked like the identical twin to the revolver my ex had stolen from my bedside drawer, and it was pointed right at me. "Maybe this will make you see how important it is for me to get those photos back."

My heart leaped up into my throat and I stopped breathing momentarily. "You can't be serious."

"I am, P.J. I must have that DEA job. My wife's life is at stake, and your involvement with Vivian Remington has already put me at extreme risk." He crossed the room and yanked the phone jack out of the wall. "The only evidence that I ever sold drugs at UVA is those photos you took when you vandalized my apartment."

"You don't have to threaten me with a gun."

"Apparently I do since you don't seem to be able to take a hint—several in fact."

"You're the one who's been making those weird calls?"

"You should have heeded the advice, P.J. Now, please give me the photos."

"They're not here. Go ahead and search if you don't believe me."

Gareth stood there, the corners of his mouth turned down. "No. I was pretty thorough when I—"

"You're the one who broke in?"

His smile was humorless. "You could call it a fair turnabout, P.J. It was easy enough to follow you back here after the reception. You're lucky you weren't stopped for speeding."

"Why didn't you just ask me for the damn things?"

"I did. Several times. But you keep saying no. I must have those photos, especially since Vivian told me she'd found out about my wild-and-crazy past."

"*You* killed her." I couldn't stop the trembling in my arms and legs. My heart was racing, and a cold sweat broke out on my brow. But then an uneasy calm replaced the panic. I knew Gareth was going to kill me. It was almost like I'd already died and was standing outside my body observing how P.J. Smythe reacted to the threat of imminent death. So far, she seemed to be holding her own, her mind racing to buy time, wondering if anyone in the apartment above had heard the loud voices and would be coming to her rescue. And that's when I remembered that it was currently vacant.

Gareth lowered the gun. "Actually, no, although I'm sure you think I'm lying since you've always thought the worst of me."

"It makes too much sense. Vivian died of a drug overdose. You're the one who knows drugs. And you apparently had a motive—although I swear I never said one word to Vivian about your college sideline."

"Now look who's lying. C'mon, P.J., tell me where you keep those photos. I promise you I won't hurt you if you hand them over."

I thought about telling Gareth I'd stashed copies everywhere, but I figured that would drive him over the edge. "In my uncle's safe. At MoneySource."

His brow lifted. "Okay. Let's go." He lifted the gun, pointing it skyward like one of those FBI agents in a TV show.

"I don't have a key."

"When did that stop you?"

With a heavy sigh, I stood up. "The combination's in my purse."

Gareth followed me into the bedroom where I retrieved my purse from the floor beside the dresser. I pawed slowly through the junk inside until I found what I was looking for, then aimed the perfume tester right at his eyes and let her rip.

There was an ear-splitting boom as the gun went off, and a piece of ceiling plaster clattered down onto my back. I threw myself underneath the dresser, expecting any moment to be engulfed in excruciating pain—or to slide into an immense void as my life slipped away to nothing.

Still deafened but feeling neither pain nor its much worse alternative, I stared at Gareth. He kept coughing while wiping his eyes with the back of the hand that held the gun. We both sneezed, not that either of us could hear it, but I ducked my head out of sight anyway trying to shrink myself down to the size of a dust bunny. The gun was aimed at my bed, and Gareth's finger kept jerking at the trigger. Only nothing happened. He flipped open the chamber. I couldn't actually hear what he said, but it looked like, "The fuck?" He tossed the gun onto the bed and, in two strides, crossed the room, slamming the front door behind him as he left.

Oh no, you don't. Scrambling from beneath the dresser, I ran into the living room, grabbed the telephone, and punched in 9-1-1 only to be greeted by silence. Shit. I ran out onto the street. Gareth had disappeared.

After I plugged the jack back in, it occurred to me that, as much as I wanted the police to come to my rescue, they would probably think I was as guilty as Gareth, considering how uncooperative I'd been when they'd invited me to rat him out.

Chatterton. I would call her. But I only had an office number, and it was after ten in the evening.

I stood there, ears ringing, trying to wrap my head around the realization that I'd nearly been killed. Then I called Alicia.

"Get out of there. He could be coming back to finish the job!"

"With what, Alicia? The gun misfired. Besides, he left it here."

"Still," she said, "he could try something else . . . You did call the police, didn't you?"

"No. They would want the whole story, and then they'd arrest me."

"No way. You were attacked and nearly killed."

"Omigod! I told Gareth the photos were at MoneySource. You don't think he'd try to break in there, do you?"

"Why not? The guy's crazy enough to threaten you at gunpoint. He's clearly desperate. You better tell your uncle."

I groaned. "You realize what'll happen to me? No. What'll happen to *him*. A heart attack. I can't take that chance."

"You don't have to spill the beans, P.J. Tell your uncle one of your deadbeats threatened to trash MoneySource. He'll have his muscle stand guard. End of story."

CHAPTER TWENTY-SEVEN

How I wish that had been the end of the story. But, no. There was more to follow, and it had nothing to do with Gareth Swenson trying to break into MoneySource to get the photos that were not in my uncle's safe or anywhere on the premises. Like I'd give Uncle Alex a chance to peek into the darkest secret of my college days? Hah.

Maybe I was still in shock—or maybe I'd become inured to the idea of having people point guns at me, since it seemed to be happening a lot lately—but for some reason I was not afraid that Gareth would come back. He'd been desperate enough to try threatening me at gunpoint. He'd even fired the gun, although I think it was more likely a reaction to being sprayed with that toxic perfume than an attempt to actually shoot me. But now he was probably sitting in a bar somewhere in Washington, wondering how he'd let things get so out of hand. If he had a shred of class—highly doubtful—he'd turn himself in to the police. Except that wouldn't be at all good for his wife. I thought about calling him to tell him I would not pursue the matter if he'd stay away, but I only had his home phone number and couldn't figure out how to leave a message that wouldn't make things even worse for Sarah.

"I'm not going to do a thing," I told Alicia as we stood in the Banner Building office, trying to decide where best to start on the packing-up operation.

"What *is* it with you and the police?" Alicia wrestled with one of the flattened boxes she'd had delivered the day before. "Damn, these things are hard to put together."

"Here. Let me do it."

She scooted aside, checking one of her nails. "The police are here to protect us, remember? Gareth Swenson needs to be taught a lesson."

I sat back on my heels, shoving the assembled box toward Alicia. "Not going to do it, girl. You might think the police are nice guys, but you aren't somebody they suspect of murder."

"True. And speaking of which, if Gareth didn't kill Remington and the Senator from Hell didn't do it, maybe it really *was* a drug overdose . . . not that I'm saying they have the right suspect, of course."

"Sutherland could have arranged it," I reminded Alicia. "She has the resources."

"What does Chatterton say? I don't think you've told me about your session with her."

I raised an eyebrow. "Haven't you heard of lawyer-client confidentiality?"

The corner of Alicia's mouth turned up. "Translation: She told you to talk to the police."

I threw a box of paper clips at her, missing by about six inches. "Speaking of cops, let's get cracking before they show up, wondering if I'm trying to do a runner."

We managed to fit everything—picture, calendar, phone book, note pads, envelopes, and other small items—into two boxes, leaving only the Underwood typewriter, the ditto machine, and the adding machine.

"Those are too heavy for the boxes," said Alicia, rubbing two fists into the small of her back."

"So we'll just carry them."

"Not me, Ms. Muscle-bound." Her gaze roamed around the office, searching for a solution. "Ah. We'll just put them in the filing cabinet. The movers will be using dollies, so a few more pounds won't be a problem."

The typewriter wouldn't fit, but the other two machines did. As I closed the top drawer, I noticed the mangled warning label. Well, too bad. I wasn't about to lift a heavy machine out of the top drawer and lower it into the bottom. We'd just warn the movers the thing might be a little top-heavy.

"Let's go eat," said Alicia when she returned from washing her hands.

My cell buzzed, and I flipped it open. Uh-oh. Uncle Alex.

"What on earth is going on, P.J.?" He sounded furious. "First your office is overflowing with work you can't be bothered to do. Then I get a call from that fuckin' Bobby Crane, after which I see this disgusting picture of you in the Crabwrapper!"

"What?"

"You deaf or something? Where are you? You said you were gonna get caught up. You promised!"

"I'll be there this afternoon."

There was a heavy sigh at the other end of the line accompanied by the sound of fingers drumming on wood. "One hour, P.J. You get back here in one hour, or you're fired. Got it?" He slammed the phone down.

As soon as I ended the call, I got another one. It was Neal.

"Where are you?" he said. "We need to talk. Somebody named Bobby Crane called me, claiming to be your ex-husband, of all things, and insinuating all sorts of sleazy things about you."

"He is my ex, and I'm sorry he bothered you. Everything else is probably a lie since we're not exactly on good terms."

"Well, whatever. But then Marguerite Sutherland called me too. And, I must say, I sure hope she's also lying. But we need to get this straightened out."

Shit. Shit. Shit. That bitch! "Okay. Well, right now, Alicia and

257

I are packing up the office, and my uncle's on my case about missing work, among other things—"

"What office?" The anxiety level in his voice zoomed. "What's going *on?*"

I took a deep, calming breath, noticing that Alicia was shaking her head, mouthing "Tell him everything." Then she pointed at her watch and said, "Thirty minutes, okay?"

"Look, Neal. It isn't as awful as Sutherland probably indicated. I'm the victim, as a matter of fact. And I'd be happy to tell you all about it." I gave him directions to the Banner Building, explaining that Alicia had rented the fourth-floor office for one of her film projects and that I'd been helping her clear it out.

"Don't you move, P.J. I'm coming right over." He too slammed the phone down.

"Oh, shit," I said, plopping into the chair.

Alicia stood there, gazing at me, her eyes narrowed to slits. "You know, I think you need help. Instead of telling your uncle that Gareth nearly killed you last night, you let him get all over your case about missing work."

I held up my hand, but she was on a roll. "Shit. If he'd known what happened to you, he'd have given you the day off!"

"I don't want Uncle Alex to have a heart attack."

"Uh-huh? You don't want him—or Neal, I suspect—running over here to take charge of things—starting with *calling the police!*" Her cell rang, and she pulled it out, peering at the message. "Damn. I have to meet Mother for lunch. If the movers show up before I get back, you'll take care of things?"

I nodded, but I guess it wasn't too convincing, mostly because I was trying to figure out how much I could tell Neal about my episode with Senator Bitch without ruining what remaining chances I might have with him.

"I'll eat fast, okay?"

"I'll be all right." Not at all believing what I'd just told Alicia, I waved her away. Then I stared up at the ceiling. Perhaps I should get some legal advice from Neal about how best to handle the police inquiries, especially since Chatterton wasn't going to be much help.

Then Tall, Dark, and Handsome walked through the door, and my mood brightened. He was wearing a black cashmere coat and leather gloves, neither of which he bothered to remove. Well, we'd left the window open while we were packing, so it was kind of chilly. I stood up and lowered the sash.

"Good grief, P.J." His head swiveled as he took in the threadbare condition of the office. "This looks like something out of the Great Depression."

I shrugged, suddenly longing to be safe in his sheltering embrace. "That guy you saw me talking to at the D.C. Reception—Gareth Swenson?" Neal nodded. "L-last night he threatened to k-kill me," I said, my voice beginning to tremble. "Didn't work."

Neal leaned against the doorframe. "Okay. Start at the beginning. Then we'll call the police."

As I glossed over the incident of my arrest in Charlottesville and how it had led to last night's confrontation, I could practically see the wheels turning in Neal's head as he figured all the angles, the way a good lawyer would.

"So I guess my main concern is that I won't get much sympathy from the cops, considering if I'd 'fessed up the first time they asked me, Gareth would already be in jail."

"Why would he give Vivian Remington an overdose?"

"I'm not saying he did. He denied it when I asked him. But the point I'm trying to make is that, if the cops here knew what I know about Gareth, they wouldn't be so suspicious of me."

Neal rolled his eyes. "You sure seem to know a lot of people who don't have a very high opinion of you."

"It's not my fault!"

He sighed. "Look. Let's forget your ex-husband's accusations for the moment and focus on Marguerite Sutherland. She told me you visited her in D.C. last week under the pretext of photographing her for God knows what purpose and that, while you were there, you feigned illness, and—"

"It's true. I feigned illness, and she was late to the theater, so she told me to let myself out. And I was just about to do that when the two of them—her and Juan Carlos Francisco—showed up. He accused me of trying to steal something that might cause some kind of trouble to her or maybe him or possibly both of—"

"Wait." Neal held up his hand. "Back up a minute. Why did you visit her in the first place? Are you really a photographer?"

I hesitated, wondering if one more lie would tip the scales against me, and then I thought what the hell. "I was returning a piece of jewelry that Sutherland lost in the ladies' room at the Cosmos Club. So her story about me being there to steal something of hers is bogus."

"Then why pretend to get sick?"

Oops. "Why don't you take your coat off and sit down? I feel like you're grilling me, and you're not even my lawyer."

Neal shoved his hands into his pockets. "I'm sorry, P.J. You know I can't represent you when I already have dealings with Marguerite Sutherland."

Wrong answer. I shoved my chair back and stood up as a red haze formed in front of my eyes. "Then just forget it. Think whatever you like about me. This conversation is over."

"Whoa." Neal held his arm out to keep me from pushing past him. "Don't get so upset."

I slumped back into the chair. "You're not the one who was threatened at gunpoint. Twice, I might add. The first one to do that was your client!"

Neal put up a hand to calm my outburst. "Okay. I know you're upset. Obviously you think Gareth Swenson and Marguerite Sutherland and Vivian Remington are all somehow connected. And, in fact, they are—not that it's in any way a sinister connection. But when one of them winds up dead, and the other two threaten you at gunpoint—"

"Exactly. Maybe Gareth didn't do it, but Sutherland hated Remington—going way back, I might add."

"But murder is such an extreme thing." Neal paused, thinking. "I wonder what would make her overreact. What makes you such a threat?"

I put my head in my hands. "Oh, Neal, I am so confused. At one time, I thought Vivian was trying to blackmail Sutherland, maybe even planted that coat. But now, I just don't know. There was nothing in her apartment, and Sutherland claimed she—"

"So you did search her place." Neal was rolling his eyes. "What in hell did you think you'd find there?"

My face began to turn a little pink. "An ocelot coat. It's what Vivian hired me to do. She claimed Sutherland stole it. I thought there'd be a connection between that and Vivian's death."

"You even looked in that bedroom that Marguerite's turned into a closet—" He coughed, muffling the sound with his hands.

"Yep. I pawed through every single one of those—oh." Two thoughts collided at once in my frozen brain. First, the photograph of Neal among the guests at Marguerite's apartment. If he'd only been there as a guest—even in the guise of work—how come he knew about the closet-room? Then there were the words I'd overheard Sutherland saying to Juan Carlos Francisco, something about Neal being expensive.

Crossing the room to stand in front of my desk, Neal reached into his coat pocket and pulled out a small plastic bottle, the kind you get at the pharmacy. "I really hate to do this, P.J., but . . ."

Oh. My. God. "Do wh-what?"

He tossed the bottle from one gloved hand to the next. "I'm really sorry, P.J. I thought you were such a straight arrow. But that business at UVA, dealing drugs—"

"I didn't!"

"—and now giving Vivian Remington what turned out to be an overdose . . . well, I'm sure you regret it now—so much so that you're going to kill yourself, I'm afraid."

My heart skittered to a stop. "You're *glad* I went snooping all over the place—not to find anything, but to incriminate myself!"

He shrugged, still tossing the bottle back and forth. "Had to be done, I'm afraid. But don't look so frightened. This won't hurt. You'll just drift off."

"But *why?*"

"I have to, P.J. Vivian found out I was funneling Wetlands stuff to Marguerite Sutherland. She threatened to tell Get-rich. I couldn't let that happen."

"You killed her?"

There were tears in the sky-blue eyes. "I really hate this, P.J. It's just that everything's snowballing now, and I need to get things back under control."

"But how? Why? People like you, they don't—"

"Yes, sometimes, they do. I needed the money. You already figured that much out, even though you didn't know why. I was so sure I'd make partner that I started living like I already was one, and then the bastards told me it was never going to happen. What was I going to do?" Crossing back to the doorway, Neal peered up and down the hall and then closed the door. "Marguerite Sutherland was the only one willing to help me get caught up—well, that and the loan from Alex—so I did whatever she asked."

"And Vivian found out."

"Vivian knew it was an egregious conflict of interest. I would have been disbarred—probably put in jail. Not an option."

"So you killed her and made it look like a drug overdose."

"I thought they'd finger Swenson because Vivian had been in touch with him recently."

"You knew about Gareth's past dealing?"

"Marguerite told me. She was lobbying to get him a position with the DEA because she's got some issues in Florida that he could handle in her favor, if you get my drift."

Why was I not surprised? "I know you're upset, Neal, but this has gone far enough, hasn't it? You don't want to add another mur—"

"Shut up. All I need to do is take care of one last loose end."

"Don't do this, Neal. *Please.*"

He shook his head. "Sorry. But look at it this way: Pretty soon, you won't care. And if you're one of those people who believe we are all eventually reunited in heaven, then think how happy your mother will be."

That was the wrong thing to say. She would have been furious. Don't be a victim, sweetie. Stand up for yourself. How callous could the guy get, tossing that pill bottle back and forth as if it were full of vitamins? The red haze reappeared, blocking out rational thought—such as he's much bigger than you are. I lunged forward, trying to knock the bottle from Neal's hand. He jerked backward out of reach, and I leapt from the chair and ran to the window.

But Neal was too quick. He moved around the desk and, with a lunge, grabbed hold of my sweater, pulling me toward him.

I aimed a kick at his balls, but missed. He jerked his hips backward, which gave me a clear shot at his legs. With as much force as I could muster, I scraped his shinbone with my shoe, jamming my heel into the top of his foot. With a howl of pain, he toppled over, pinning me to the desk. My hand scrabbled frantically for some kind of a weapon—a letter opener, scissors, even a pen—all now safely packed away.

"Shit!" He said as the prescription bottle fell from his gloved hand. He leapt to his feet, scurried around the desk, and dropped to his knees in front of the filing cabinet. The cap had come off the bottle, and tiny white pills were strewn across the floor.

I sat up, wondering if I could make it through the door before Neal tackled me. Not likely. But he would need every single one of those pills . . .

Vaulting over the desk, I yanked open the top drawer of the filing cabinet. Looping my arms over the edge of the drawer, I hung there, adding my weight to the already overloaded drawer. The cabinet slowly tilted forward and then landed with a crunch on Neal Patterson's back. I heard a loud grunt, and then he collapsed, one leg twitching.

My hand flew to my mouth. Stepping across his motionless body, I opened the door and ran for the stairs.

CHAPTER TWENTY-EIGHT

"Looks like you got yourself in some big trouble," said Detective Peabody. The ambulance had gone, carrying the man who'd almost killed me. The crime scene folks were still doing their thing, and I was trying to stop shaking like an aspen in a mountain breeze.

"He w-wanted to kill me," I croaked.

"Let's go downstairs," said Fitzhugh, shooing the three of us into the hallway where Alicia stepped off the elevator, looking as cool and unruffled as an ice-covered pond. "I'm sorry, miss," said the detective. "You'll have to leave. This is a crime—"

"Well, P.J., good to see you've finally called the police."

Peabody gave Alicia a puzzled look. "You were here when it happened?"

"Excuse me?"

"Alicia," I said, gripping her arm. "Neal tried to . . . I think maybe I killed him!"

Fitzhugh looked confused. "I thought you said he tried to kill you."

I nodded and then found myself unable to stop my head from bobbing up and down. Alicia put her arm around my shoulder and squeezed. "It's all right, babe. I'm right here."

And she was, her arm never leaving my shoulder as I recounted the incident. My head was beginning to pound from the adrenaline rush, and my knees felt rubbery. "I need to sit down."

Even in that shaky state, I couldn't handle the elevator; so Alicia and I, accompanied by the two detectives, trooped down the stairs to the lobby. I plopped into the scratchy horsehair sofa, raising a cloud of dust in the process. Alicia moved off to a corner where she could observe but not participate. Fitzhugh, who'd been about to join me on the sofa, changed her mind and remained standing, notebook and pen in hand.

"So this Patterson fellow, the lawyer? He was going to make you take an overdose of those pills we found on the floor, and you—" Here her eyes widened in disbelief. "You managed to push a filing cabinet over on top of him?"

"It's not that hard," I said. "The top drawer was full of machines."

That required a bit more explanation on my part, at the end of which the two detectives seemed to be at a loss for words. But I was suddenly feeling very sleepy. My throat hurt. The foot that had stomped Neal didn't feel too good either. "He more or less told me he killed Vivian Remington."

"Who the hell is she?" I looked up to see Uncle Alex standing there, wearing white socks, black oxfords, and a huge frown.

"Who are you?" asked Peabody in irritation.

"I'm her boss."

The detective shot me a puzzled look. "I thought you were self-employed."

"It's okay, Unc. We'll be finished in a minute or two."

Uncle Alex backed away and grabbed Alicia's arm. Over Peabody's shoulder, I could see the two of them in intense whispered conversation.

". . . if we can tie him to Remington," the detective was saying.

Fitzhugh moved to stand beside Peabody, effectively blocking my view. "We need your full attention here, Ms. Smythe."

"Sorry. Could you repeat what you just said?"

"When—uh, if—Patterson comes to, we'll check out his story. We'll also have the pills tested, by the way."

"Okay," said Peabody. "You wouldn't happen to know why Patterson might have wanted you dead, would you?"

I nodded. "He said he had to get things under control. That was pretty much it."

"Wanna tell us what you know that would make a guy like that resort to attempted murder?"

I sighed, rubbing my eyes with my fists. "It's a long story, really. I'm not sure where to begin . . ." Nor was I sure I still didn't need a lawyer.

Fitzhugh shut her notebook and shoved it into the pocket of her sky blue blazer. "You're looking pretty shocky there. Not that I blame you. But you might want to get yourself to a hospital for a checkup. We'll get a more complete statement from you in the morning."

Her words called up memories of my interview all those years ago with the skeptical Charlottesville detective who'd made me go over and over and over my story, hoping to trip me up in a lie.

My lies of omission—all in the misguided name of loyalty to a one-time lover—had not fooled that guy for a nanosecond. But worse, by keeping those pictures, I had unwittingly planted the seeds of desperation that had nearly resulted in my own demise. My face reddened as I contemplated the astounding degree of naiveté that had not prevented, but merely postponed, the inevitable consequences of Gareth Swenson's past.

The two detectives headed for the elevator, their task only just beginning.

I looked around the lobby and spotted Alicia repairing her lipstick. "Where's Uncle Alex?"

"Went to get his car," she said. "I called him, by the way. But you two go on without me. I need to handle the movers."

"I need to get out of here," I said, trying to keep the jitters out of my voice. "Anyway, you'll probably have to reschedule the movers, considering . . ." I waved my hand upward as a reminder that a piece of police tape was still stretched across the doorway of what easily could have been the last office I ever saw.

We headed out onto the sidewalk. "You've got some serious explaining to do, girl."

"He'll never forgive me."

"Oh. I think he's pretty okay with that." She jerked her head backward in the direction of the Banner Building lobby. "You did, after all, survive. And I sort of suggested that the best way to handle it probably was not to lock you up and throw the key away."

"As if he'd listen to you. And by the way, where were you when Neal Patterson was trying to kill me?"

She looked stricken. "You have no idea how bad I feel. To think I might have been able to stop him from—"

"But?" I jumped in.

"I had to move my car. The parking police are so overzealous in this part of town. I didn't think I'd be gone that long, but it took a while to find a space."

I patted Alicia's arm. "Don't worry. How could you have known? How could I? I still can't believe Neal Patterson is a murderer. And poor Uncle Alex. They were friends. He'll think it was all my fault."

Alicia laughed. "I doubt it. He knows you had your heart in the right place. You two just need to work out some trust issues. Besides, I threatened to sic the fashion police on him if he didn't lighten up. Of course, he's still plenty steamed about Bobby's call, not to mention the scandalous item in the *Capital.*

"You mean it's not about what just happened?" I should have realized the paper couldn't print the story practically as it was unfolding. "So, tell me, what is it?" A familiar silver sedan rounded the corner and pulled to the curb.

"Oh, no," said Alicia. "You need to see it with your own eyes. We'll pick up a paper somewhere on the way."

I opened the car door and climbed in, sitting next to my uncle. "I'm sorry, Uncle. I should have told you all about it a long, long time ago."

"P.J." He drummed his fingers on the steering wheel.

"I know. You have a right to be upset. Next time, I won't be so—"

"How about no next time, huh? You nearly got yourself killed by someone I had a lot of respect for."

"I'm afraid we were both fooled."

He turned toward me. "You know that thing about fool me once, shame on me? Well, you've fooled me more times than I can think of. So how about explaining yourself, missy?"

"Stop the car," said Alicia from the back seat. Uncle Alex pulled to the curb in front of a drugstore and waited while she went inside to buy the newspaper.

The more I talked, the redder his face got; but by the time I'd reached the end of my story of the Present Consequences of Past College Misadventures (leaving out the part where Gareth also threatened to shoot me—my uncle's heart could only take so much, after all), I could detect a slight release of the tension in his shoulders, and at least one of his clenched fists relaxed.

"I felt I had to unmask Vivian Remington's killer before I ended up facing criminal charges," I explained. "I guess I believed that if I told you what was going on, you'd lock me away or send me off somewhere and then I would never find out. Besides, Uncle Alex, it wasn't really my idea to—"

"P.J. . . ."

"Hear me out. Maybe I was wrong to go along with Alicia. Okay. It was exceedingly poor judgment. But she is my very best friend, and I owed her from—"

"What is it with you, P.J?" A muscle twitched in his jaw as the man sitting across from me got a speculative gleam in his hazel eyes. He didn't say another word, just shaking his head every now and then and heaving a sigh of . . . what? Surrender? Relief? A little of both? "Okay. Right now I think you're kinda crazy. Going toe-to-toe with a fella who's a helluva lot bigger and heavier than you isn't my idea of—"

"—I didn't have much choice, Unc. You weren't there, so you don't know."

Alicia opened the back door and climbed in the car. "Mission accomplished," she said.

"Wait," said my uncle, holding his hand up. "It still bothers me that—"

"Charlottesville. I should have told you at the time, right?"

"Yes, and your explanation now sucks."

"Oh, lordy, lordy," said Alicia, accompanied by the sound of rustling pages. "The things I don't know about P.J. Smythe."

My uncle wasn't finished. "Why in hell did you give that scumbag my telephone number?"

"Gareth Swenson? I didn't."

"Your fucking ex, dammit. He's the one who called."

"Bobby did ransack P.J.'s apartment," said Alicia. "Maybe he took your number 'cause he wanted to hassle you. Not the first time that's happened."

"Okay," said Uncle Alex. "You're probably right." His jaw was still clenched, though. Which made it hard to think he really meant it.

"So, if you're not upset about me trashing Gareth's apartment—"

"Forget that. If what your fuckhead ex tells me is true, your mother will be rolling in her grave."

"Wait! What exactly did Bobby say?"

"You worked in a strip joint."

"No way, Uncle A. I found a neat gig that would help pay my college expenses. It was back when I was a junior and, well, I just couldn't stand the idea of waiting tables or flipping burgers or answering telephones."

My uncle crossed his arms and sighed, waiting for the punch line.

"I sang in a bar, okay? That's the absolute worst you can say about it. I was fully clothed the whole time." And using the Paula Jo stage name, just in case one of Uncle Alex's Baltimore buddies happened to wander into the place and noticed a torch singer in a skin-tight dress, belting her lungs out, and then wound up telling my uncle she looked vaguely familiar . . .

Uncle Alex's jaw was twitching again.

"It was a nice place." Sort of. "Chadwick's Landing on the outskirts of Charlottesville? They paid good money too." That was because there weren't many people who could carry a tune who were willing to wear body-hugging, low-cut gowns and drape themselves across the Steinway while performing. "I only did it for a while, and then I decided it wasn't worth the hassle."

"Ah," he said. The twitch in his jaw became more pronounced as he struggled to control his temper. Or was he trying not to laugh?

"I knew you could sing," said Alicia. "But I just can't picture you performing on a stage."

"I made really good tips." Justification enough, as far as I was concerned. Reaching for the paper, I searched for my name.

"I don't know what it is about you," said Uncle Alex as he flipped the paper over to page seven. "But I'm sure you'll have an equally amazing explanation for this too."

Underneath my photo was a title that said, "Local Loan Clerk Auditions for *Playboy.*" The caption read:

Annapolitan P.J. Smythe hopes to supplement her income as a clerk for MoneySource by posing for Playboy *magazine. The* Capital *obtained this photo from one of the magazine's editors. Parts of the photo have been masked off to protect innocent eyes. Ms. Smythe could not be reached for comment.*

There I stood in my birthday suit, far taller than I could ever hope to be, draped in a very familiar spotted fur coat, my private parts "shielded from innocent eyes" by a judiciously placed black rectangle.

CHAPTER TWENTY-NINE

It was a dark and rainy Thursday, two weeks after the arrest of Neal Patterson for the attempted murder of P.J. Smythe, and I was still trying to balance the ledger of what Alicia Todd Ritchie owed me versus what I owed her. I was no less angry that she'd dragged me so deeply into her film project that I'd found it nearly impossible to extract myself—reputation intact, that is. I was still furious that Marguerite Sutherland was going to get away with that humiliating body search and coercing me into signing a false confession, not to mention whatever mischief she and her Latin lover had concocted to sabotage Everglades restoration.

If I had been a real private investigator, I would have gone after the two of them until I had enough evidence to get them in really bad trouble. But I wasn't. Or, to be really honest, I was a dismal failure at playing private eye. Again, Alicia's fault.

I might have been driving a practically brand new powder blue BMW, but I was broke. Fortunately, my uncle had decided not to give me the axe, but there would be no bonus under the Christmas tree either.

Alicia was in Gstaad—a wise move, considering my current feelings. Gareth Swenson was no longer in Washington—or at least no longer at the number on his business card. I'd called to see how Sarah was doing and to tell him I was willing to forget (if not forgive) his transgressions. Oh. And the incriminating photographs? I still can't remember where I stashed them.

I did have one other meeting with my lawyer—to wrap things up and to get her guidance on how I should conduct myself as a witness in Neal Patterson's trial.

"Feeling better?" she asked as I plopped into the chintz chair opposite her desk.

"I suppose," I replied, plucking an invisible piece of lint on my jeans, "although I've had to make some pretty tough decisions lately."

"Such as . . . ?"

"Sucking it up in a job I really hate."

"Welcome to the real world."

"What? You hate what you're doing?"

She laughed. "I love what I'm doing. But most people, as you might recall from your college exposure to literature, lead lives of quiet desperation. I just meant you're not alone."

I sat back. "At least I know what I don't want to do."

"Besides the job."

"Yeah." I ticked them off on my fingers. "Private investigations. Snooping. Stirring up trouble."

"Excellent."

"Not to mention appearing in so-called documentary films."

This got another laugh. "It's hard to say no to Alicia Todd Ritchie."

I nodded. "And it's real hard to figure out what I'm going to do with the rest of my life—after the, uh, trial."

Chatterton walked me through a description of what usually happened and told me the prosecutor would be interviewing me about my testimony "so there won't be any surprises during her examination."

"I'm more worried about Neal's lawyer. He'll probably drag all my sins into public view, and I'll be publicly humiliated, not to mention jailed."

"With any luck, he'll cop a plea."

"Why would he do that? I mean, it's my word against his, isn't it?"

Chatterton's hose made a swishing sound as she crossed her legs. "Put yourself in Patterson's place for a moment. He tried to kill you. It looks premeditated since young, healthy, respectable civil attorneys don't usually walk around with enough Oxycontin in their pockets to sedate a herd of horses. He doesn't want to die by lethal injection. He certainly doesn't want to be locked behind bars with a bunch of people who have a rabid dislike of lawyers. What does he do?"

I shrugged. "I don't know. Kill himself?"

"P.J. Think. What would *you* do if somebody had been paying you to acquire documents in an illicit fashion, and you're suddenly facing a murder charge?"

A huge grin nearly split my face. "You mean it? You're not just saying it to make me feel better?"

Chatterton shook her head. "It's what I would do. And I'm sure Patterson's lawyer has mentioned it to him."

"Oh, if he could help put that bitch in jail, it would make me so happy!"

"Well, we're not there yet. And, who knows? I could be wrong."

"But she's the one . . . I mean, yeah, he tried to kill me and he should pay for it, but that woman—what she did to me—there ought to be a law!"

Chatteron rolled her eyes. "You can be sure that there is now no record that you ever typed up that note she made you sign. In fact, if I were you, I'd call it even. You did conduct an illegal search of her house, after all."

"Oh." My face grew hot. "It's not that. It's the other thing."

"Which was . . . ?"

I told Chatterton about Marguerite Sutherland's all-too-thorough search of my person the night I'd been caught snooping. By the time I finished, she was leaning forward, scribbling a note on her legal pad.

"You were fully clothed during this, ah, search?"

"Except for my jacket. Look, I know I wasn't raped or anything like that, but I feel so violated!"

"Just so you know. Rape and sexual assault are defined—" She moved to the bookshelf and pulled down a legal tome, flipping through the pages. "Here we go. A person is guilty of sexual assault in the first degree when that person engages in sexual intercourse or sexual *intrusion* with another person and either inflicts serious bodily injury upon anyone or employs a deadly weapon in the commission of the act." She closed the book. "Did Sutherland penetrate your vagina? Panties or not?"

My face was crimson. "No."

"Or your anus?"

"That didn't—No."

"Well, then you weren't raped—legally speaking, that is. Your privacy was certainly violated, and I understand how you must feel. If it continues to really upset you, therapy might be an option."

"Or just get over it. Only I feel so angry all the time. I just can't seem to let it go! I keep telling myself, you know, come on, P.J., you put yourself in that position, so suck it up! But, frankly, it's spilling over into other parts of my life. For example, Alicia. The rational side of my brain tells me not everything was her fault, but that doesn't seem to do anything to help."

"Therapy might."

When I could afford it. Which meant not any time soon enough.

"Or try the old-fashioned remedy: counting your blessings." Chatterton held her hand up, ticking her points off, finger by finger. "First, you're still alive. Second, your uncle didn't fire you. Third, Marguerite Sutherland might—just might—get her comeuppance in the halls of justice and, if not, you can console yourself by remembering that she still thinks that diamond hair clip you returned to her is real."

She had a point. Why sweat the small stuff? "Yeah, and then there's my uncle. You wouldn't know about it but . . ."

"He *did* fire you?"

I shook my head, smiling. "Maybe you saw it in the papers. My uncle's name is Alexander Boyd Smythe, and he has just been named Annapolis's Volunteer of the Year."

On Saturday, the day before Alicia fled the country, she and I had accompanied him to Maryland Hall where he was honored for his work finding legal employment for women of a certain age whose ability to make a living plying their trade was disappearing as fast as the physical charms that had once got them noticed by their potential customers. I thanked my lucky stars that I'd never accused Uncle Alex of seeking illicit sexual thrills. But then how could I? If he knew what I'd been up to on Clay Street that night, his opinion of me would have been worse than the one I'd have earned if the embarrassing photo in the *Capital* had turned out to be authentic.

"Okay," I said, when the giggles finally subsided. "I should try to have a more positive outlook. But I have to tell you: My uncle is not at all as nice as everybody in town seems to think."

"Let me guess. You weren't fired, but demoted."

"No, thank God. It's just that Uncle Alex is probably guilty of vandalism."

"I thought Gareth Swenson was. He confessed to searching your house, after all."

"This is something else. Really not connected to the Vivian Remington thing—or at least, I'm pretty sure. Just some mischief that got a little out of control."

Chatterton fiddled with her pen. "Speaking of mischief, what was the deal with those weird photos?"

"I can only guess some of it. I know the one of Vivian was a birthday joke. At some point, she must have decided that she could get the same thing done using Marguerite Sutherland's head."

"But why?"

"Probably an alternate tack." I paused, a light bulb finally going off in my head. "Actually the primary one. Second choice was the big lie about the stolen coat, which as we know now, was just a ruse to get me into Sutherland's house where Vivian figured I'd find a way to search for the coat and, in the process, find something that would prove Sutherland was sharing Wetland Protectors Alliance strategies with her boyfriend."

"The woman must have been nuts. There are much simpler ways to trace an intelligence leak. Sheesh." She paused, running fingers through her hair. "So. The kinky photos?"

"I think Vivian was planning to use the doctored photo to embarrass Sutherland by showing her wearing an endangered garment and engaged in some kind of dominatrix hanky-panky. It wouldn't even have to be true to cause a furor on YouTube. And the more Sutherland tried to defend herself, the more likely it would appear she was lying. By the time the dust settled, it would be too late for her to clear her name."

"And the picture of you?"

"I'm guessing Marvin Ross couldn't help indulging in yet one more piece of digital mischief." It had only taken a rather long and involved phone call from me to persuade the *Capital* to publish a prominent retraction.

With Gareth Swenson still presumably at large, I'd kept the gun he'd abandoned. I had my own thoughts about where he'd obtained it, which I didn't plan to share with Alicia or Uncle Alex. You see, the last time I'd held my own gun—the one without a permit, the one that had disappeared right before Gareth's visit—I had loaded only one bullet into the chamber.

Which reminded me of the one remaining puzzle: Who destroyed my 1971 Volkswagen? It had to have been someone who clearly didn't want me driving the car. That narrowed the suspects down to five. It might have been my ex-husband, although my beloved Beetle had already been compacted into a slab of metal by the time Uncle Alex and I were involved in the boat wreck that would have made Bobby angry enough to seek vengeance. It might have been Gareth Swenson, except he probably didn't think trashing somebody's car would put him any closer to getting his hands on those pesky photos. Marvin Ross? Naw. He was too slightly built—and definitely not enraged enough—to be able to wield a hammer over and over again.

That left two others, but only one of them had friends in East Baltimore. Some fine day, but not until I'd paid off my car loan, I was going to have to have a little talk with Uncle Alex.

I left Chatterton's office feeling a little less consumed with anger. For one thing, I figured maybe Alicia had already suffered enough—financially, that is. Discounting the expenses associated with the Banner Building and the actual filming, she'd had to bribe Marvin Ross *and* pay for the faux diamond hair clip. She was also covering my legal expenses. But then, what are friends for?

ABOUT THE AUTHOR

P.J. Smythe first showed up in *Futures Mysterious Anthology Magazine* in a story titled "Beginner's Lessons." She made a second appearance in *Orchard Press Mysteries* in a story titled "Growing Pains." Caroline Taylor's short stories have also appeared in *A Fly in Amber, The First Line, The Greensilk Journal, Strange Mysteries 2, The Dan River Anthology 2009,* and *Workers Write Tales from the Capitol!*